PROJECT
ENTERPRISE

PROJECT ENTERPRISE

H.J. "Walt" Walter

Dedicated to the patient one, my wife, Dolores

Order this book online at www.trafford.com
or email orders@trafford.com

Most Trafford titles are also available at major online book retailers.

Printed in the United States of America.

ISBN: 978-1-4669-6226-2 (sc)
ISBN: 978-1-4669-6225-5 (e)

Trafford rev. 12/12/2012

 www.trafford.com

North America & international
toll-free: 1 888 232 4444 (USA & Canada)
phone: 250 383 6864 ♦ fax: 812 355 4082

Acknowledgements

To my wife Dolores, for always being there when I needed guidance. For being so patient when things went wrong. For always supporting what i was doing no matter how much time it required writing alone in my study.

To a dear friend, Edie Fleeman, for helping in editing my book and making welcome suggestions to improve its content.

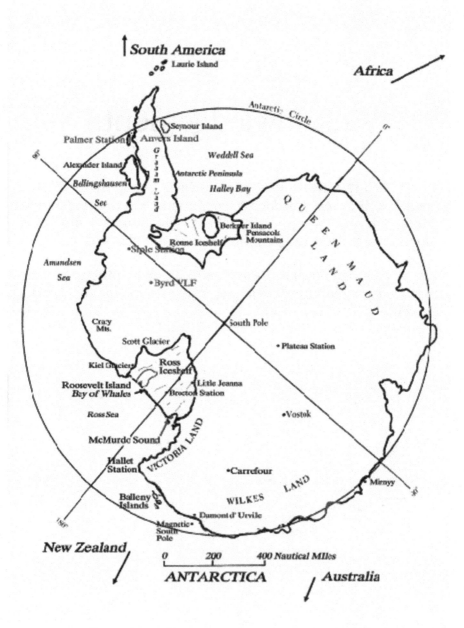

PROLOGUE

"Emergency in Space"

Houston, TX

The day shift at mission control had just come on duty and the mission control commander, former astronaut Pete Crown, was finishing his briefing before the controllers manned their stations. Suddenly over the loud speakers in main control the space shuttle Enterprise Mission Commander broke the relative silence with the words, "Houston this is Enterprise. We have a problem. Over."

All hands froze in their tracks as if stunned by a laser gun. It was not something anyone ever wanted to hear. They were prepared for almost any emergency but still the words were chilling to hear. The controllers reacted by immediately checking their consoles to see if anyone could determine the problem.

Pete keyed his mike and responded to Enterprise. "Enterprise, this is mission control. What is your problem? Over."

Paul Anderson, Enterprise Commander, in a clear and concise voice reported, "We have lost all the fuel to our maneuvering thrusters and our main engine. We have the vehicle under control and have stabilized it in a neutral position."

"Roger," Pete responded. "Give us a minute to check our calculations and confer on the problem."

Pete's heart rate was well up over 150 beats per minute and he immediately knew this was going to be a serious

1

situation. He switched over to intercom and started an inquiry with all the controllers. Shuttle systems monitor was the first controller to report.

"We observe that all indications from our telemetry concur with Paul's initial observation. All fuel on the shuttle has been lost for some unknown reason."

Human resources next reported that all astronauts appeared to be okay except of course their heart rates were outside the normal range due to the nature of the emergency. The controller reported that oxygen supply was measured at 96 hours remaining based on normal usage.

There were 7 astronauts on board Enterprise and all were experienced space travelers. They would remain calm in the face of danger and hopefully NASA's Houston team would solve their problem. Reentry or lack of capability for reentry would be their main problem.

Washington, D.C.

Communications officer for the Office of Polar Programs at the National Science Foundation, Ken Nichols, burst into Director Jack Forester's office shouting for Jack to turn on his television and tune to Fox News. As he did the newsman was just reporting that there was a problem with the space shuttle and describing the nature of the problem.

It had been a busy week for Jack Forester at the National Science Foundation. His main assignment was managing the Office of Polar Programs but additionally, his real responsibility was for the operation of the Antigravity Flight Vehicle Program (AFV), a top-secret program whose vehicles were often identified as UFOs. Jack had been the chief architect and manager of the program since his retirement from the U.S. Navy. While on active duty with the Navy he had been an Antigravity Flight Vehicle (AFV) pilot with Antarctic Development Squadron Six (VXE-6). The AFVs had been shadowing the space flight and Jack asked Ken if he had any reports from operations in Utah concerning anything the AFVs might have observed on their flights. He directed Ken to contact Jack Shepard, operations director in Utah for the AFV program, and obtain any information they had and report back to him.

Ken left Jack's office for the communications center to deal with Jack's request. As Jack watched the television his mind drifted back to the early days of the AFV program. One of the responsibilities of the program was to shadow the United States space flights in case trouble developed. The AFVs were passive but could become active if needed for rescue or just for observing and making suggestions on solving problems.

He recalled John Glenn's first orbital flight in the Mercury program. On his first orbit while moving onward above the Pacific over Canton Island, Glenn experienced a short 45-minute night and prepared his periscope for viewing his first sunrise in orbit. As the day dawned over the island, he saw literally thousands of "little specks, brilliant specks, floating around outside the capsule." Glenn's first impression was that the spacecraft was tumbling or that he was looking into a star field, but a quick hard look out of the capsule window corrected this momentary illusion. He definitely thought the luminescent "fireflies," as he dubbed the specks, were streaming past his spacecraft from ahead. They seemed to flow leisurely but not to be originating from any part of the capsule. As Friendship 7 sped over the Pacific expanse into brighter sunlight, the "fireflies" disappeared.

They were in fact particles from one of the AFVs, which unbeknownst to Glenn, was escorting him just in case of a problem. The AFV pilot called it "Search and rescue of the third kind." The AFV had stayed out of visual sight of the periscope, which was mounted in the Friendship 7 spacecraft, and continued to monitor the flight from a longer distance.

Subsequently, on the very next orbital flight, Scott Carpenter flying Aurora 7 experienced trouble with his automatic flight control system. At the retrofire event, the pitch horizon scanner malfunctioned, forcing Carpenter to manually control his reentry, which caused him to overshoot the planned splashdown point by 250 mi.

Harvey Elkington was shadowing the flight that day and followed the spacecraft all the way to splash down. He fixed his position to be 19deg 29min North 64deg 05min West. The spacecraft was intact and Carpenter appeared to be okay except for the 45° list of the capsule. The recovery task force was some 250 miles from this point so Harvey climbed for altitude and broke radio silence transmitting the capsule's geographic position to AFV flight operations. John Kats was on duty and after receiving the message retransmitted it to his contact at CIA via radio teletype.

It can only be assumed that this information was somehow transmitted to NASA Mission Control and then passed on to an Air Rescue Service SA-16 amphibian aircraft from the Puerto Rican Air National Guard. Visual contact was established with the spacecraft 39 minutes after landing and the USS Farragut, located it about 90 minutes later.

Harvey stayed on station out of visual range just in case he was needed. After Scott was picked up by helicopters from the U.S.S. Intrepid, Harvey returned to base. It was a tense time for the AFV program. Shadowing the space program was not a job for sissies. Jack knew this was going to be a long day.

Jack was so engrossed in the scenario enfolding on the television that he barely heard the red security phone, which was a direct link to the Director of Central Intelligence. Jack picked up the receiver and spoke into it. Admiral Bill Reynolds was on the other end of the line.

"Jack, have you been listening to the reports on the television." He asked.

"I sure have," responded Jack. "What do you make of all this, Bill?"

"I don't have any newer information than the news reports but thought you might have further info from one of your pilots."

"Bill, we're working on it. I have Ken Nichols querying Jack Shepard in Utah. Should have a report any minute now."

"Jack, let me give you my take on this up to the present. Because the shuttle has lost all its fuel there is going to be a reentry problem. NASA may even try to mount a possible rescue mission. From what I know they do not have the capability to complete any rescue in time before the crew's oxygen runs out. That leaves a possible AFV rescue mission."

"Those are not words I like to hear, Bill. If we were to do this we once again risk exposing the program to the world and you know what that will bring. However, I realize this is what we have been working for all these years. I knew if we were ever needed in such a case as this we would be ready."

"Right Jack. But it is something we need to consider. Let's have dinner tonight in my dining room and discuss the possibilities. Be sure to bring all your up-to-date information when you get it from Utah."

"Ok Bill I'll see you at 7:00p.m. Take care, Bill."

Jack hung up the phone and went over to his safe. After opening it he retrieved the contingency plan for protecting the AFV program from exposure. He thought, here we go again, remembering the fiasco they had four years earlier with "Swede" Larson, the Antarctic explorer.

1

"Close of an Era"

Hibbing, Minnesota: Four years earlier

It was March and still exhibiting signs of winter in Minnesota. The weather was threatening snow. Temperatures were in the mid twenties with wind chills approaching the teens. Susan Larson had returned to Hibbing just a day earlier from Texas where she had been living since her separation and divorce from Swede.

The Office of Polar Programs in Washington, DC, had located her through the court divorce papers she had filed in Hibbing while Swede had been on his snowmobile trek to the South Pole. They had notified her of Swede's death because she was the only known living relative albeit an ex-wife. She had already known of Swede's fate through the TV coverage of his rescue and subsequent demise on the flight from the Antarctic to Christchurch, New Zealand. Planning for his funeral had fallen on her shoulders and through her grief she had accomplished it with some difficulty. Her love for Swede had never waned but she had made her decision concerning his life style and when she couldn't bear it anymore had divorced him. The return to Elm Street in Hibbing had been traumatic. When she had first entered the old homestead she was overwhelmed by the emotions of the flashbacks she had of their good times together. Their restoration of the old house had welded their love for eternity and she couldn't help but remember it all. Their ski trips to the slopes and the parties afterward with the huge fires in the living room fireplace were all etched in her mind. The laughter, hugging, kissing and love making all touched her and helped he overcome some of the grief she felt in losing Swede.

Now she had to face life without him and this afternoon would be the hardest time of the whole ordeal. She would have to say goodbye to Swede for the final time.

Her good friend Becky from just a couple of houses down the street knocked and startled her back to some semblance of reality. She opened the front door and greeted Becky.

"How are you holding up?" asked Becky.

"I'm doing okay I guess," replied Susan.

"That's great, Lars Swenson told me we needed to be at the funeral home by 1:00 p.m. because he wanted to get the memorial service started by about 1:30 p.m. and get to the cemetery by 2:30 p.m."

Becky stayed close to Susan almost since she arrived in Hibbing for the funeral. She had been her friend for 12 years and had been emailing and communicating by telephone with Susan since she left Hibbing after separating from Swede.

"Let me run upstairs, get my purse, put on my hat and I will be ready to go," said Susan.

"Lars said he would send a limo to pick us up around 12:45 p.m." She looked at her watch. "Its almost that time," Becky replied.

Susan went upstairs for her purse and hat and descended the stairs ready to depart for the funeral home. As she reached the bottom of the staircase she put on her coat. Just then the limo pulled up and they walked out arm in arm. This was going to be one tough ordeal and they both knew it. They would need each other for moral support to get through it.

Meanwhile, Jack Forester, Head of the Office of Polar Programs, had arrived in Duluth, Minnesota, and rendezvoused with Commander Jeri Perriman, U.S. Navy, the Commanding Officer of Antarctic Development Squadron Six. Jeri had flown in from Point Mugu, California, home base for the squadron when not deployed to the Antarctic. Jeri had been on the rescue mission and the fateful flight where Swede had died enroute to New Zealand. He harbored a sense of loyalty and a little responsibility to Swede to see that he was properly honored for his accomplishments. He was aware of the recklessness with which Swede planned and carried out

8

his Antarctic expedition but that was water over the dam and he couldn't change it. He knew only that with the squadron's involvement he owed it to any survivors to comfort them and assure them that Swede died peacefully in search for his quest for fame.

He greeted Jack as they met at the Hertz rental desk in the airport. They picked up their contract and proceeded to the area where the rental cars were parked and loaded their luggage for the drive to Hibbing.

Along the way they stopped at the Outback Restaurant for lunch and still had plenty of time to arrive at the funeral home in Hibbing before the start of the memorial service.

Jack had been stunned by the swift change of events. The news of Swede Larson's death had reached him during the news conference in Washington, DC, and he had not been prepared for it. Executing the plan to cover-up Project Galaxy activities and keep Swede Larson from exposing the Antigravity Flight Vehicle program to the world had occupied Jack's every waking hour and he had not even anticipated Swedes death. During the past few days he had been trying to regroup and organize his thoughts and schedule to proceed with routine things. As a courtesy to Susan Larson and to give her a feeling of closure over Swedes death he felt as Jeri that his presence at the funeral would support what Swede had tried to accomplish even though it had given Jack many tough days and a lot of heartburn.

Jeri and Jack arrived at the funeral home a little early, which was good because Jeri had brought an American flag to be draped over Swede's coffin. He had died while on a military aircraft and had been in the care of the U.S. Navy since his rescue so it was only appropriate that he be given the honor of the flag. They met Lars, introduced themselves and stated their association with Swede. Lars took the flag and placed it appropriately over the closed coffin with the stars over the left shoulder of Swede, as was tradition.

Susan and Becky arrived a short time later and were greeted by Lars. He introduced them to Jack and Jeri. They all sat down for a few minutes and Jeri described the rescue of Swede, his physical and mental condition at that time and the situation surrounding Swedes death. The words seemed to comfort Susan and she thanked him for making the effort to attend the funeral and show the Navy's respect for Swede. Jack in turn offered his condolences and expressed the National Science Foundation's extreme sorrow in her loss.

A few local people wandered into the room and sat down to participate in the memorial service. All in all about 17 people were present for the service. The pastor of the local Lutheran Church, Reverend Kjell Sunderland, performed the service, which lasted about 30 minutes. Afterward Susan and Becky led the congregation from the chapel to the waiting vehicles lined up outside on the street. The hearse was first in line and after all the vehicles were loaded Lars and his associates brought out the coffin and loaded it in the hearse. The funeral procession proceeded east on Main Street and traveled about 1 mile where they turned into the cemetery. Concordia Cemetery had been established by Gethsemane Lutheran church where Swede and Susan had attended services. They had purchased two burial plots for themselves. Little did Susan realize that one would be occupied so quickly?

Lars had erected a small white tent over the gravesite with covered sides to prevent the wind and cold from blowing through the tent. The coffin was wheeled from the hearse and placed over the open grave. The mourners gathered and sat in the chairs provided. Reverend Sunderland read the last rites and the ceremony ended with a lone bugler from the local American Legion located just outside the tent playing taps. Lars then gave each person in attendance a red rose and they placed it on the flag-draped coffin as they passed then departed the tent. Susan and Becky were the last ones present and that's when Susan broke down sobbing and crying saying she couldn't leave Swede like this. Becky and the Reverend comforted her and spoke quietly to her saying that they had done all they could for Swede and that she should remember him as he was in life, full of vigor and exuberance. Still sobbing she was led from the tent to the limo. As she passed Jack and Jeri she thanked them once again for coming and expressed her gratitude to them for making the effort to attend the funeral as they did. They shook her hand said their goodbyes and departed the scene.

They drove quietly for a while towards Duluth where they would board their plane back to Minneapolis and then home. Some miles down the road Jeri broke the silence.

"Well Jack," he said. "That was a tragic ending for what could have been a productive life. Too bad he was such a poor planner and had such a big ego. If he had followed procedures his expedition may have been successful."

"You're right Jeri, but his expedition was doomed from the beginning and he paid the ultimate price. How many times do we know of where poor planning and execution of Antarctic expeditions has ended tragically?"

"Too many I'm afraid," responded Jeri.

Jack wanted to discuss the possible catastrophe Swede could have caused had he exposed the AFV program, which he had observed accidently in Antarctica but Jeri wasn't privileged to that program so Jack remained silent. The remainder of the conversation during the drive to Duluth was taken up with the past Antarctic flying season and what the future holds for the squadron, the U.S. Navy and the United States Antarctic Research Project. (USARP)

They arrived in Duluth and turned in their rental car then proceeded to the airline check-in desk for their flight to Minneapolis. They boarded the 50-passenger Canadair regional jet and were off to Minneapolis. Upon arrival they deplaned and walked into the terminal. Jack had 2 hours and Jeri had 2-1/2 hours before making their connections to their destinations so they went into the sports bar for dinner. Conversation was a reliving of old times flying great planes off carriers, flying helicopters off ice breakers and generally just flyboy talk centered on the navy.

After dinner they sat for a short time and then Jack said his goodbyes and headed to his gate for his flight to Dulles. He would be glad to get home to Fairfax and Kate, his ever faithful, patient wife.

Jeri boarded his flight 1/2 hour later headed for Los Angeles. He would have to drive the 75 miles up the road to Naval Air Station (NAS) Point Mugu before arriving at his quarters on the base and his family. He was lucky though, he would gain 2 hours passing the 2 time zones enroute to LA so he would not be quite so late and the family might just be up waiting for him. He looked forward to spending some quality time with them after his harrowing season deployed to Antarctica with the squadron.

2

"Honoring the Heros"

NAS Pt. Mugu, California: Four years earlier.

The squadron had been off duty for thirty days. An old navy tradition known as "cold iron." The men of Antarctic Development Squadron Six were currently reporting back for duty. They had many tasks to perform while getting back into the northern summer routine. First would be delivery of the three UH-1N "Huey" helicopters to overhaul at Pensacola, Florida, then on to Lockheed Aircraft Corporations overhaul facility in Marietta, Georgia, to deliver the LC-130 "Hercules" for their annual maintenance checkup and update of equipment. While at Marietta the Naval Air Training and Operating Procedures Standardization Program (NATOPS) Officer, Maintenance Officer and Operations Officer would attend an update conference making suggestions on how to improve the LC-130s for Antarctic operations.

NATOPS officer, Lieutenant Commander Bob Avery, would lead the group headed for Lockheed and the update conference. Things went smoothly and the three UH-1Ns as well as the six LC-130s were successfully transferred.

Meanwhile back in the squadron spaces all departments were readying their final Deep Freeze report for the previous season. The first week back after all-hands had returned for duty, the squadron had their annual full dress parade. During this parade all personal decorations would be awarded. The parade began on a Thursday morning at 8:00am All-hands mustered on the hangar deck and were accounted for. The uniform for this formation was full dress blues with medals and swords for officers. The divisions for each department made up the platoons while the department heads acted as company commanders. The Executive Officer mustered the departments and when that was completed, he reported squadron ready for inspection. The first dignitary to arrive was the Commander Fleet Air (COMFAIR) Pt Mugu. The Commanding Officer of NAS Pt. Mugu, Captain Edgeworth, accompanied Captain Peabody. Next to arrive was Commander Naval Air Forces Pacific (COMNAVAIRPAC), Vice Admiral Robert J. Fitzsimmons. Last to arrive was Commander in Chief Pacific Fleet (CINCPACFLT), Vice Admiral Gordon Nakajima. The skipper, Commander Perriman, greeted all these VIPs. Also in attendance were Jack Forester, Office of Polar Programs, and Commander Antarctic Support Force, Rear Admiral John C. Boland.

All honored guests and other VIPs took their respective places on the dais. The squadron was called to attention and colors sounded. The color guard marched the colors front and center. Upon arrival the national anthem was played and honors rendered to the flag. The colors were posted and the Commanding Officer, Antarctic Development Squadron Six, walked to the podium. The skipper then asked the Executive Officer if the squadron was ready for inspection. The Executive Officer (XO) replied in the affirmative and the Commanding Officer (CO) asked CINCPACFLT to accompany him on the inspection. The inspection party began on the extreme left of the formation and moved quickly to the right trooping every rank and looking at every sailor standing there for inspection. After completing the inspection of the squadron the CO again mounted the dais. He introduced the guests of honor and finally introduced the guest speaker, Vice Admiral Gordon Nakajima. Admiral Nakajima was a former skipper of NAS Pt. Mugu during the Reagan years. He was a naval aviator and had flown the A-6 extensively. He had been captured during the Vietnam War after being shot down on a daring raid on North Vietnam. His remarks were brief but inspirational. He praised the squadron for its professionalism and unbelievable accomplishments. He closed his remarks wishing all hands well in the future endeavors in naval aviation.

Next came the individual personnel awards. First called front and center was Lieutenant Commander Bob Avery. As he approached center he stopped at attention and saluted very smartly. The salute was returned by the Commanding Officer, Commander Perriman. The skippers yeoman, Master Chief Joel Adams approached the microphone and began to read the following citation:

> *"The President of the United States takes great pleasure in awarding the Distinguished Flying Cross to Lieutenant Commander Robert H. Avery, United States Navy, for meritorious service in the Antarctic during operations with Task Force Forty-Three. His performance of duties as Officer in Charge of rescue operations regarding the crew of the sunken ship Maverick Explorer and his subsequent rescue of Antarctic Explorer Edvard T. "Swede" Larson, a United States citizen, were in keeping with the highest tradition of Naval Aviation and the United States Navy. His outstanding ability as a naval aviator and his application of leadership skills resulted in the operations being carried out in an effective and efficient manner without further loss of life. His dedication to duty and perseverance will go down in the annals of Antarctic flight and place him among the great icons of naval aviation. His performance was in keeping with the highest traditions of the naval service. Well done Lieutenant Commander Avery."*

With the reading complete the Commanding Officer pinned the DFC on Lieutenant Commander Avery's lapel saluted him and invited him to join him in the presentation of further awards. Bob took his place next to Commander Perriman.

Next called front and center were Lieutenant Commander Larry Beck, Lieutenant Commander Mark Hastings and Lieutenant Commander Jim Brandies. Each in turn was awarded an Air Medal for their part in the rescue of the crew of the Maverick Explorer as well as some participation in the rescue of Swede Larson.

Lieutenant Junior Grade Jeff Ring and Ensign Oscar Huerto were then ordered front and center. Their award was the Navy/Marine Corps Medal for heroism. These two intrepid naval aviators had checked out in United States Antarctic Research Project's (USARP) Air Cushion vehicles (ACV) in less than one hour of "stick" time and then performed flawlessly while participating in the rescue of the Maverick Explorer crew in the Bay of Whales. Their performance was in the highest traditions of naval aviation even though they flew ground vehicles.

Finally all the flight crews, maintenance personnel and any others who participated in the rescues were presented with the Navy/Marine Corps Commendation Medal.

COMNAVAIRPAC was next introduced and he delivered brief remarks concerning the professionalism of the squadron in carrying out their assigned mission. His most memorable remark centered on the fact that the squadron had performed in such an outstanding manner for so many years. He paused briefly in his remarks as if pondering the reasons why the squadron had been so successful. Anyone associated with the squadron however, knew the reason. It was because of the enlisted personnel along with a few officers who had been with the squadron for so many years. The leading chief, Master Chief Bingham, had been there 18 years. The chief flight engineer, Master Chief Lenny Boardman, flying LC-130s, had been there 17 years while others had been there continuously for more than 14 years. They all knew their job well. They loved the duty because the routine was the same from year to year and they had lots of time off in the northern summer. Once qualified in a job they needed no further training so it was easy to keep up on their performance. The admiral continued. He turned to the chief yeoman who handed him a folder. He removed a paper and began reading.

> *"The Secretary of the Navy takes great pleasure in awarding Antarctic Development Squadron Six the Navy Unit Commendation for outstanding service on the Antarctic continent. Operating in a demanding and challenging*

environment, directly enhancing U.S. Navy, scientific and national objectives. The squadron displayed exceptional skill, tenacity and perseverance while operating under extremely challenging conditions to support Antarctic scientific research. Antarctic Development Squadron Six's acumen was further displayed by their highly successful participation in the rescue of the crew of the Maverick Explorer and of Edvard Larson, Antarctic Explorer".

All-Hands were dumbstruck that they had been so honored by SecNAV. Commander Perriman was called front and center. Vice Admiral Robert J. Fitzsimmons pinned the ribbon on Commander Perriman's right breast symbolizing the award for all-hands.

After Admiral Fitzsimmons finished the ceremony, Commander Perriman called the squadron to attention. All honored guests departed the hangar area in the reverse order from how they had arrived. After the last VIP departed the XO ordered the department heads to dismiss the squadron. Each department head in turn passed the order on to the division officers who then dismissed the men.

The other half of the hangar from the inspection area had been turned into a picnic setting. All hands including family and guests were invited to a picnic feast. It included bar-b-que, hot dogs, "penguin" burgers, other assorted food and of course as much free beer as one could drink.

During the festivities, Jack Forester, Admiral Boland and Commander Perriman conferred on plans for the upcoming recovery of the Pararescue team from Palmer Station in the Antarctic. They were stranded at Palmer Station because they had made a jump onto Anvers Island, rescued two scientists and then trekked to Palmer Station. Because it had been late in February, no sea ice was yet available for an LC-130 "Herc" to land to pick them up. No other runway was available in their vicinity so the plan was to wait until the bay off Palmer Station froze over and the ice reached the proper thickness to support a Herc and then send a plane to recover them.

The three men were in agreement that the ice would reach the proper thickness in a few weeks and that daily ice readings from Palmer were now indicating 23" of ice.

The following Monday Commander Perriman called Bob Avery into his office and they discussed the upcoming rescue of the pararescue team. Commander Perriman informed Bob that he would once again be called upon to lead the rescue mission. He also assigned the Executive Officer Commander Pete Vernon and Lieutenant Commander Larry Beck as the other two Aircraft Commanders for the mission. Bob Avery scheduled a meeting of the three of them for the next morning to begin the planning process.

Anvers Island, Antarctica

Palmer Station had been overcrowded since the Antarctic Development Squadron Six pararescue team had made their jump and subsequent rescue of the two scientists on the Gadout Glacier then trekked to Palmer Station. Team leader Lieutenant Russ Parker ensured that the team was kept busy to try to make the time pass more quickly. He had asked permission and had received it from the station Officer-in-Charge to put two of his team on the ice thickness patrol. This required the patrol to snowmobile out on the ice once a day to a distance of 2 miles and then take ice thickness readings at ¼ mile intervals while working their way back to the station. It was a fairly simple task, which he assigned to Dick Spalding and Jake Gorsham. The patrol would drill a hole with their hand auger and then measure the thickness with a special tape measure, which had a hook on the end to enable them to find the underside of the ice. Their report of the day's ice readings were then forwarded to Task Force Forty-Three's headquarters back in Washington, D.C. The latest readings indicated an average depth of about 23 inches. At the present growth rate it was estimated it would reach a safe thickness for an LC-130 landing in about three weeks.

Meanwhile Doc Kealey, another member of the team, immersed himself in assisting the station doctor with all his tasks. In Antarctica very few assigned personnel ever got sick. This was due to the cold and not having any germs or bacteria being able to survive. Doc Kealey involved himself in a photographic study of the firmament. He assisted one of the astronomers with his scientific study taking photos of the sky and kept busy developing film, which he exposed nightly. Ken Koenig another team member was a squadron aircraft maintenance officer. Before his commissioning Ken had been a ground equipment repairman. He hooked up with the station equipment maintenance specialist and between them they were in the process of overhauling every large piece of machinery at the station.

The fifth member of the team, Sean McKenna, specialized in survival equipment and he too assisted the station personnel in bringing the survival equipment up to an A-1 condition. The pararescue team officer was pleased with his team in the way they were making themselves useful in upgrading the station to a high level of readiness to meet their mission. He busied himself with the planning of the station responsibilities for the upcoming flight to the station to pick them up. Task Force Forty-Three headquarters was keeping the station advised of the requirements necessary for preparation when the flight would arrive at the station. The station was also coordinating its requirements that the LC-130s would be tasked with to deliver from the States.

Pt Mugu, California
Lieutenant Commander Avery called a meeting of his task unit who were charged with planning the recovery of the pararescue team. He advised them of the tentative schedule being considered. They would depart Pt Mugu in three weeks and fly to Howard AFB, Panama. Overnight, then fly to and remain over night in LaPaz, Bolivia, fuel the aircraft and proceed to Punta Arenas, Chile. From there they would wait for the best weather forecast for Anvers Island and then mount the flight to Palmer Station. After loading their passengers and cargo they would proceed to Seymour Island for fuel if necessary, then fly back to Punta Arenas after which they would retrace their flight path back to Pt. Mugu.

The mission called for three LC-130s with augmented crews so that crew duty time would not be a factor. Augmented crews consisted of three pilots, two navigators, two flight engineers, a loadmaster and a scanner. Before they could plan their aircraft assignments they would need to pick up the three Hercs from Marietta, Georgia, at the Lockheed repair facility where the Hercs were even now undergoing overhaul. The repair schedule called for three to be completed in seventeen days.

Bob Avery had also asked the CO if they could have Lieutenant Paul Eskew from Task Force Forty-Three staff as a meteorological observer. He was the best Antarctic weather forecaster in the business. The CO made the request to Task Force Forty-Three and it was approved.

As a meticulous mission planner and also being on the conservative side, Bob Avery knew that the best chance of success for this mission was three aircraft. Flying into the Antarctic in the middle of winter was as dangerous as flying becomes, then having to land on sea ice and possibly refuel at a strange base then fly back to Chile, he knew it would take the best Antarctic experienced pilots the squadron could muster. Bob knew Larry Beck was just one of those people but he wasn't quite certain of Commander Vernon. Commander Vernon was about to become the commanding officer in a month or two and the current CO had assigned Commander Vernon to be one of the pilots for this mission so Bob Avery had to adjust to what was handed him. He would keep his eye on Commander Vernon and try to make him one of the best as they progressed through the mission. Other than the aircraft commanders, Bob had a free hand to pick whatever crew members he wanted for each of the aircraft. For his lead navigator he selected his old friend Bill Grammercy. He and Bill went way back to the time of flight training when they first met. Bill was a naval aviator who had lost his flight status due to his eyesight but he had requalified as a naval flight officer and Bob was glad to have him on board. He would ride herd on the other navigators assigned to the mission and make sure the I's were dotted and all the T's crossed before they left Pt. Mugu. For his other lead navigators Bill Grammercy picked Billy Joe Springer known to his friends as the "Bounder". Billy Joe had been on the aircraft with Commander Vernon, which had crashed the previous year in East Antarctica. They had both recovered from that experience and had been solid crewmembers ever since. For the third lead navigator Bill selected Ivan Wheaton. Ivan was a third year crewmember and was highly experienced in the Antarctic.

The selection of the remaining pilots, navigators, flight engineers, loadmasters and scanners Bob left to the aircraft commanders. As for himself he chose his crewmembers from the previous years deployment. They had been with him, some for one year others for two years. All were Antarctic experienced flight crew personnel.

3

"The Meeting"

Washington, DC: The present

Jack had been keeping himself busy during the day with his normal routine. Shuffling papers and writing reports had come to be an easy task and he was finally realizing that he had become a Washington bureaucrat. During the day his mind had wandered and he tried to figure out what they were going to do with the problems being experienced by the space shuttle. As an old naval aviator he knew there was no fix for the loss of maneuvering fuel and the lack thereof for the space shuttle's engine. Retrofire and eventual reentry was out of the question. Depletion of the oxygen supply would mean loss of the entire crew. A rescue mission had to be mounted before this occurred and it appeared that the only capability, which existed was the Antigravity Flight Vehicle Program. Exposure of this program once again loomed on the horizon and would rear its ugly head. Jack knew he would be on the hot seat because once exposed he would never hear the end of it from the media who would hound him for what would seem like an eternity. His life would be a public spectacle on daily television and his entire career would be scrutinized over the public airwaves. Somehow he had to figure a way to not let this happen and he hoped his meeting that evening with Bill Reynolds and the emergency contingency plan they could come up with a solution.

Six o'clock approached and Mary McGuire, Jack's secretary, came up on the intercom telling Jack she was leaving and that he should also be on his way to his evening appointment with Admiral Reynolds at the CIA. Jack acknowledged and wished her a goodnight and told her he would see her in the morning.

Jack packed up his briefcase, put on his suit jacket and headed out the door. He took the elevator to the first floor. As he passed the security desk he waved to Jim Knowles, the guard on duty, and wished him a goodnight. Jim waved back and told Jack to take care and have a nice trip home. Jack walked down to the parking garage, which was under the building. He thought, "Isn't it nice not to have to walk a couple of blocks to get to the car." The move from Washington, DC to Arlington, Virginia, had been carried out a few years back and, being located just off Glebe Road and I-66, was very convenient to access all routes in and out of Washington. Jack however, knew the back streets of Arlington from his early days at the Navy's Bureau of Naval Personnel so he took them over to the Key Bridge and onto the river parkway, which would lead him to McLean and the headquarters of the CIA.

Jack arrived about 6:40pm, parked his car and walked to the main entrance. He entered and signed in at the main security desk. He had no trouble since he already had the proper credentials and was readily admitted. He took the elevator to the floor where the director's office was located and proceeded to the office location. As he entered the director's office, his administrative assistant Susan Clark greeted him and told him he could go right in as the director was expecting him.

Bill looked up from his paperwork as he entered, "Evening' Jack, I was expecting you. Just finished a review here so have a seat while I put my John Henry on this thing and we can order some dinner."

"Thanks Bill." Jack responded. "I famished so don't take too long. Guess you had as busy a day as I did. I saw the report concerning the developments in Iran."

"Yeah Jack, that's been on the front burner all day and we are just about to wrap up our assessment of the situation. As usual we couldn't have gathered as much Intel without your AFV missions. The close-up photos of the nuclear sites have been spectacular. I have to give the President his usual morning intelligence briefing tomorrow morning so I need to get this back to the analysts for final proofing and printing."

With that, Bill signed the report he had been working on and came around the desk to sit with Jack in the lounge area of his office where Jack had taken a seat.

"Willie Sutton, our chief cook, has prepared us a great dinner of pork roast, mashed potatoes, sweet corn and a tossed green salad. Tell me your pleasure of dressing and I will get him to send it up to us on the dumb waiter."

"Tell him to make it French dressing, Bill. That will be great, sounds like a good dinner." Jack replied.

Bill rose, hit the intercom button for the galley and asked for Willie. Willie responded and the admiral told him to send up two orders of dinner and salads, one with honey mustard and the other with French dressing.

Soon they were both munching on dinner and Jack brought up the current situation with the space shuttle.

"The report from Utah is Bruce Fleming was shadowing the shuttle when he observed gas clouds escaping from all the thrusters and the vent on the engine fuel tank. He reports that this made the shuttle unstable for a short time but it steadied out after a short time. He was not exactly sure what the crew was doing to correct the venting but it stopped and the shuttle steadied down again.

"I am at a loss on how to solve this problem," said Jack. "I know NASA is working feverishly trying to come up with a solution, Bill, but from my experience I can't come up with any solution other than to mount a rescue with the AFVs. You know what that will bring on. Unless the Emergency Contingency plan has a blueprint the AFV program might be exposed to the world and we will be on the hot seat trying to muffle the din we can expect from the media."

"Let's look at the other possibilities, Jack. How long would it take NASA to mount another space shuttle for a rescue mission?"

Jack thought a minute. "Even if NASA accelerated their procedures it would still take them a little over 72 hours to get one to liftoff and from my calculations the astronauts only have 86 hours of oxygen remaining and that's if NASA starts right this minute to get the next space shuttle ready."

Bill chimed in. "That would leave NASA 14 hours. Let's say they make the decision and start in the next 6 hours that would leave them 8 hours after lift off, achieve orbit and rendezvous with the Enterprise and complete the rescue. It's doable but that's cutting it very close."

"What about a possible Russian rescue?" Jack asked.

Bill answered. "Their only reusable capsule is currently at the space station and does not have the capability of intercepting Enterprise from there. The Russians would need to recover the capsule and then reset it on a rocket and go through launch procedures which would probably take a week to do so that is out of the question. In addition they could rescue only six of our astronauts from the shuttle as that is all the capsule will hold in addition to the one Russian astronaut required to pilot the capsule."

Bill continued "The Chinese have a capsule but it is not mounted on their rocket and is being stored in a hangar near their launch pad and I am sure they could not possibly mount a rescue in time and once again their capability to rescue all seven of our astronauts in not within their capability. I think our best course of action at this point is to wait until tomorrow and see what NASA will do Jack. How much lead time will your guys need to mount a rescue?"

"Give us about 6 hours to be on the safe side." Jack answered. "We can launch four of our vehicles and take on up to two each of the shuttle crew on three AFVs and one on the final vehicle."

"Okay then, plan on that just in case we are needed but keep our guys on the Iran missions so we know just what is happening there. Meanwhile I will inquire with Winston Perry at NASA and see what plans develop there. The plans to keep the AFV program from being exposed are almost useless although it is something we planned for. Why don't you take the plans and study them and see if they are doable. MJ-12 will not have time to be consulted and you and I will be saddled with the decision as to whether we rescue the astronauts or let them die up there to keep the program secret. That is barring a miracle with NASA and they rescue them in time."

The two old friends continued their dinner and chit chatted about other projects presently underway and how they could help each other complete them. Dinner had lasted about two hours and Jack was about ready to get home.

"Well, Bill, I have plenty of work on my plate for tomorrow so I think I will get going and try to get some sleep. I will talk with you first thing on getting to the office in the morning." With that Jack shook Bill's hand and proceeded out the door and down to the parking garage.

On his drive back home to Fairfax Jack's mind wandered and it was filled with all sorts of recollections. Over the years there had been many crises and somehow the people he had worked with made them all a success.

He remembered the mission four years ago mounted by VXE-6 to retrieve the pararesuce team from Palmer Station, Antarctica.

It was early April and the squadron had picked up the three Hercs from Marietta, Georgia, and had returned them to Pt. Mugu.

The squadron was in the process of winterizing the Hercs and gathering the necessary survival equipment for the aircraft. Crew personnel were finalized and they were acquiring personal survival equipment for the mission. Their normally issued gear had been left in storage in Christchurch, New Zealand, because the squadron did not know at the time who would be mounting the rescue so all new gear had to be issued. Because of the lack of Navy survival gear, the United States Antarctic Research Program (USARP) provided the survival gear. When it was issued to the Navy men they were all smiles, as they had never seen such great gear. It was a far cry from what they had been using and much advancement had been made since the Navy had purchased theirs. The new Japanese Mukluks were really great compared to the huge white rubber boots they had been used to. Three layers of protection from the cold while still so light they weighed hardly much more than normal flight boots. The bright red USARP Parkas were also a great improvement from the squadron-manufactured birdcloth parkas they had been wearing during the regular Deep Freeze season. All in all the crews were very pleased with their gear.

The planes were finally winterized and ready for the Antarctic. The crews were prepared for departure with navigation planning complete and all survival gear loaded aboard. Final preparations would take only a day or two to complete once the word to go was received. LCDR Avery checked the ice thickness reports daily as well as the weather over the Antarctic Peninsula. Lieutenant Eskew remained at his base at Pt. Hueneme but traveled over to Pt. Mugu daily for the weather briefing. As the days passed the ice thickness began approaching 30 inches, the calculated safe-ice thickness. Bob figured another 10 days and they would have a safe ice runway on which to conduct their operation.

Those days would pass very slowly for the flight crews. Bob notified the operations officer of his planned departure date who in turn relayed this info to the Task Force Forty-Three staff so that all cargo destined for Palmer station could be at Pt. Mugu and loaded prior to departure for Anvers Island. Bob Avery, Larry Beck and Pete Vernon all scheduled flights in their aircraft while checking out their crews and maintaining their flight proficiency.

Meanwhile some of the AFV crews were on Temporary additional duty at Nellis Air Force Base flying missions out of Area 51 and relieving those pilots who were temporarily operating out of Siple Station, Antarctica. Lefty Wardhill, former AFV pilot and VXE-6 commanding officer had recently retired as liaison officer at Nellis and George Pilkington had taken his slot and was coordinating AFV pilot's movement between Pt. Mugu and Nellis. They were conducting missions keeping track of the U.S.S.R., and their activity and preparations for conducting nuclear tests at Eastern Kazakh, Semipalatinsk.

These crews were at Siple for about two weeks at a time, then relieved by other crewmembers flown in from Area 51. Operating in 24 hours of darkness was a challenge and approaches at Siple were usually instrument in nature but made easy by the 10 mile VLF antenna that was stretched out on the surface. VLF approach instrumentation had been available and developed some six years earlier and proved very reliable in the AFVs. A couple of years earlier Siple station had been upgraded to accept the new three place AFV-2 which was slightly larger than the—1s. The large horizontal sliding hangar doors had been made to open wider to accommodate the new craft. Below the snow the hangar area had also been made larger so the new fleet of six AFVs could be stowed and worked on with ease. Choyce Proulx had been brought aboard to run operations at Siple and he was a crackerjack at his profession. With this many machines to deal with Choyce had as many as 36 VXE-6 crewman to work with as well as four station personnel to assist him with all the operations tasks that needed to be accomplished. For Jack Forester it was becoming a nightmare. With this many people being involved over the years it was always a possibility that the program details would leak out and the media would start snooping. Jack however, had done a great job of screening personnel and thus far the secret of the AFV program was being kept safe.

The crews at Siple were asked to assist with the Palmer mission by overflying that station and reporting the general situation, which they observed when returning from an AFV mission.

4

"The Detachment"

Point Mugu: Four years earlier

Lt Paul Eskew was at the squadron spaces when the CO arrived for work. Bob Avery arrived a short time later and was called immediately to the skipper's office. Paul had brought a message from TF-43, which included a report from Palmer of the status of ice thickness. It read, "ice thickness now 34 inches. Commander Perriman put it to Bob Avery, "What is your schedule, Bob?"

"Looks like departure for Punta Arenas in 48 hours. I will alert all necessary agencies and personnel, Skipper," Bob reported.

"Great Bob," the skipper replied, "If you need assistance you have it."

"Roger that Skipper."

Bob and Paul left the CO's office and consulted on what Paul needed prior to departure. NAS Point Mugu weather office would provide the briefing folders for the trip to Panama while Paul would get a six-day forecast for the Antarctic specifically for the Antarctic Peninsula and Palmer Station. Paul had access to the satellite images of Antarctica and also the polar forecasts from the National Weather Service. Bob Avery would get Bill Grammercy to request the weather briefings from Panama to Punta Arenas. He then went to the Communications office and drafted an itinerary for the trip to Punta Arenas. The return trip would be planned after the trip to Palmer Station was complete.

Task Force Fourty-three was notified of the intended departure time and they in turn would activate the request for diplomatic clearance and landing request for Bolivia and Chile. Their staff would also activate the cargo and mail plan for transport from Punta Arenas to Palmer Station. The Embassy at Santiago had been accumulating the mail and would transport it to Punta Arenas on their DHC-6, a turboprop DE Havilland Twin Otter. Cargo for Palmer was already being accumulated in Punta Arenas and being held by a bonded storage company.

All VXE-6 crew members assigned to the mission were notified and put on alert status as well as all department heads. The squadron was geared up preparing the planes and crews for departure. All planes had been test flown the previous day and maintenance was in the process of working off the gripes. Aircraft survival as well as personal crew survival gear were stowed and in place for the flight. All that was necessary now was to fuel the aircraft and they would be ready for the mission.

Twenty-four hours passed and a briefing was scheduled for all crewmembers at 0900. The crews gathered in the squadron training room, which also doubled as a briefing room. Small groups were drinking coffee and reliving old Antarctic experiences. They had all been hand picked and there were no newcomers. All had one year's experience or more of Antarctic flying. The crew lists had been published and operations had tried to keep crewmembers that had been on the same aircraft together as much as possible. This would add to the efficiency and productivity of the crews.

As Commander Perriman and Lieutenant Commander Avery entered the room someone called the room to attention. All hands snapped too and stood at attention. Commander Perriman directed all-hands to be seated.

Commander Perriman thanked everyone for accepting this assignment and the positive attitude exhibited by all-hands. He indicated this would not be an easy mission since an LC-130 had never landed on the ice at Palmer Station. He wished everyone the best of luck. He then called on Lieutenant Commander Avery. Bob took the podium and gave the crews the general plan. They would depart tomorrow morning at 0800 and fly to Howard AFB, Panama, remain over night and then depart the next morning at 0800 fly to LaPaz, Bolivia, where they would refuel and then continue on to Punta Arenas, Chile. From there, when the weather allowed he would lead the assault on the Antarctic accompanied by Lieutenant Commander Beck, backed up and standing search and rescue by Commander Vernon. They would depart Punta Arenas so as to put them at Palmer Station at midday to take advantage of the best light as possible, since it would be daylight for only a few hours. Once the mission was completed on the ice at Palmer he and Lieutenant Commander Beck would fly to the Argentine base at Seymour Island, if necessary, refuel and then proceed back to Punta Arenas. After sufficient crew rest they would then retrace their route back to NAS Point Mugu. If everything worked correctly they should return to Point Mugu in 7 to 8 days. If any aircraft had a problem along the way all aircraft would remain wherever they were and wait until all planes could proceed together.

Bob Avery indicated that was the end of his general brief and asked for questions before they proceeded. Wally Glennon, the flight engineer on aircraft 321, raised his hand. After being recognized he asked if they were taking JATO bottles from Mugu or whether they would have some available at Punta Arenas. That was Larry Beck's area of expertise so he stood and answered the question. They had considered it but since this would be an ice runway landing no JATO would be required but they would carry it just in case it was needed.

Next question came from J.C. Friend, flight engineer on aircraft 917. "What kind of fuel is available at Punta Arenas?"

"Good question, Friend," Bob Avery responded. "There is only JP1 available. We will be able to climb only to 10,000 feet on our trip to Palmer. As you know JP1 doesn't give us the BTU's we need to get to a higher altitude. Our fuel consumption will be greater than normal and that is why we are planning on refueling at Seymour Island, JP4 is available at Seymour since the Argentineans fly their C-130s there all the time."

Ivan Wheaton, navigator of Aircraft 319, raised his hand, "What kind of accommodations do we have in Punta Arenas?"

Lieutenant Bill Springer was the accommodations coordinating officer. He stood and spoke. "We will be staying at the Best Western Finis Terrae. It is located downtown as are all the hotels. There is nothing close to the airport. We are planning on getting rental cars for local transportation. Also for those of you that need cash we have arranged for base disbursing to give you an advance. They will be open today at 1300 today and I think Mr. Avery has arranged for you all to be off this afternoon to spend some time with your families."

Next Bob Avery called on Paul Eskew to give the flight crews an Antarctic weather briefing.

Paul turned on his projector connected to his laptop. He projected the latest infrared image of the Antarctic Peninsula and surrounding seas. He began his briefing. "Generally the weather at Palmer Station is comfortable Antarctic weather. Temperatures have been running from the low 20s Fahrenheit to a high of 32°. Winds generally out of the west to southwest 8 to 11 miles per hour. Barometric pressure has been running near 29.30 inches of mercury. Cloud cover is generally high, broken to overcast cumulus at 10,000 to 11,000 feet. During the past week a low-pressure system passed over the station moving from west to east and the station experienced wind gusts to 52 miles per hour with some snowfall, which resulted in whiteout conditions for a short period of time. This is typical for April weather at Palmer. As winter approaches more lows will be moving across the Antarctic Peninsula, temperatures can be expected to continue to drop but no extremes will be experienced. Flights will be able to proceed in good weather conditions as the lows are moving quickly across the area and our satellite images will give us plenty of time to complete the mission between times of expected bad weather. Sunrise is now around 8:00am and sets at about 4:00pm. That gives us a large window to complete our Antarctic portion of the mission during daylight hours. That completes my briefing. Any questions?"

There were no questions from those assembled. Bob Avery once again took the podium. He asked if there were any more items to cover or if there were any questions about the mission. "Alright team," Bob said, "muster at 0600 tomorrow and we'll be on our way. Dismissed."

With that all-hands departed for their respective offices and assignments to complete last minute tasks. Bill Grammercy asked Bob Avery, Larry Beck and Pete Vernon if they wanted to have lunch at the O'club. They all agreed to meet around 12:00 noon. Bill also asked Bill Springer if he would like to join them. With that they dispersed to their respective offices.

Morning came early for the men of VXE-6. The flight crews reported in, many before the 6 o'clock hour. When Bob Avery arrived Bill Grammercy was already working on the flight plan for Howard AFB in Panama. He had obtained the winds for the route of flight and was in the process of calculating time of arrival. Bob met with Larry Beck and Pete Vernon. They discussed the flight plan to Panama. It was decided that Bob would depart first followed at five-minute intervals with Pete second and Larry bringing up the rear. Bob would file for 31,000 feet with Pete at 29,000 feet and Larry at 27,000 feet. Each crew had two copilots assigned. After checking with their respective Aircraft Commander they proceeded to the aircraft and conducted the preflight, which included an external inspection as well as an internal one. Each plane had been assigned some cargo for the flight including scientific equipment for the station as well as machine parts needed to repair some of the Palmer Station support equipment. Mail as well as perishables would be loaded at Punta Arenas just before the flight departed for Palmer.

All navigators completed their flight planning documentation and joined the Aircraft Commanders. The duty officer provided transportation in the form of a van to base operations for a weather briefing and for filing a flight plan. Paul Eskew joined them. As they entered the weather office the meteorologist on duty espied Paul.

"Hey Paul how are things going?" He asked.

"Great Al!" Paul replied.

"I have your briefing folders and have worked up your enroute and Howard AFB arrival weather."

"That's what we need," said Paul. "This is Lieutenant Commander Bob Avery, mission commander. How about giving us the enroute and terminal weather forecast."

"Pleased to meet you sir," Al said as he extended his hand. They exchanged handshakes and Bob said, "Pleasure is all my mine. Hope you have some good weather for us."

"Yes sir. Here is your enroute chart and weather. You can expect mostly scattered to broken high clouds until you reach the Mexico City area and then clouds layers lowering to scattered to broken cumulus with bases in the Panama City area of 2500 to 3000 feet. Possibility of an isolated thundershower in the Panama City area. Visibility will remain greater than 10 miles except in thundershowers. Winds will be light and variable. Looks like typical tropical weather," he added.

"That sounds like a piece of cake, Al. Thank you. Looks like we will have a pleasant flight," responded Bob.

With that he turned to Larry and Pete. "You guys have any questions?"

"Nah. Looks good to me, Bob. Should make for a great flight," said Larry.

Pete nodded his approval and added, "Looks like an easy time, for the first leg anyway."

With that said they thanked Al for the briefing and proceeded downstairs to the Operations Duty Officers desk to file their flight plans.

Lieutenant Commander Cliff Gross, a former super constellation pilot in the squadron, had the duty.

As the pilots approached his counter he said, "Where you guys off to today?"

"Headed for Punta Arenas, Cliff, but just going as far as Panama today." Bob observed.

"Here are our flight plans. We hope to get off by 0800."

"I know you guys have probably checked the NOTAMS (Notice to Airman) but just a reminder our TACAN is down for maintenance until 1000 local today," said Cliff.

"Roger, Cliff. Our Navigators have it in their planning documents. Don't think we will need to worry about that, however, what with the weather being severe VFR (Visual Flight rules) today.

Having completed their business at base ops they all got back into the squadron van for the trip back to the hangar.

When they got out of the van the skipper was there to greet them.

"Morning men," he offered.

They all saluted which the skipper returned

"Morning Skipper, you're up early," Bill replied.

"Yeah, I just wanted to see you off and wish you a good trip. How's the weather look for the first leg?"

Pete Vernon chimed in. "Things look good all the way to Panama Skipper. Typical tropical weather for this time of year. We should have a good trip today."

"Sounds great." The skipper answered.

With that the crews shook his hand and turned to proceed to their aircraft.

After a normal startup, taxi and run-up the crews were ready to depart Point Mugu.

They all received their air traffic clearance, switched to the tower frequency, were cleared for take-off and were airborne. Los Angeles center cleared each direct to the San Diego VORTAC station, the NavAid serving San Diego.

Bob Avery leveled off at 31,000 feet and headed direct for San Diego. Pete Vernon was at 29,000 feet with Larry cruising at 27,000 feet. After passing San Diego each in turn was handed over to Mexico City control center for the trip across Mexico. They were in and out of high clouds, which dissipated after passing Mexico City, leaving them with low broken cumulus all the way to Panama. Landing at Howard AFB was normal where they would remain over night. Bill Springer suggested a trip to the local watering hole but they all decided to have dinner at the O'club and settle in early.

The next morning all crews were off early to La Paz, Bolivia, where they refueled and were quickly on their way to Punta Arenas, Chile.

Cruising along in the bright sunlight at altitude was really enthralling. The Andes were mostly clear and the mountains were beautiful in the fall sun, which was streaming across the peaks and valleys, a serene scene, which would soon turn ugly. At LaPaz the NOTAMS had indicated that the VOR NavAid was out of service at Punta Arenas and radar coverage was intermittent because of electrical surges due to bad weather. Passing Santiago Bill Grammercy reported passing the VOR station at 31,000' at 1630 local time. Santiago center responded with a roger. Bill then asked for the Punta Arenas weather with estimated time of arrival about 1830, which would be 6:30pm local time in Punta Arenas. It would be dark by then as sunset was 6:13pm. Shortly, Santiago Center asked, "Navy 48321 are you ready to copy the Punta Arenas weather?"

Bill responded, "Santiago Center. Ready to copy. Go ahead."

"Roger 48321. Punta Arenas weather 4:05pm local time: 1200' overcast, light rain, visibility 2-3 miles in showers, wind west at 45mph gusts to 60, altimeter 29.30 inches of mercury. Forecast for 6:00pm to 7:00pm local time, 800' overcast, light to medium rain showers, visibility 1-3 miles, wind west 40 gusts to 50mph, altimeter 29.28 inches."

Bill responded, "Roger Santiago Center. 48321 copied all."

Everybody in the cockpit was listening. Bob Avery was the first to speak up. "I guess we can't get a break. If everything goes well we shouldn't have a problem." He asked Bill who was still listening. "Bill, ask the center what the current status of the electrical power is at the airport."

"Roger Bob," said Bill

"Santiago Center. Navy 48321. Request the status of the electrical power at Ibanez Airport, over."

"Roger 321 stand by will check with Ibanez."

After a couple minutes delay Santiago Center called, "Navy 48321 over."

Bill answered. "Santiago Center. Navy 48321. Go ahead."

"Navy 321, Ibanez Approach control reports electrical power is still intermittent and excepted to remain that way until 10:00am tomorrow."

"Roger Santiago copied all. 321 out."

About that time Pete Vernon in 917 reported passing Santiago and reported he had copied the Punta Arenas weather and status of electrical power. In short order, Larry Beck in 319 also checked in over Santiago and reported he had also copied the weather and power status.

This sparked a discussion by all three aircraft commanders on the squadron common ultra high frequency. Bob told Pete and Larry that if power were out upon arrival that they should join up in 1 mile in trail and they would decide from there what to do. Bob also discussed the situation with Bill. Bill already had a plan that would take close coordination but was doable so that all three could get into Punta Arenas. Bob approved and alerted Pete and Larry to follow Bill's instruction closely as they approached Punta Arenas.

Bob Avery was now 30 minutes out of Punta Arenas and his copilot Charlie Black was calling Punta Arenas approach control of UHF. He had no success so Bob directed him to return to squadron common. He switched and Bob called the other two aircraft. He directed Pete and Larry to switch to 235.5 MHz, which was Punta Arenas approach control. Both checked in with Bob on that frequency.

"We will operate on this frequency until touchdown unless Punta Arenas comes up and is able to direct us through approach and landing. Backup frequency will be 15,500 kHz on HF radio." Everybody acknowledged.

Bill Grammercy took over as the air traffic controller. He instructed 917 to take-up a position three miles in trail on 321 and 319 to follow 917 at three miles. All navigators were now responsible for maintaining position with each other using the aircrafts' radar. Both aircraft shortly reported in position. Bill announced over the frequency that 321 was descending to Flight level 23,000' maintaining 250 knots indicated airspeed and instructed 917 to descend to FL 23,500' and 319 to descend to and maintain FL 24,000. Within a couple of minutes all aircraft reported level.

Bill was now aiming for a point due south of Punta Arena on the coast. As they were approaching his imaginary Initial Position (IP) he briefed the other two aircraft.

"We will simulate a jet penetration. On my mark 321 will turn to heading 230° magnetic and start down at 250 knots. Each of you in turn upon reaching the IP will do the same. Reverse course passing 11,000' and turn to the port, rollout on a heading of 340° and continue your descent to 3500'. Your altimeter is 29.28in and begin slowing to 160 knots." He paused then said, "Now." Upon reaching 3500' level off and slow to 150 knots. Maintain your 3 miles in trail all the way to touchdown."

It was silent on the radio for a few minutes and everyone listening was intense and focused. This would be no easy task but these pilots were the best naval aviators for this job and all hands were certain of that.

As 321 approached the coast Bill gave the command to Bob and broadcast to all "321 turn right to 230°." Bob complied and made a beautiful ½ standard rate turn, rolled out on heading 230°. Bill announced over the radio, "Commencing penetration, leaving FL230 for 3500' on my mark. "Mark." Bob immediately retarded the power levers to flight idle and pushed the nose over. The rate of descent needle started down and Bob stabilized it at 6000' per minute. He called for the descent checklist and when his speed reached 250 knots he once again stabilized it.

The other two aircraft mimicked 321 and were also in their jet penetration. Bill had predetermined that 3500' would take them clear of the terrain which would be about 2500'.

As Bob passed 11,000' he began his course reversal and once again rolled out on heading 340°. Bill reported to the other two aircraft that they were passing 11,000'. As Bob approached 3500' he began to raise the nose attitude, and slowing the aircraft. He stopped his descent at 3500' and continued to slow to 150 knots. They were now passing the coastline and Bill gave him a correction to heading 345° pointing the aircraft toward the northern point of Dawson Island. He transmitted that corrected heading to the other aircraft. They had been in the clouds since leaving FL 24,000 and were now in a rough choppy turbulence probably cause by the terrain and the strong winds blowing over it. The other aircraft reported level at 3500' and established 3 miles in trail. Bill briefed the other aircraft navigators telling them that they were heading for the northern tip of Dawson Island and once passed it should try to maintain a distance of 12 miles from the mainland and 6 miles from Grande Isle. At this point the Straits of Magellan were 18 miles wide and this would keep them well clear of land and mountains.

Bob asked the copilot to read the before landing checklist. He complied and they both ensured each item was as it should be. The copilot announced that approach speed would be 125 knots, threshold speed 115 knots and touchdown speed at 105 knots. Bill passed these speeds on to the other aircraft. Halfway across Dawson Island he instructed Bob to descend to 1000'. Over the air he proclaimed. 321 out of 3500' for 1000'. He cautioned the others not to descend until halfway across Dawson Island. He reported over the air that 321 was passing the northern tip of Dawson Island descending to 1000' at 500 feet per minute. It was now 36 miles up the straight before intercepting the centerline of runway 25 at Ibanez. Bob leveled off at 1000' at 150 knots. The other aircraft, in turn, reported out of 3500' descending to 1000'. Turbulence was still bad. Rain was light to medium and intermittent in the clouds. Bill now had a couple of minutes so he briefed the other crews once again. He started his stopwatch and planned to fly 14 minutes on this heading before turning onto runway heading. He keyed the mike telling the other crews to time the leg and turn on final at the 14-minute mark to heading 260°. He also indicated that they would slow to approach speed upon completing the turn. At the 14-minute mark he instructed Bob to turn to heading 260 and slow to approach speed. As Bob rolled out he slowed the plane to 125 knots and called for flaps to 10%. Now was the moment of truth for Bill. He set his radar antenna at 3° down and started to look for the airport. They were approximately 10 miles from touchdown and Bill knew there was a highway on the north side parallel to runway 25. He had also obtained an overhead photo of the airport, which had been taken two years earlier by a crew in 321. There were two fighter revetments on either side of the approach to runway 25 which had taxiways angling into the runway. Bill knew if he could pick them out they could find the runway. He was shooting for a point about halfway between two nodes sticking out into the straights, which were prominent on the shoreline. As they approached 6 miles from the end of the runway he told Bob to prepare for descent to the runway recommending 400 feet per minute. It would be a tough job as they were really being jostled by the turbulence. Bob called for gear down, skis up, lowered the nose and trimmed the aircraft for a 400-foot per minute descent. The copilot started to call out the altitude. "Out of 1000', passing 900'." Everybody was hanging on for dear life. This was a dangerous move, in the dark without runway lighting and guidance by ground radar. The copilot continued, "800'." Bill gave Bob a correction to 255°. Approaching 700' they appeared to be out of the layer of clouds with scud below them. "600' I can see the ground," called out the copilot. Bob continued on instruments but turned on the landing lights. Bob continued the descent. Suddenly Bill called out, "Come to heading 245° I have the revetments at the end of the runway. Now turn back to 255°. Runway is 1-1/2 miles dead ahead." As they passed one mile, Bob transitioned to visual and looked dead ahead. "I have the runway in sight."

Bill chimed in, "Roger. Field elevation is 144' but altimeter could be off and radar altimeter now reads 85 feet while the pressure altimeter reads 200'." Bob slowed to threshold speed and after crossing the numbers slowed to 105 knots and began to flare the aircraft by raising the nose. The wind appeared to be blowing 270° at 40 knots with gusts to 55 miles per hour. Bob touched down slightly right wing down and left rudder. It was smooth and firm. A safe landing. He could see the centerline and kept the aircraft lined up on center while he put the power levers in full reverse.

Meanwhile Bill reset his radar antenna to 3° up and told Bob to roll out to the intersection with runway 13 and then stop off the runway heading 070°. That way he could assist 917 and 319 to line up on runway 25. Bob did just as Bill recommended. As his radar swept the forlorn skies searching for 917, Pete's copilot Lieutenant Jerry Elliott reported they were 6 miles out. At 6 miles Bill picked up 917. He keyed the mic and told 917 he was about ½ mile left of centerline and to come right 10°. 917 reported out of 1000'. Bill gave them a weather report with ceiling at 700' and scattered scud beneath. Bob left his lights on as a beacon for 917. 917 reported out of the clouds at 700' and at 500' he reported 321s lights in sight. 321 advised 917 of his ground position to give 917 a sense of their relationship to the centerline. The crew of 321 spotted 917's lights at 1 mile and 917 reported runway in sight.

It was now Larry's turn in 319 to run the gauntlet. He reported on heading of 255° leaving 1000'. 917 was now parked on the north side of runway 25 parked on runway 13 in a similar fashion as 321. They both had their radars working and were trying to find 319. Ivan Wheaton, navigator in 917, first reported that he thought he had 319 at 9 miles but 3 miles left of centerline. Bill answered that he now also had 319 in the same place. Bill gave 319 a course correction of heading 275°. As 319 approached centerline Bill corrected his heading to 255°. The copilot of 319 had reported that they had copied the weather when it was relayed to 917. Both aircraft now had their landing lights on and at 1-1/2 miles 319 reported he had their lights in sight and at ½ mile he reported the runway in sight. Larry put the props in reverse and stirred up a large cloud of rain. Bob came on the air and told the other aircraft to follow him. He started down runway 13 and while looking for a taxiway he saw an emergency vehicle with its flashing lights coming out to meet them. He continued and in a minute the vehicle picked them up and led them to the Fixed Base Operator (FBO) terminal. They completed all their checklists and shutdown the aircraft engines. They left the gas turbine compressor running so as to have lights inside while they got organized to deplane. Bill Springer went inside the terminal to talk with customs and immigration. He identified himself with his passport and suggested customs and immigration come out to the airplane where they had lights. The agents thought that to be a great idea and they followed Bill out to the aircraft. After clearing both agencies the crews shutdown the aircraft completely and went into the terminal to rent a couple of cars. They had no success since all machines used for car rentals were off line. They found a 30-passenger bus sitting in front of the terminal and offered the driver enough money that he agreed to take them into the city and their hotel. All crewmembers piled in and were soon off to the city. They arrived at the Best Western, checked in had a quick shower and met in the bar for a well-earned libation. Dinner was in the hotel dining room. They were boisterous as only Navy flight crews can be. They were not rude or out of order but they were just glad to be on Terra Firma and in a warm place with good food.

5

"Mission Preparation"

Punta Arenas, Chile: Four years earlier

All the flight crews were up early for a briefing in the dining room at 9:00am. Most arrived around 8:00am so they could finish breakfast and be ready for the briefing. The wind outside was still howling and rain was coming down heavily at a 45° angle. It was a driving, bitter rain for an early fall day in the southern hemisphere. The dining room was almost void of patrons as the tourist season had ended and few were wanting to travel to Punta Arenas when the bad weather began. It was definitely a dull day and a good one to stay inside and just catch up on planning and paperwork.

Bob Avery was up early and went into the business center of the hotel to logon the Internet to contact the squadron. It was the best way to communicate because there was no military communication site available through which to send a message. Bob discovered the electricity had come on around 6:00am, which turned out to be earlier than the 10:00am expected time. He had the squadron communications officer's email address and after the EarthLink site came up on the computer he logged into his own email account and sent a message. It was short and to the point. Bob reported that all planes were safe on deck in Punta Arenas and in an up status. He indicated that he would be checking the weather forecast for the next couple of days for Palmer Station as soon as he and Paul Eskew had an opportunity to get out to the airport that morning. He asked the squadron to direct the bonding company to contact him as well as the embassy in Santiago so he could make arrangements for delivery of the equipment in bonded storage as well as delivery of the U.S. Mail currently being held for the personnel at Palmer Station. He also needed to arrange for fresh veggies and eggs for Palmer Station. He told the communications Officer where he could be reached and the telephone number of the hotel. After hitting the send button he logged off and left the business center for the dining room.

All the crews were already eating breakfast so he joined Larry Beck and Pete Vernon. Good mornings were exchanged all around. The waitress took Bob's order, departed and the three began discussing details of the mission. Bob filled them in on the email he had just sent and what could be expected in the next 24-48 hours. Pete suggested a duty officer and assistant duty officer to monitor any of the expected contacts so that someone was available at the hotel at all times to take calls and answer questions. Bob was taking notes for the upcoming briefing and he didn't want to miss any items, because everyone should be aware of them. He was following instinct, as this was the Navy way. Every officer should be able to take over and lead the mission should the next senior officer be unable to do so. The three of them discussed what the plan was for the next two days and what the options were. Bob's immediate plan for the day was to get out to the airport and check the weather for the next two days enroute to and from their destination Palmer Station. Larry suggested powering up one of the aircraft and attempting to contact Palmer Station directly on one of the HF transceivers. Bob and Pete both thought that to be a great idea if it would work. They finished their coffee and Bob took a position on one side of the room so everyone could face that direction and participate in the briefing.

Bob asked everyone to quiet down so he could start the briefing. He thanked them for making the effort to be there. He acknowledged that the previous day had been long and difficult and said he realized most people had had very little sleep. He started his briefing with the email he had sent to the squadron communications officer. His brief included his email address, password and web site needed to log on to receive email. He asked everyone to copy down that information in case it was needed. He included the phone number of the hotel on which he expected to receive calls and who he expected to call. He told the crews what he, Larry and Pete expected to do at the airport and what they expected to do about ground transportation. He stated that they would need six rental cars to transport all crewmembers to and from the airport. Billy Joe Springer, lead navigator for Larry Beck, spoke up.

"Why don't we see about the minibus we came in from the airport? If we can arrange that we can save a lot of money and driving by the crew."

Bob replied. "That's a great idea Bill. Anybody want to run that down and see if it can happen?"

Lieutenant Charlie Black raised his hand, "Ivan and I will do that," Charlie answered.

"Great, Charlie," Bob said. "We will call the hotel when we are ready to depart the airport and before we rent cars to check on the status of transportation."

Bob continued. "For all hands, we are expecting calls from the bonded storage company which is holding the cargo for Palmer. Also expect to hear from the embassy in Santiago concerning the U.S. mail for Palmer. I don't know what arrangements have been made for the fresh produce and eggs we are going to be delivering so perhaps anyone who takes that call from the embassy needs to ask that question. Now for the mission itself."

Bob called on his navigator, Bill Grammercy, to give the briefing.

Bill started. "When everything looks right for the mission to proceed, we will attempt to depart Punta Arenas about 0800 local time and land on the annual ice off Palmer Station about 12 noon. Distance is 746 nautical miles and flight time will be approximately 3 hours, 26 minutes while cruising at 10,000' altitude. Altitude is limited due to availability of only JP1 at Ibanez Airport. On deck time for Lieutenant Commander Avery's aircraft is estimated to be not more than 1 hour. Return flight time estimated to be approximately the same as the flight to Palmer Station. Lieutenant Commander Beck's crew will accompany Lieutenant Commander Avery to Palmer and will circle until it is determined that conditions are safe for a second aircraft to land. After off-loading and reloading northbound cargo, both aircraft will depart for Seymour Island if refueling is necessary. Fuel will be a full load, which will allow a sufficient margin of safety with point of no return calculated to be over Palmer Station. After completing the mission on the ground at Palmer we will proceed to the Argentinean Base at Seymour Island for refueling to provide sufficient fuel for an alternate airport should weather conditions preclude landing back at Punta Arenas. Commander Vernon's crew will depart Punta Arenas at approximately 0845 and proceed to a point halfway to Palmer Station where they will act as search and rescue and communications relay. If necessary they will orbit until both planes are on their way back from Seymour Island. Fuel for Commander Vernon's plane will be a full load with 1000-gallon auxiliary tanks full. This will give them eleven hours projected flight time. UHF (Ultra High Frequency) will be squadron common 315.6mhz. HF (High Frequency) will be Palmer Station's frequency of 4735khz on at least one HF radio at all times and you navigators set your other HF radio to McMurdo Control on15,250khz. Commander Vernon will monitor Chile's Flight Information Region to whom he will make our position reports as the controlling agency for our flight plans. We will relay our position reports to him on the Palmer Station frequency. Are there any questions?"

Nobody had a question so Bob Avery continued.

"Bill," he asked. "Would you take on the task of setting up a watch bill? I think we need at least one officer and one petty officer on duty during the daylight hours. Break it into four-hour shifts and indicate to the front desk they should call Pete, Larry or me after dark. We should advise the hotel's front desk who is on duty. If we provide them a copy of the watch bill they will know who to look for."

Bob continued the briefing covering what the plan was for the day. The three Aircraft Commanders along with two flight engineers and Paul Eskew would be going out to the airport to check the weather forecast for the next few days and also going to try to contact Palmer of HF radio through one of the aircraft's radio. They would attempt to make contact with the bonding company and find out the status of the cargo being held by them. Raytheon Corporation had given Bob the name Pacific Feeder Services SA, Punta Arenas Branch Office: Pedro Montt 969, Punta Arenas.

"Those who have the duty we are expecting a call from the Embassy in Santiago regarding the cargo for delivery to Palmer. You all have my email account and duty personnel should check that account once each hour for a possible email from the squadron. Are there any questions? I see none, the rest of you who do not have an assigned task for today can just relax or take in the sights although the temperature and rain will probably keep you inside most of the day."

The briefing was complete and some of the crewmembers went back to drinking coffee and discussing what they might do with the rest of the day. Bob Avery went to find the hotel manager and see about some transportation for seven of them to the airport. Shortly thereafter he was ushered into hotel manager Hector Rodriquez' office. He explained there predicament telling him about being unable to rent cars when they arrived due to the power outage. Hector was sympathetic because the hotel itself was without power for the same period of time. He told Bob they could use the hotel's airport shuttle for as long as they wanted it and that he would check with the other hotels about possibly using their airport shuttle busses since the tourist season was over and many would have them sitting idle. Bob explained that their schedule was flexible but Hector insisted everything would work out and not to worry about it. He scheduled the bus for a 10:00am departure and went out to round up those who would be going with him to the airport. Soon they were on their way to the airport along the costal highway. It was still cool outside, rain coming down heavily and the wind blowing about 25mph with gusts. The land was barren and the vegetation was turning brown in the fall weather. Snow was beginning to appear on the upper levels of the mountains to the west of their route. Winter was fast approaching in this southernmost city in the world. Upon arrival at the airport they proceeded to the fixed base operator (FBO). They would be responsible for servicing the aircraft and providing transportation on the ramp to and from the aircraft. Bob directed Pete Vernon to see if he could find the bonding company's airport office and to determine how much lead-time they would need to deliver the cargo to the aircraft prior to departure. Larry would be responsible for aircraft readiness so he and the two flight engineers went out to the aircraft to begin that procedure. Meanwhile Bob and Paul went over to the main terminal where air traffic control and the weather office were located. They found the weather office first, walked in and Paul introduced himself. Meteorologists were always glad to share their given profession with each other and Paul perked up as his Chilean counterpart introduced himself. Jose Jimenez was a forecaster with the weather service, a man of small stature but lean and fit. Not too many people in Punta Arenas were overweight as the harsh environment and available food kept them that way. This was a result of the requirement to ship in much of the food as the harsh environment prevented the natives from growing a wide variety. Paul briefed Jose on where they were going and what the mission would be. They poured over the current weather and latest forecasts for the Antarctic Peninsula. Palmer was a normal reporting station on their net. The current weather was a low overcast with visibility restricted due to blowing snow, temperature 28°F with winds out of the southwest at 35mph gusting to 50mph. The forecast called for the low pressure area producing this weather to remain in the area of Palmer for another 24-36 hours then improving slightly with higher ceilings, greater visibility and winds diminishing. They would need ceilings above 3500' to carry out the mission since Palmer had no navigational aids and no instrument radio procedures were available at Palmer. Islands with low mountains stuck up everywhere around Palmer and radar descent and visual approach were a must to do it safely. Bob pointed out that they were in no hurry and could wait for good weather to attempt to complete this mission. Jose pointed out that 48 hours looked like a good weather window to attempt the mission. After 48 hours the forecast was calling for high scattered clouds, visibility better that 10 miles and winds out of the East at 10 mph. Paul reserved his assessment and stated he would need to talk directly with Palmer before committing to weather go. Paul and Bob thanked Jose and set out to find the Air Traffic Control (ATC) office for Chile's Flight Information Region (FIR). They stopped to ask and were directed to the building just below the airport control tower. The building housed local approach control as well as the FIR communication's center. They entered the building and just inside a sign on the wall directed them to the 2nd floor where the FIR communications center was located. As they entered the room they observed a large magnetic map which was ceiling height where flights were tracked through the FIR. Bob noticed that their area of responsibility ended at 60° south. Once again they introduced themselves and explained where they were headed. Hans Berkstcher, a German immigrant, was the manager and he welcomed them into his control center. He spoke perfect English as well as Spanish, they presumed, as that was the official language of Chile. Of course English was the official language required by the International Civilian Aviation Organization (ICAO). The Navy men explained what their flight plan would be, and elapsed times enroute and delays so Hans's organization could keep track of them within his area of responsibility. Bob and Hans exchanged HF frequencies so that all planes could communicate if necessary with the FIR controllers. Pete Vernon's crew would have this responsibility for most of the mission. With their business complete Bob and Paul departed and returned to the Fixed Base Operations. It had taken them the better part of two hours. Pete was already there and Larry and the flight engineers were in the pilot's lounge drinking coffee. Pete, Bob and Paul joined Larry in the lounge.

"What did you find out, Pete? Asked Bob.

"I located the bonding company's office in the third hangar down from here. Their bonded warehouse is located in town, down on the waterfront. They called downtown and located our cargo and can have it out here for us on four hours notice but remember that notice would have to be given during normal working hours, 8:00a.m. to 4:00p.m., local time," Pete responded.

Bob began, "Paul and I received a weather briefing on Palmer forecast and enroute weather. It's Monday and looks like we have a go for Wednesday morning. We also visited the Chilean FIR Communications center and briefed them on our proposed flight plan. We copied the primary and secondary HF frequencies, which we can use for our flight. What did you find, Larry?" Bob asked.

"Bob. We inspected all aircraft and found no maintenance discrepancies. All survival gear is in place and secured. We each have two sets of JATO (Jet assisted take-off) bottles; our aircraft have parachutes for a direct airdrop or for a LAPES (Low altitude parachute extractions system) extraction as a backup and three cargo pallets compatible to the aircraft rail system. Pete has a SAR (Search and Rescue) kit on board, one set of JATO in case of an emergency on the ice. All aircraft have ½ dozen red smoke flares for use in case of airdrop. We checked out all aircrafts' HF radios so we can use any one of them to attempt to contact Palmer Station."

"Great work, Larry," Bob replied. "Let's go out to 917 and see if we can contact Palmer. Pete you're welcome to go with us or stay here and we'll be back in about ½ hour."

"I think I'll just stay here and drink some coffee," said Pete.

With that Bob, Larry and the two flight engineers asked the FBO to take them out on the ramp to LC-130 #917.

Bob, Paul and Larry climbed the entry steps and went up into the cockpit and occupied the pilot's seats with Paul in the navigator's station. Senior Chief Randall and Petty Officer Glennon followed them. Randall had Glennon take the flight engineers seat. Bob instructed Glennon to get electrical power on the aircraft. Glennon started the Auxiliary power unit and brought the bleed air driven alternator on line. The aircraft jumped to life with all electrical busses powered up. Larry turned on both HF transceivers and tuned them to the primary and secondary frequencies of Palmer Station. There was already some chatter on the net with McMurdo and South Pole Stations joining in the chatter with Palmer. With a short break in the transmissions Larry keyed his microphone and called Palmer.

"Palmer Station this is Navy Aircraft 50917 do you read, over." After a pause of 10 seconds with no response he tried once again.

"Palmer Station this is Navy Aircraft 50917 do you read, over"

Immediately after releasing the key they heard, "Navy 50917 this is Palmer read you loud and clear, over."

Bob then keyed his mike and asked to speak to the Officer-in-Charge. Lieutenant Junior Grade Lud MacKay came up on the frequency and indicated he and his staff were standing by for a communications conference. He also had invited Lieutenant Russ Parker, Officer-in-Charge of the pararescue team, to listen in on the conference. Bob briefed the Palmer crew on the schedule of events detailing all activities, which would need to be carried out before, during and after aircraft operations at Palmer. Bob asked for the ice runway to be marked with smoke pots every 2 thousand feet for a length of at least 6000'. He indicated that the aircraft pallets should be unloaded while still on the aircraft and reloaded with outgoing cargo and mail as necessary. Paul Eskew asked for the station meteorologist to give them a rundown on the current weather and the forecast. Aerographers mate Jason Matthew confirmed the weather and forecast that Jose Jiminez had briefed them in the Punta Arenas weather bureau. Jason added that with the strong wind they had out of the Southwest the sea ice had appeared to shift slightly and might be a little rough on landing. Bob told the station personnel that the forecast wind would be out of the northeast and planned landing was to the east-northeast. That would put them closer to the shore and the station. Lieutenant Junior Grade MacKay indicated that the grid heading of the runway layout had been determined to be grid 050°. Just before signoff Lieutenant Russ Parker came on and with anticipated enthusiasm told the pilots that they were really looking forward to getting home. It had been almost nine months since they had deployed with the squadron and were getting mighty homesick. Bob tried to assure them they would be on their way soon. Bob and Larry signed off, shut down the HF radios and instructed the flight engineers to secure the aircraft. After that task was completed they hopped into the ramp vehicle and made their way back to the FBO where Pete was waiting for them. The hotel's bus had been standing all day and they piled in for the ride back to town and the hotel.

6

"A Change in Plans"

Punta Arenas, Chile: Four years earlier

The embassy in Santiago had called the hotel while the Aircraft Commanders had been at the airport. The embassy indicated that their plane would deliver the cargo destined for Palmer station to Punta Arenas about noon on Tuesday. The duty officer reported that to Bob on his arrival back at the hotel from the airport. Bob told the duty officer to ensure that all-hands were notified that there would be a meeting in the dining room at 9:00am Tuesday.

Tuesday Morning

Most everyone from this detachment was in the dining room by 8:00am having breakfast to be ready for the 9:00am meeting. At 9:00am Bob rose to conduct the briefing for the meeting. He outlined the plans for the day. Bill Grammercy would meet with the navigators in the hotel where they would plan the flight. He would review the procedures to be used for grid navigation and decide where they would switch from magnetic to grid. Pete Vernon was directed to contact the bonding company and arrange for delivery of the cargo to the aircraft during the afternoon. The aircraft commanders would be at the aircraft to supervise whatever needed to be done. They would load cargo, meet the embassy aircraft from Santiago and transfer the cargo to the Hercs. The Flight engineers would refuel the aircraft and assist the loadmasters and scanners where necessary. He asked the copilots to visit the FIR center and make themselves knowledgeable on the flight procedures and frequencies. A personal touch with the controllers would always help the mission go smoother. He also instructed them to check with the airlines to see if they could get twenty-eight in-flight lunches. If so, some crewmembers would pick them up before 7:00am Wednesday.

Bob decided they should arrive at the airport before 11:00am have lunch and then be available to meet the embassy aircraft due to arrive about 12 noon. Paul Eskew would request weather-briefing folders for all the aircraft from the airport weather office. Bob concluded the briefing and asked it there were any questions.

Mike Brenner, 917 copilot, raised his hand. "Will we need to clear customs and immigration on our return from Palmer?" He continued without waiting for an answer. "If so we will probably need to take our passports with us since we are not checking out of the hotel."

Bob responded. "Mike, that's a great question. Why don't you inquire at their offices at the airport when you all are visiting the FIR communications center."

"Any more questions?" Bob asked. "We'll meet in the lobby at 10:30am to go to the airport."

All-hands departed the dining room to prepare for the afternoons activities.

The crewmembers gathered in the lobby just before 10:30.am for departure to the airport. Bill Grammercy cornered Paul Eskew and asked that he relay the forecast winds enroute for the flight back to him at the hotel so his navigators could apply them to their flight plan. Paul said he would, as soon as he had a handle on them at the weather office.

Two shuttle busses pulled up in front of the hotel one from the Los Navegantes Hotel and the Best Western shuttle. Los Navegantes had agreed to let the crews use the shuttle as long as they were in Punta Arenas. Bob Avery, in turn, had agreed to keep the gas tanks full while they were there. The crews piled into the busses and they departed for the airport. On arrival the crews entered the airport terminal and found a small deli where they were able to get a sandwich and a drink. There were a few passengers waiting for flights but for the most part the terminal was quiet since the tourist season was over for the year. After partaking of lunch the groups divided and went their separate ways to complete their assigned tasks. Most went over to the FBO. The flight engineers, loadmasters, scanners and pilots procured transportation out to the aircraft waiting for the embassy plane to arrive from Santiago.

At about 12:15pm a turboprop equipped Twin Otter appeared on final for runway 25. That would be the embassy flight they were waiting for. After landing, the aircraft was directed to taxi over to the LC-130s on the ramp. After shutdown the pilots exited the aircraft and low and behold they were old friends of Larry Beck. Ralph Touch and Bill Marsh had both served together with Larry as flight instructors at Naval Air Station Corpus Christi, Texas, in the early '80s. They greeted each other as old friends and Larry introduced them to Bob and Pete. Pleasantries were exchanged all around and Bob and Ralph discussed the transfer of cargo to the Hercs. The two hercs scheduled to land at Palmer were already powered up with their cargo ramps in the down position and were ready for loading. The FBO had provided a small luggage vehicle, which was backed up to the Otter and the process of off loading commenced. Larry suggested they go over to the pilots lounge at the FBO and relax while the off loading was taking place. Ralph and Bill could also file their return trip to Santiago from there. Bob talked with Chief Randall for a minute and then they all departed in the crew bus for the FBO. It was only ½ mile but the Chilean Air Force, which shared the airport, preferred unauthorized personnel not wander around the ramp unescorted. The pilots all had a cup of coffee in the lounge and Bill Marsh filed a flight plan for their return to Santiago. After about an hour Chief Randall sent word that the Otter was unloaded and ready for departure. They all went back out on the crew bus to the aircraft. Ralph and Bill said their goodbyes, and climbed into the Otter and in short order departed the ramp for their return trip. Bob, Larry and Pete inspected the cargo in #321 and #319. The mail was in #319 and the produce in #321. That left two pallets for the cargo yet to be delivered from the bonding company. Pete had called them early that morning and delivery was promised by 2:00pm. It was nearly that time so they just relaxed and waited for the cargo to arrive.

Shortly a large 8 x 8 truck approached flying a ramp flag. The markings on the side of the cab confirmed that it was from the bonding company. The crew had him back up to Herc #319 where they began off-loading part of the cargo. When they had about half of the cargo on #319 they moved over to Herc#321 and loaded the remainder of the cargo on the remaining two pallets. All-hands helped in this evolution and then the loadmasters took over and secured the cargo on the pallets. About that time a fuel tanker, loaded with JP1, arrived on the scene where Glennon directed them to the starboard side of the first aircraft, just aft of the wing where the refueling panel was located. Ensuring that the aircraft was grounded he began refueling the first aircraft. When finished they moved to the next aircraft where the same procedure was completed and finally the third aircraft was refueled.

While all this was taking place the copilots were busy visiting with the controllers in the FIR control center. They briefed them on their route of flight, time enroute and return information. The controllers were pleased that the copilots would take the time to visit with them. Having finished their visit the copilots went down into the terminal and went to find the catering manager for American Airlines to inquire about in-flight lunches. They were directed to the manager's office and were finally introduced to Macaria Alarcon. She was an immigrant from the Philippines who was a 19-year employee of American Airlines. The copilots layed out the situation and Macaria agreed to provide twenty-eight in-flight lunches and to fill the coffee containers from the C-130s galley. They agreed on a price of $5.00US per lunch and she said they could pay when they picked them up the next morning.

Mike Brenner told the other copilots that if they wanted to go over to the FBO to go ahead as he still needed to check with customs and immigration about clearance on their return to Punta Arenas. Charlie Black said he would accompany Mike, so the two of them took off to find the customs and immigration offices. It was located on one end of the terminal concourse and was easy to find.

Upon entering the office Mike identified himself and asked to speak to the supervisor. One of the agents told him to wait and he would announce him with the supervisor. Shortly, Mike and Charlie were ushered into the supervisor's office. Mike described the situation and also explained that they were bringing back eight members of the squadron who were all U.S. citizens but were stranded at Palmer Station without clothes or identification papers. The supervisor advised them that when they arrived back from Palmer that his office would work with them and iron out the details but they would be admitted into the country on a temporary basis. He also told them that all crewmembers would be required to produce their passports. Having finished their assigned tasks they wandered down to the FBO to meet with everyone else to go back to the hotel.

Paul Eskew had spent the two hours he had with Jose in the weather center. They had discussed the forecast enroute and destination weather. Paul also asked about the forecast for Seymour Island where the Hercs were planning on refueling. When he had first arrived he was briefed on the enroute winds and had called them back to the hotel so the navigators could finish their flight planning. Jose promised flight folders would be available for all aircraft upon their arrival at the airport in the morning. Paul said he would pick them up around 7:30am. He thanked Jose for the great afternoon and departed for the FBO to catch the bus.

With all-hands accounted for, the crews piled on the busses and during the twenty-five mile trip back to the city they exchanged the information each had gleaned during their time at the airport.

Some of the officers decided to have dinner out and settled on the Beagle Restaurant. The Beagle specialized in barbeque, Chilean and seafood and that seemed to be okay with everyone.

About 6:30pm Bob, Larry, Pete, Bill Grammercy and Bill Springer gathered in the lobby of the hotel. The hailed two taxis and departed for the Beagle. It was a short drive and on arrival they stood in front of the restaurant and just took in the architecture. What stood out was the white stucco building with a brightly colored red roof. They quickly went inside as the temperature on the street was dropping rapidly and the chill in the night air was quite brisk.

Once inside Bill Grammercy spoke to the Maître-d' and asked for a table for five. They were seated in a booth near a sidewall in a restaurant that would hold approximately eighty people when full but being the off-season there were only twelve people currently in the room not including the staff.

A perky middle-aged waitress appeared and introduced herself in Spanish. Bill Springer being from south Texas was quite fluent in the language and responded. He was the designated translator for the night and so this group of young American naval officers got along quite well in coping with the language barrier. They started off with a round of drinks and whiled away the time talking about the upcoming mission the next morning. There was no doubt amongst them and no fear but that the mission would be successful. They were confident in their abilities and all had been trained to deal with any adversity which may arise.

Bill passed on the order of food to the waitress which all had decided on while consuming their adult beverages. Bob Avery and Larry Beck had decided on the seafood while Bill Gammercy and Bill Springer were trying the barbeque. Pete, however, had settled on a local Chilean dish made from pork.

After consuming their dinner and while lingering over their coffee they all agreed that the food was delicious and with a par to most American restaurants. While still discussing the next day's activities, Bob Avery began complaining about severe pains in his lower right abdomen. In the space of an hour he was now almost doubled over in pain and it had gotten worse. He told his companions that it was isolated to that one area and he got up to try to walk it off. As he did he collapsed on the floor of the Beagle restaurant. His companions rushed over to assist him. Larry Beck picked him up and sat him on the nearest chair. When he touched his skin he realized Bob has a very high body temperature and that something was seriously wrong. The staff of the Beagle also rushed over to see what was wrong. Bill Springer was invaluable at this point. Speaking in Spanish, he directed the manager to call a taxi so they could take Bob to the hospital as quickly as possible. A taxi arrived in short order and Bill along with Larry put Bob into the vehicle and Bill told the driver to get to the nearest hospital ASAP. The driver drove them to the Naval Cirujano Guzmán Hospital, which was just a few blocks away. They arrived at the emergency room and Larry practically carried Bob inside. The hospital staff wheeled Bob into a cubicle and then asked what were the symptoms. Bill in his best Spanish told them of the severe pain in the lower right quadrant of the abdomen and of the high fever. The staff already knew about the high fever as they had already taken his temperature. The doctor on duty came in and examined Bob and after a short time turned to Bill and told him that Bob had acute appendicitis and needed an immediate operation. Bill consulted with Larry, who at the time was busy trying to get the appropriate information to the person registering patients for admission. He spoke no Spanish and the other person spoke very little English. Larry consulted with Bob who was slightly incoherent but both agreed that they should go ahead and operate. After a short delay for paperwork with Larry helping Bob, he signed the release papers allowing the hospital staff to perform the surgery.

Within minutes they wheeled Bob into pre-op to get him ready for the surgery. Bill accompanied Bob acting as his interpreter. Larry waited in the designated waiting room. Meanwhile Pete and Bill Grammercy had proceeded back towards the hotel. During the ride they discussed the mission. They decided a discussion with Larry was in order before they could come to a conclusion on what should be done. They directed their driver to divert to the Naval Cirujano Guzmán Hospital. After arrival and some wandering they found Larry in the waiting room. Larry brought them up to speed on events and what the current situation was. A discussion was held on whether the mission should go or no go the next morning. A consensus was reached that the mission should be delayed for at least one day but should go forward. Bob Avery's participation was out of the question so the next problem was who could replace Bob flying 321 as aircraft commander. The name of Mike Brenner was bandied about. He was a well-qualified 1st pilot and had almost completed his aircraft commander training. The three determined that Mike should replace Bob as the aircraft commander. Next was the method on how to carry out the mission. They could not ask Mike to do the same job Bob was slated to do which meant there would have to be a reassignment of tasks. Bill Grammercy told the group he would take care of notifying the detachment personnel so he left the room to try to locate a telephone. At the main information desk in the hospital lobby he was able to commandeer the phone. He dialed the hotel and asked for Lieutenant Joe Rogers. Joe was the duty officer. The hotel rang his room and shortly he answered. Bill briefed him on the events of the evening and told him to notify all personnel about the delay and that a meeting would be held in the dining room of the hotel at 10:00am the next morning. He hung up and returned to the waiting room.

Two hours had passed since they had taken Bob to pre-op. The surgeon appeared in the door with Bill Springer at his side. He briefed them on the results of the surgery through Bill doing the translation. The bottom line was that Bob had come through the operation with flying colors and was in recovery and resting quite comfortably. The surgeon indicated they could see Bob in about a half hour and would be called in by the recovery room nurse.

The surgeon departed and Bill Springer sat down after drawing a cup of coffee. He was exhausted and needed a break. Pete told those assembled that Bill should act as liaison for Bob with the hospital and should not go on the mission. Bill Grammercy volunteered his 2nd navigator to replace Bill Springer on his crew and he would navigate by himself on his crew. They decided that all the details could be worked out over breakfast and the detachment personnel briefed at the 10:00am briefing. They also decided that only Larry should visit Bob before they left for the hotel. Finally the nurse came in and told Bill Springer that they could visit Bob for a short time. Larry went into the recovery room and saw Bob for just a few minutes. He was still a little groggy from the anesthetic but indicated to Larry that he was concerned about the mission. Larry assured him that everything was under control and that Bill Springer would brief him the next day. He told him to try to rest and that everything would work out just fine. With that he squeezed his hand and told him to take care. Larry rejoined his companions and after briefing them on Bob's concerns and condition they departed for the hotel.

7

"Disaster"

Punta Arenas: The next morning

Dawn had not even broken yet over the city when most of the detachment personnel were already milling around the hotel lobby awaiting the dining room to open for breakfast. Rumors had been spreading all morning about what had delayed the mission. Larry, Pete, Bill Grammercy and Bill Springer came in to the dining room about 8:30am having gotten to bed about 1:00am. They knew the rumors would be flying but felt that they could calm them all at the 10:00am briefing. During breakfast Paul Eskew came over and asked what they wanted to do about the weather folders being made up today's flight. Larry, who was now the mission commander, told Paul to cancel the weather folders for today but to get a briefing on tomorrow's weather and be prepared to give the flight crews an updated briefing at the 10:00am meeting. Paul acknowledged and left the dining room to take care of Larry's request.

Much coffee was being consumed after breakfast. Larry, Pete and Bill Grammercy discussed the crew changes and other aspects of what neeeded to be done to meet the mission requirements for the next day.

The 10:00 o'clock hour approached and all hands were getting anxious. Finally at 9:51am Larry stood and called for the room to be quiet. Immediately all hands stopped what they were doing and sat up to listen.

Larry began, "Good morning, men. Last night after a fine dinner at the Beagle restaurant, Lieutenant Commander Bob Avery was stricken with acute appendicitis and was taken to Naval Cirujano Guzmán Hospital where his appendix was safely removed at about 10:30pm. Some of us where there and when we left him he was in recovery and doing just fine. He is lost to us for this mission so I have assumed the duties of mission commander. Lieutenant Springer, who you all know speaks Spanish, is assigned to be our liaison officer with the hospital for the remainder of our stay in Punta Arenas. If there are no specific questions concerning Lieutenant Commander Avery I will proceed with the new mission briefing."

Petty Officer Rodman raised his hand and asked, "Sir, will he be seeing any visitors today?"

"As far as I know, Rod, he can have visitors most anytime." Larry answered.

"Any more questions?" Larry asked.

"Okay then, here are some of the revised details for the mission. First new crew assignments. Lieutenant Mike Brenner will take over as aircraft commander of crew 321. Lieutenant Commander Grammercy will go to Commander Vernon's crew as 1st navigator and Lieutenant Junior Grade Dick Beers will take his slot with Lieutenant Brenner's crew as 2nd navigator. Lieutenant Tom Harger will move up to 1st navigator in that crew. My crew will still fly aircraft #319 Commander Vernon will take Aircraft #321 and Lieutenant Brenner will pilot #917. Commander Vernon and I will make the landings on the sea ice off Palmer Station while Lieutenant Brenner will act as Search and Rescue and communications relay for the mission. Commander Vernon and I will monitor Palmer Station on 4755khz and McMurdo Center on 15,250khz on our high frequency transceivers. Lieutenant Brenner will monitor Chilean Flight Information on 6535khz and Palmer Station on 4755khz. Aircraft 319 and 321 will relay all position reports to Lieutenant Brenner who in turn will pass them to Chilean FIR control. 321 and 319 will communicate interplane on squadron common Ultra High Frequency (UHF) 315.6mhz.

"We expect to spend minimum time on the ice off Palmer Station. We should have enough fuel on board to make the round trip without refueling but if needed we can still land at Seymour Island and take on enough fuel to return to Punta Arenas. Take off time will be 8:30am local time tomorrow with the other two aircraft to follow shortly thereafter. Mike, how about you arranging once again for the in-flight lunches. You can take a government voucher and pay for today and tomorrow's lunches all at one time. I am sure American Airlines will want it that way. Lieutenant Eskew is currently getting a briefing on tomorrow's weather and arranging for weather folders for all three aircraft. He will be back in here shortly and give us that brief. Commander Vernon will be working on advising the squadron and Task Force Forty-Three of the recent developments and the projected new dates and times for the mission. I will be working with the local airport people and the FBO coordinating our new departure and arrival times. Mike while I think of it, contact Customs and notify them of our new plan and indicate that we will arrive back here around 1730 local time tomorrow evening."

"Lieutenant Harger, how about you liaise with the Flight Information controllers today and brief them of our intended flight times."

Lieutenant Harger responded with, "That's a roger sir."

Mike Brenner acknowledged and gave Larry a thumbs up.

Larry turned to Pete and asked him if he had anything to add to the briefing.

Commander Vernon stood up and reminded all-hands to be sure to pick up their passports from the front desk before departing the hotel in the morning, as they would be needed to show to the immigration people upon arrival back in the country.

Paul Eskew had reentered the room and Larry turned to him and asked for the weather briefing for the next day.

Paul began, "Weather enroute to Palmer forecast to be stratus layers up to 21,000'. Temperature at expected flight altitude of 10,000' forecast to be 15°F with medium to heavy snow in clouds. We will have to transit through the area of low pressure, which is sitting a few hundred miles northwest of Palmer Station. It is affecting the Palmer weather but forecast for Palmer at ETA expected to be better than 3500' broken, with higher overcast. Visibility 10 miles and winds, grid 070 at

10 to 15 miles per hour. They have had improving ceilings all day and night for the past fourteen hours with the trend the same. I have the winds for the navigators at cruising altitude for flight planning purposes. Are there any questions?"

No one raised a hand.

Larry stood up and spoke. "Everyone has their assignments for today. Does anyone have anything further to add?" Larry glanced around the room. No one seemed to have a question or comment but he espied Bill Springer, who had just reentered the room.

"Bill, would you like to give us an update on Lieutenant Commander Avery?" Larry asked.

Bill walked up front and began. "Lieutenant Commander Avery is out of intensive care and is doing just fine. He has been transferred to Room 125, has had a light breakfast and has been asking questions about the mission since he got out of intensive care. I am sure he would welcome visitors today so I have set up a small bus to take any of you who wish to go, leaving the hotel around 1:00pm this afternoon." With that he nodded to Larry indicating he was finished.

Larry asked if anyone was interested and about six members of the crew indicated they would be interested.

"Bill," said Larry. "Commander Vernon and I will visit Lieutenant Commander Avery this evening so please tell him that and also that I will brief him on the mission when I get there and not to worry, everything is progressing just fine."

Bill acknowledged.

Larry concluded the meeting and dismissed everyone but not before indicating that a bus would be available around 11:15am for departure for the airport for those needing to go to complete their assigned tasks.

Commander Vernon proceeded to the business center in the hotel to send an email to advise the squadron and Task Force Forty-Three of the new plans for the mission. A few of the officers and men stuck around the dining room and ordered another pot of coffee. Just a little time to kill and chat about things in general.

11:15 arrived and a small group gathered outside the main entrance to board the bus for the ride to the airport. It arrived in short order and all hands climbed aboard. It was a routine ride to the airport, as they were becoming old hands at this particular evolution. After arrival each man went about his business like a well-oiled machine and within an hour had completed their tasks. They had agreed to meet at 12:45pm at the main terminal for lunch. After lunch they once again boarded the small bus bound for the hotel.

The members of the detachment spent the remainder of the afternoon relaxing. Some of the junior officers had started a bridge game while the enlisted personnel had broken out an acey-ducey board and were hard at knocking each other off the board.

Larry, Pete, Bill Grammercy, Bill Springer and Tom Harger had dinner early at the Rosita Conchita restaurant and then proceeded to the hospital to visit Bob Avery. The city was quiet with few people stirring. Sunset had occurred around 3:30pm this dark winter day. There had been light snow falling all day but not enough to cause any kind of traffic problems. They had the 10-passenger bus standing by which they boarded and took off for the hospital. Upon arrival they walked into the main entrance where Bill Springer greeted the receptionist in Spanish telling her they were going down to Bob Avery's room for a short visit. She smiled and reminded them that visiting hours ended at 9:00pm. It was a short walk to room 125 where they found Bob sitting up in a chair having just finished his dinner.

Bill Grammercy spoke first. "Nice job here, Bob?" He asked. "I guess you were born for goldbricken' just sittin' here relaxin' having people wait on you."

Bob took it in fun as it was intended and responded, "Yeah, Bill, only thing is I have to get out of bed to eat and go to the head."

With that each man present shook his hand and offered a short comment that he was looking good and asked how he was feeling. Larry was the last to greet him and they both looked at each other knowing just what each was thinking.

Larry started, "Yeah, I now you are worried about the mission but remember your job is to get better so we can take you back home with us when we get ready to depart this burg. As for the mission we made a few changes with Mike Brenner taking over your crew. He is well qualified and he will fly 917. Pete here is taking 321 and he and I are going to make the landings on the ice off Palmer Station. All the details have been taken care of and aircraft are loaded and ready to go. We are set to go at 8:30am tomorrow."

Bob responded, "Larry, I know the mission is in good hands with you in charge, I just hope everything goes smooth tomorrow. I look forward to hearing from you tomorrow evening after you get back."

Bill Grammercy chimed in, "I know, Bob, you don't know how we will do it without you but you taught us well and we can handle it."

"I have all the confidence in the world in you guys. I just worry about your safety. You know how the Antarctic can jump up and bite you in the ass once in a while," Bob answered.

Pete Vernon broke into the conversation. "Bob, I notified the squadron of your predicament and all the changes necessary to carry out the mission. I presume they have notified your family and are awaiting further word. I gave them the phone number of the hospital but it may be hard to get a call through to this isolated place. When I get back to the hotel I will send them an update and try to keep the worry factor to a minimum."

"Thanks, Pete," said Bob.

The group passed the next half hour with the usual naval aviator banter just trying to keep Bob's spirits high. Finally Larry indicated that it was time to leave and get back to the hotel and get some sleep. He reminded them they had a big day tomorrow. With that they all once again shook Bob's hand and wished him a speedy recovery and departed. The bus took them back to the hotel where they bid each other a goodnight and headed for their respective rooms for a good nights sleep.

The Mission

Morning came early for the enlisted crews. They were up and having breakfast by 5:30am. The hotel had been good enough to serve them early. They were already boarding the bus when the officers came down and entered the dining room. Larry stopped and talked with Master Chief Randall just before he boarded the bus. He told Randall they would be at the airport by 7:00am, file their flight plans and be at the aircraft by 7:30am for their scheduled 8:30am departure. Randall confirmed that all the men had their passport before departing for the airport. The FBO had been notified of their departure time and were going to provide ramp transportation as necessary. All officers were finished with breakfast, retrieved their passports, gathered their flight gear and were ready for departure to the airport by 6:30am.

Upon arrival Mike Brenner double-checked on the in-flight lunches and American Airlines personnel assured them that they were in fact already on their way to being delivered to the aircraft. The navigators put the finishing touches on the flight plan, plugging in the enroute winds and filling out the ICAO flight plan paper work. Pete suggested to Larry that only the aircraft commanders, 1st co-pilots and 1st navigators in addition to Paul Eskew attend the weather briefing. He figured ten people crowding into the weather office would be sufficient. He was correct, ten people barely made it into the small office. The Chilean weatherman greeted Paul as he entered, gave him the flight folders, which he in turn distributed to the aircraft commanders.

Paul then commenced his briefing. Current Punta Arenas weather was 1200' overcast, visibility ½ mile in fog, temperature 34°F, and altimeter 29.45 in of mercury. Winds were out of the southwest at 2 mph. Enroute weather expected to be layers up to 21,000' with in-flight conditions IFR at 10,000' snow showers in the clouds. Approaching Palmer Station some clearing was expected with scattered layers down to 3500', visibility 10 miles, temperature 29°F, winds grid 070° at 10 gusting to 15 mph, altimeter 29.38 in of mercury.

Larry asked if there were any questions. Everyone was satisfied so they went into the Chilean Flight Service office to file their flight plans. Tom Harger confirmed with the controllers that they would use 6535khz as the primary frequency and 8655khz as the backup.

Having completed their task they proceeded over to the FBO for transport to the aircraft. On the way Larry reminded the aircraft commanders that they were operating on JP1 and their expected performance would not be what they were used to with JP4. Co-pilots were reminded to double-check their takeoff performance data using JP1.

Everything and everyone were now in a serious mode and had on their game day faces. Each crewmember went about their assigned duties with professional precision. The flight engineers had completed all their preflight checks; aircraft was heated and powered up ready for engine start. Loadmaster reported that pallets were locked in the rail system, cargo was secured and in-flight lunches were aboard. The copilots completed their external preflight while aircraft commanders carried out the internal preflight checks. Navigators were already in the cockpit checking out their navigation instrumentation and high frequency radios. UHF radio was set to channel 14, squadron common, 315.6 MHz.

All-hands manned their positions in preparation for engine start. The before starting engines checklist was completed. Larry Beck called 321 and 917 for a radio check. Both responded and reported ready to start engines. Larry then called for the "Start Engines Checklist." Copilot Charlie Black began reading the checklist and in short order all engines were started and operating normaly. Shortly thereafter 321 and 917 reported ready to taxi. Charlie acknowledged the transmissions and Larry told him to direct the other aircraft to switch to ground control frequency 121.9mhz. Charlie responded as directed, switched the VHF to ground control and keyed the mike.

"Ibanez ground Navy 48319 request taxi for three, over."

Ground responded, "Navy 48319 cleared to taxi runway 25, winds 240 at 2 mph, altimeter 29.45" hg."

"Roger ground runway 25 and your altimeter 29.45" hg.

Larry reached the approach end of runway 25, set the brakes and went through his engine check. After completing the check he called for Charlie to request clearance.

"Ibanez Ground, Navy 48319 requesting clearance."

"Roger Navy 48319, you are cleared to the Ibanez Airport via 64°54' south, 64°45' west. After takeoff, passing 1500' turn left to 155° intercept 175° radial of the Punta Arenas VOR, climb to and maintain 10,000' contact Punta Arenas departure control on 128.9mhz."

Charlie read back the clearance; ground acknowledged and directed 319 to switch to Ibanez Tower on 118.7mhz.

Hercs 321 and 917 checked in and reported ready for takeoff.

Charlie switched to tower, "Ibanez Tower Navy 48319 ready for takeoff."

"Navy 48319 is cleared for takeoff. When airborne switch to departure control on 128.9 MHz"

Charlie rogered as Larry taxied onto the runway. Full power was added, brakes released and takeoff roll started. Charlie backed him up on the power levers while Larry released the nose steering wheel. Charlie called out V1 as they passed reject speed then V2 and the reached liftoff speed. They used up 7900' of the 9154' available. Larry called for gear up, then flaps up as they were passing 750'. Charlie indicated to Larry he was switching to departure control. He called departure control, reported airborne passing 1000' for 10,000'. Departure control responded with "radar contact, upon reaching 1500' cleared left turn to heading 155° to proceed on course." Charlie acknowledged and Larry called for "After Takeoff/Climb Checklist." It was competed in short order and at 1500' Larry turned left to heading 155°. Charlie verified the VOR station set to 114.1mhz and identified as call letters "NAS."

Herc 321 followed five minutes later with Herc 917 as tail end Charlie six minutes later.

All three aircraft settled down cruising at 10,000' and departure control turned them over to flight following with the Chilean Flight Information Regional Center. They all reported passing 100 miles out of Punta Arenas. Herc 917 took over the communications watch on 6535khz. In-flight conditions were fairly smooth with lots of frozen precipitation in the clouds and multiple layers of stratus clouds. Things went normally and all aircraft reported leaving the FIR about 1-1/2 hours out of Punta Arenas. Herc 917 proceeded another 50 miles and then took up an orbiting position while 319 and 321 continued on to Palmer station. As they approached within 100 miles of Palmer the weather began to improve as Paul Eskew had forecast. Communications had been interesting since the flight began. As Mike Brenner had begun his orbit he was contacted by Collins Radio from their corporate headquarters in Cedar Rapids, Iowa, telling him that they were relaying all communications to the squadron in Point

Mugu, California. On the Palmer Station frequency, South Pole Station had checked in as well as McMurdo Station. Larry and Pete had also checked in with McMurdo Center. Deep Freeze Control in Christchurch, New Zealand, chimed in and indicated they were relaying all information to Task Force Forty-Three as well as the communications center at the National Science Foundation. Seems like everybody and his brother was interested in this mission. At seventy-five miles out of Palmer, Larry began his descent with Pete following as he passed seventy-five miles out. Palmer passed the weather, which was just as Paul had forecast with the altimeter of 29.38' HG. Larry's crew began seeing the ice surface intermittently passing 5000' and broke out below all clouds at 3800'. He leveled at 3500'. Ivan Wheaton reported his radar was working and he had the Antarctic Peninsula on his scope. Pete reported to Larry that he was also level at 3500' and was about twenty miles behind him. At fifty miles Ivan reported he had Anvers Island on his scope. Larry instructed Pete to switch to 243.0 MHz. They would try to communicate with the pararescue team, as it was the emergency frequency on their survival radios. The O-in-C Lieutenant Junior Grade MacKay had indicated they would set up at the shoreward end of the ice runway they had laid out and try that frequency. Charlie Black keyed the mike,

"Pararescue this is 48319 do you read, over?"

Weak but clear 319 heard a response, "319 this is Pararescue how do your read? Over."

Charlie confirmed they could read them weak but clear. Team leader Lieutenant Russ Parker came on and confirmed the weather with winds grid at 070° at 10 gusts to 15 mph. He also indicated that they would light the fires in the 55-gallon drums marking the limits of the runway they had laid out. He confirmed with Charlie that they had 6000' of clear smooth ice runway and a safe wheeled landing could be made. He reported that, during the storm which had just passed, the ice had showed signs of some cracking but thickness remained in the safe range. The runway was oriented on a grid heading of 050°, which he passed to Pete and Larry.

They had stationed themselves at the end of the runway on the south side with one pickup and two larger trucks to put cargo, mail and veggies on board. There were the six members of the team, Lieutenant Junior Grade MacKay and two other petty officers in the pickup with about four people each in the larger trucks.

As Larry approached nineteen miles out some of his crew spotted the smoke from the fires marking the runway in their 11 o'clock position. Larry indicated to his crew that they would make a low pass up the right side of the runway just to double check conditions and ensure everything was in order for landing. The crew was not surprised by Larry's decision. An overhead view was sometimes better than a surface view. This would also allow Pete to reach the area overheard to observe and advise as necessary before attempting landing himself. Pete checked in with Larry and they discussed how they would proceed. Pete rogered, descending to 2000', while Larry descended to 500 feet over the ice. He made a wide circle to the southwest turning left toward the east-northeast while lining up parallel to and just to the right of the runway. Pete reported overhead. All-hands' eyes were on the runway and each in turn reported that everything in the landing area appeared good. Pete reported the same.

Larry's crew reported the before landing checklist complete. Larry turned downwind, climbed to 1000' and rolled out parallel to the runway. He called for flaps 10% and wheels down skis up. The landing checklist was completed and Charlie reported speeds at approach 121 knots, threshold 114 knots and touchdown at 105 knots. The air was smooth and on final at 3 miles Larry called for flaps 35%. He was now descending at 400-500' per minute, slowing to 114 knots. As he passed thirty feet at ¼ mile from the runway he slowed the aircraft to 105 knots. Touchdown was smooth but immediately the aircraft felt like it was still descending. Instantly over the UHF radio he heard Pete Vernon shouting in his mike, "WAVE OFF, WAVE OFF, WAVE OFF." Charlie had already started the flaps up to 10%. Larry's right hand exploded forward with the power levers in hand and calling over the intercom for max power. Charlie backed him up and stopped them at max turbine inlet temperature. The four Hamilton Standard propellers bit into the cold dense air clawing at it with a passion to accomplish their designed purpose. The Herc lurched forward with only one thing in mind, get some speed and altitude. Pete was still shouting over the UHF,

"Larry, the ice began breaking up as you touched down and a shock wave is moving toward the shore, if it bounces back there's going to be all hell breaking loose." Just as Larry got it airborne he spotted the wave coming back at him with the ice breaking up into large pieces, turning on edge, twisting and throwing debris in all directions. In fact Larry thought it looked like a 2000 pound bomb had gone off and this was the result. At that point a large chunk of ice broached and impacted the starboard ski and wheels.

Pete circling overhead couldn't believe what he was observing. As far as he could see in all directions, the ice was breaking up apparently from the wave Larry had started when he touched down. It was moving in an ever-increasing arc outward from the shore. First cracks then ice chunks broaching followed by water sprays from impact. He saw Larry getting airborne when his view was directed toward the trucks at the end of the runway. The two large ones were sliding towards an open lead in the ice and the pickup was already in the water up to the running boards. Apparently the large oversize tires were keeping it afloat. People were bailing out of the trucks in all directions. His attention was drawn back to Larry and he called 319 to see what their status was. Charlie reported they took one hell of an impact from the broaching ice but that the gear retracted normally and hydraulic pressure was normal. Larry discussed things with Pete and they decided Pete should join up and see if he could determine whether they had suffered any damage. Larry started a left turn and leveled at 1500'. Pete joined up on Larry, below and slightly aft of his starboard side. Shortly, Pete reported he could see some damage to the starboard ski and the rear tire punctured. He couldn't tell whether the front tire had sustained damage or not. They decided it best to proceed to Punta Arenas and abort the mission. An ice landing was now out of the question. Ivan called Palmer Station and advised them of the mission abort and asked for a status report of the people trapped on the ice. The station personnel had no idea about the status since all portable radios on the trucks had been lost and they could only report that they were launching a small boat to try to reach those stranded personnel. It would be a little time before that would know what the status was. They would call 319 when they had an update.

8

"Unforeseen Consequences"

On *the Ice at Palmer Station*

An AFV had been inbound to Siple Station after a mission collecting intelligence on the riots in South Africa. Ian Harrison had been monitoring the Palmer mission and radioed Lieutenant Bruce Fleming who was piloting the AFV and diverted him to make a couple of passes over Palmer to evaluate the situation.

Lieutenant Fleming reported back to Ian that there were people on the ice off the station and it looked like they were trying to rescue some of the people from the trucks, which appeared to be sinking.

On the ice there was furious action taking place. When the ice had started to break up the Pararescue team, which had been in the back of the pickup truck, jumped off and moved away from the vehicle. Lieutenant Junior Grade Mackay and the driver were just a microsecond behind and the delay in getting the doors open slowed them enough that the truck was settling into the water as they leapt from the truck. Both were now in the water and the pararescue team quickly sized up the situation and moved in to try to rescue them. Some of the team had grabbed their equipment as they jumped out of the truck and were now breaking out the climbing ropes they usually carried. They tossed the ropes to each of the survivors so they could grab them and be pulled from the water. The team tried some three times but each time they could not connect with the men in the water. Finally Chief McKenna told his group to tie the rope around his waist that he was going in after them. Likewise Petty Officer Jacob Spalding did the same. They both moved to the edge of the ice and slipped into the cold icy water. As they were moving toward the men in the water both slipped under the ice and disappeared from view. Chief McKenna dove twice under the ice but failed to locate Lieutenant Mackay. Petty Officer Spalding also dove under the ice. The third time he came up with Seaman Gorchinski in his grasp. The other members pulled them both from the icy water onto the ice. Chief McKenna wanted to dive again but the team pulled him from the water as he had been in it for about three minutes. Doc Kealey had immediately begun applying CPR to Seaman Gorchinski. Meanwhile the team searched their equipment to find something to help warm those who had been submerged in the icy water. They managed to come up with three space blankets, which they normally carried for rescues in the Antarctic. The men were wrapped in them and the team stopped to assess the situation. Doc Kealy continued to give CPR to Seaman Gorchinski. Lieutenant Parker was suddenly aware that the two large trucks, which had been with them, were no longer in sight and the four men in them had disappeared beneath the Antarctic ice.

Everybody on the communications net was frustrated because there was nothing they could do but wait. After a couple of minutes of chatter most every thing went quiet waiting for a report from Palmer Station.

Larry and Pete focused on the task at hand and were even now climbing back up to altitude and proceeding back towards Punta Arenas. Bill Grammercy contacted 917 with position reports and ETA entering the Chilean Flight Information Region. 917 in turn relayed this information to the controllers in Punta Arenas. As Larry and Pete passed Mike in 917, Mike fell in trail behind them at about one mile. They were all on squadron UHF common and Larry and Pete discussed arrival procedures at Punta Arenas. Arrival would be in the dark and Larry directed Pete and Mike to land first in case of trouble on landing with a flat tire and damaged ski. Mike descended 500' to 9,500' and accelerated to pass both Pete and Larry. They had each other on radar and when Mike reported passing Pete he dropped down to 9,500' and took up a position at one mile behind Mike. Larry stayed at 10,000' and trailed Pete by one mile.

Bill Grammercy made a call to Palmer Station in an attempt to get an update on the status of those personnel who had been thrown into the water as a result of Larry's attempted landing on the bay ice. He tried a number of times with no results. It appeared that Palmer was off the air temporarily. The flight crews were concerned because they knew a communications blackout usually meant disaster in the Antarctic.

As each aircraft passed one hundred miles out of Punta Arenas they contacted Approach Control. As Mike passed fifty miles Approach Control cleared him to descend to 5000'. Pete in turn was cleared to 6000' and Larry to 7000'. Approach control was advised of Larry's problem and requested type of assistance required. Larry had decided that a foamed runway would be in his best interest to avoid a fire in the wheelwell on landing. He advised approach control that they should foam 3500' of the right side of the duty runway after the first two aircraft had landed.

Radar contact was established at twenty-five miles for all three aircraft. The weather was overcast with 3 miles visibility but the ceiling was over 1000'. The first two aircraft made a VOR instrument approach to runway 25 and landed safely. Herc 319 was held over the VOR station at 3000' until both aircraft had landed and the runway was foamed. Larry had been airborne for about 8 hours and his fuel was now down to a minimum. He still had enough fuel to make as many approaches as necessary to get the aircraft down safely. Finally, approach control cleared him for a VOR approach to Runway 25. They also advised that crash trucks were standing by in case of trouble. Charlie Black reported at 3 miles "Gear down and locked Runway in sight." Larry used every bit of his experience. At ¼ mile he slowed the plane to touchdown speed and dragged his airplane over the fence like any good navy pilot would do. As he approached the foam he reduced the power and set the plane down as gently as a mother putting her baby in a crib. As soon as the wheels touched down he forced the yoke forward, called for flaps 10%, grabbed the nosewheel steering and threw the power levers into full reverse. The plane tried to swerve right off the runway but he forced it straight ahead with the nosewheel. He came to a stop before he ran out of foam, indicating his rollout was less than 3500'. What an exhibition of pilotage! He taxied ahead just out of the foam and came to a stop. The crash trucks were gathered around the aircraft just in case. He set the brakes and directed the flight engineer to go out and inspect the aircraft for damage and determined if it could be taxied to the ramp. The control tower was calling and wanted to know if the runway could be cleared. Charlie asked them to standby that he would give them an answer shortly. Within 5 minutes Chief Randall came back aboard and reported that the right rear tire was blown and shredded and there was ski damage but the ski was not dragging and they could taxi off the runway.

Charlie contacted the tower and soon they were cleared to the parking ramp. The crews from 321 and 917 were standing by on the ramp waiting for Larry to park his aircraft. Larry taxied slowly and carefully so as not to cause any further damage. He was directed to his parking spot by the taxi director and finally shutdown and secured his aircraft. The gas turbine compressor was still running providing electrical power to the aircraft so that post flight procedures could be completed. As quickly as the forward crew entrance door lowered, Pete and Mike jumped aboard and climbed into the cockpit. They congratulated Larry and the crew for a job well done and especially Larry for the great landing. Larry humbly accepted their accolades. He directed Chief Randall to wash down the right side of the aircraft and the wheelwell to clear them of foam and prevent it from corroding the aircraft and equipment.

The crews from 321 and 917 assisted the 319 crew in completing securing the aircraft and washing down the right side as directed. Meanwhile the crash crew was also in the process of washing the foam off the duty runway. The pilots and navigators went over to the FBO, called the FIR office and closed their flight plan. They sat down in the pilot's lounge to have a cup of coffee and wait for the enlisted crews to complete their tasks in securing the aircraft. The conversation finally got around to the day they just had in the Antarctic. Larry described what he saw and felt on his approach and go around on the ice at Palmer. Pete in turn chimed in on what he saw and felt as he observed what was enfolding below him. They, as did the copilots, mused as to what happened with the stability of the ice. Paul Eskew posed that it looked like the storm from the previous few days had cracked the ice enough to weaken it but had refrozen the cracks just enough to mask them from being seen visually. When Larry had touched down the ice crashed down into the bay and started the mini tsunami wave under the ice, which caused it to break up. Running into Anvers Island and reversing direction and spreading in an arc from its point of impact reinforced it. Everyone was concerned of the fate of those thrown into the water as a result of the violent ice breakup. Commander Vernon told the officers that he would find out what had happened and let them know as soon as possible. They all concluded that once again the Antarctic had jumped up and bit them in the ass.

Washington, DC

Meanwhile Ian Harrison sent a sitrep to Jack Forester at NSF and described what Bruce Fleming had observed in his three passes over Palmer. In addition he forwarded electronic files, via his satellite setup, of the photos Bruce had taken to the CIA.

When Jack arrived at his office the next morning, the sitrep was on his desk. He quickly digested its contents and keyed the intercom.

"Mary," he asked, "give me five minutes then would you get Admiral Boland on the phone for me please?"

"Will do," Mary responded

Jack uncased the red phone and picked up the receiver. Bill Reynolds at the CIA responded at the other end.

"What's happening, Jack?" He asked.

"Did you receive the overfly photos from Ian at Siple Station yet?" Jack asked.

"Yes, Jack. I have them on my desk right now. Here is what looks like happened. LC-130 #319 made a landing on the ice, which immediately cracked and then broached. Looks like he sustained damage to the starboard side on his go around. He made it okay but on the ice a pickup and 2-4X trucks went through the ice and some of the people went under and others went in after them. That is about all we can determine from the photos."

"Anything from your end, Jack?" He added.

"Nothing yet," Jack responded. "I have a call in to Admiral Boland. He may know what happened. I hope he has some word from Palmer Station. I will keep you advised but I would suspect this would break in the afternoon news. Talk to you later, Bill. Take care."

Jack hung up the red phone and replaced it in its case and locked it in his desk. Just then the office intercom barked. It was Mary.

"Admiral Boland is on line one, Mr Forester," she stated.

Jack swung around at his desk and reached for the phone.

"Good morning, Admiral. I just got word of what happened at Palmer. Do you have any news from your end?"

"We had an intercept from McMurdo about ½ hour ago. They had contact with Palmer and Lieutenant Parker of VXE-6 passed on a sitrep of what occurred there yesterday. He described the ice breakup and the subsequent sinking of the three vehicles. He reported six men were submerged in the icy water but only one was rescued, a Seaman by the name of Grochinski was pulled from the waters by one of the VXE—pararescue team. Doc Kealey administered CPR on the ice and finally got him recesutated. Chief McKenna, Petty Officer Spalding and Seaman Gorchinski were wrapped in space blankets while the remainder of the team made some makeshift sleds out of tarps. Then they hiked the one-mile over the broken ice back to the station. Apparently they almost lost them but upon reaching the station they put all three in a hot shower for some fifteen minutes and then in the Sauna for about another twenty minutes. They are all resting comfortably. The bad news is we lost Lieutenant Mackay and four of his men.

Lieutenant Koenig as senior officer has now been designated Officer-in-Charge of Palmer Station until we get the first ship in there in late July early August. The Pararescue team will have to fill in until relieved."

"Has your staff briefed Commander Perriman yet, Admiral?" asked Jack.

"No, not yet Jack but I expect to talk with him this morning," Admiral Boland replied.

"Roger that sir. I will be in touch with Jere as necessary later in the day. Is there any more we can do from here?" Jack asked.

"No, Jack. I think we have every thing under control. Let's reevaluate a possible air drop of supplies, material, veggies and mail before we redeploy the C-130s."

"That sounds like a good plan. Why don't you have your staff coordinate with the squadron and checkout the feasibility of such an undertaking," Jack replied.

Jack then told the Admiral he would appropriate the extra money needed to cover the costs and would coordinate with Palmer Station once they had a firm grip on whether it was feasible or not.

"I'll get back to you on this one ASAP," the admiral replied.

"Thanks, admiral. I will talk with you later. Be in touch."

With that, Jack hung up the phone and immediately began writing on his note pad. It was going to take a little planning and coordination with all concerned to pull this one off.

The Department of Defense Public Affairs Officer had been getting phone calls and media people inquiring at his office all morning. He had been coordinating with Admiral Boland and at mid-morning Admiral Boland reported that he now had enough information that he could meet with the press and TV people.

A briefing was scheduled for 1:00pm at the Pentagon. Admiral Boland travelled over there from his headquarters in downtown Washington. When he arrived at the briefing room the media was already set up with their TV cameras and the press was in their seats.

Admiral Boland greeted them and thanked them for coming. He described in great detail what had happened at Palmer Station. When he finished he asked if there were any questions. The CBS reporter raised his hand and was recognized.

"Sir, were any of the planes damaged?" he asked.

"One of the C-130s sustained wheel and ski damage but was able to land safely back at Punta Arenas." He answered.

Another person raised their hand and was recognized.

"Joe Barnes, St. Louis Post-Dispatch sir. Why was the plane making a wheeled landing? I thought skis were always required to land in Antarctica," he asked.

"Because this was a landing on ice with no snow on the surface wheels were called for." The admiral replied.

"Sir, follow up question. Will there be any further operations to Palmer Station at this time and if so where will the planes land?" He asked.

"We haven't determined yet whether there will be further operations but if we do it will require air drop operations since there are no other places to land a C-130 in that area." Admiral said.

"Seeing no further questions, thank you all once again for coming we will keep you up to date as we learn anything new." Having said that the Admiral stepped down from the podium and left the room.

9

"Regroup and Reload"

Punta Arenas: Later that Evening

After a quick dinner the senior officers once again took a hotel van to the hospital to visit Bob Avery. When they walked in on him he was looking and feeling much better than the day before. Bob immediately got the vibes from the group that something was amiss. Even though they were all tired they still were not in their normal cheery mood.

"What's with you guys?" he asked, quickly continuing, "You guys look like nothing went right today."

"These guys did their best today," responded Bill Springer. "No matter what they did the Antarctic just wouldn't cooperate."

"Well lay it on me, Larry. I think I'm well enough to take anything," Bob said.

"Bob, everything went fine until I tried to make a landing on the bay ice off Palmer Station. On touchdown the ice broke, hit the water below so hard it started a wave under the ice, which caused it to start to break up. The wave hit the shore and bounced back stronger than it hit and expanded in an arc, which caused catastrophic break up. It was like a 2000-pound bomb went off under the ice. Pieces were flying everywhere. I went around immediately but got hit by a piece of ice, which had broached and damaged a ski and blew the rear starboard tire. At that point we aborted the mission and returned to Punta Arenas."

Bob shook his head, "Did you think about maybe airdropping the cargo."

Pete responded, "Yeah we did but there was chaos down on the ice. The pickup with the pararescue team along with two large 4x's slid into the water and it looked like they were in the rescue mode when we departed. They weren't in any position to concentrate on an airdrop at that point so Larry and I didn't even discuss it."

Bob asked, "What's the status of the team and the personnel who were in the water?"

Bill Grammercy chimed in, "We tried to make contact with Palmer on our flight back to Punta Arenas but there was no response. It looked like they went on communication shutdown and you know what that usually means. Some kind of trouble or God forbid a death on the ice."

Pete added, "I am going to try to contact the squadron tomorrow morning and get more information. We haven't even discussed what we think can be done at this point. A landing on the ice is out of the question so not sure what the decision upstairs will be."

"Tomorrow we will also evaluate 319 and see what needs to be done to repair the damage. That may also determine what the staff wants us to do," Larry said.

"It appears that the pararescue team is going to have to wait until the first ship makes port at Palmer before they can come home," Bob noted.

Pete added, "I don't think there is much more we can do except make an airdrop of mail and cargo. You're right, Bob, the pararescue team is stuck for the duration."

"Well guys I'm beat and it's been a long day so how about we go to the hotel, get some sleep and work these things out in the morning," Larry said.

Everybody nodded in agreement. They quickly wished Bob good health and promised to see him sometime tomorrow.

"Tomorrow you can tell me about the landing, Larry," Bob interjected.

"You got it old friend. Have a great night," Larry said.

With that they all departed his room and headed back to the hotel.

Next Morning

The crews once again gathered at breakfast. There was a lot of speculation going around the room on what was in store for the detachment. Pete and Larry were tuned in to the discussion so Larry decided on the spur of the moment to speak to it before it got rampant and the rumors turned ugly.

He stood and called for the room to be quiet. Everyone stopped what they were doing and were attentive to what Larry was about to say, knowing that this would be the straight word.

"Men," he began, "we all had a tough day yesterday but I am proud of all of you for what we accomplished despite not being able to pick up the pararescue team. Everything else about the mission was letter perfect and everyone carried out their assigned tasks in an outstanding manner, but for the fact that the ice broke up. Obviously we can't control that. We would have accomplished what we went there to do. At this point I don't know what we will be called on to do but I do know that we need to get 319 fixed and ready to do whatever we are called on to do. We need to unload the veggies and foodstuffs we were to deliver to Palmer. If we can consolidate these from both aircraft and get them packed, neatly. I am going to ask Bill Springer to contact some of the city officials and see to whom we can donate them. Maybe an orphanage or a seniors home can use them."

Larry turned to Bill Springer and asked, "Bill can you handle that today?"

Bill responded with thumbs up and said, "I'll get Tom Harger. He and I will see what we can do."

Larry replied, "Thanks, Bill and Tom."

Larry continued, "Commander Vernon will be working on contacting the squadron and Task Force Fourty-three staff to get a handle on where we go from here. I will have transport out front to go to the airport around 10:00am. Let's just take it easy today and do what is necessary. Lunch around 12:20pm and then try to leave the airport for the hotel around 4:30pm. If we finish our tasks before then maybe we can start back here earlier. When we get back to the hotel let's meet in the hotel Conference room one for just a few minutes where Commander Vernon can brief us on where we're going.

Anyone have a question or comment? Good, no questions. Right now I plan on everyone standing down tomorrow and resting. See you out front at 10:00am."

Larry sat back down with Pete, Mike Brenner, Bill Grammercy and Bill Springer. Chief Randall stopped by the table. He and Larry discussed what parts they might need to fix 319. There was no question that they needed a fully mounted tire from the squadron. There was the possibility of wheel damage, which might not be visually detectable, and they needed a tire with a tube in it. The squadron was one of the few organizations which used tubes mainly because of the skis. They weren't intending to make a ski landing any time soon so the damage to the ski could wait to be repaired. With their discussion ended, Chief Randall left the table and those remaining continued their discussion over a cup of fresh coffee.

At 10:00am they were all out front of the hotel when the van pulled up. They piled in and proceeded to the airport. The mood of the crews was still down as they were all disappointed in the way the mission went the day before. When they arrived at the FBO Larry spoke up and told the navigators to reconnoiter the weather for Palmer Station for the next couple of days just in case they were going to be required to fly down that way. He also instructed them to get a handle on the enroute weather back to Point Mugu should they be recalled to home base.

The pilots and enlisted aircrewman gathered out front while Larry commandeered a ride out to the aircraft. Soon a small bus arrived and they proceeded out on the flight line. Mike Brenner volunteered to contact Bill Springer back at the hotel to check on progress on disposition of the veggies and foodstuffs.

Mike got in touch with Bill on the phone. Bill indicated that a truck would soon arrive at the airport from the Santa Marino Senior Citizens Home to pick up the veggies and foodstuffs. The pallet from 319 was brought to the fence just outside the FBO and soon the truck arrived. The cargo was quickly transferred to the truck with many thanks all around. The people receiving the goods were very grateful to have these things and couldn't thank the Americans enough for their generosity.

Meanwhile Chief Randall had been supervising the removal of the starboard ski and wheels from LC-130 No. 319. He had borrowed a wing jack from American Airlines and soon had the ski and wheels laying on the ramp. The wheel axles were inspected for visual cracks as well as damage further up the anchoring hardware. No further damage was found but it was past lunchtime so all-hands took a break and proceeded over to the terminal for lunch. The crews were loosening up from being so tense and frustrated the day before and hard work always brought out the best in the men. There was some laughter and banter, which only reinforced the notion that the crews were returning to a happy and satisfied group. After lunch they went back to work and reinstalled the forward wheel but left the rear wheel off as well as the ski. They stored the ski and wheel in the cargo compartment to await delivery of a new wheel/tire assembly. The wing jack was lowered and then returned to American Airlines. That was all the work which could be done so the aircraft was buttoned up and the crew headed for the bus at the FBO to return to the hotel. Larry reminded all hands that there would be a short meeting in Conference Room 1.

When they arrived at the hotel the time was already approaching 4:30pm. Pete Vernon greeted them as they disembarked from the bus.

"Hey, Pete. How did things go today?" Larry asked.

"Pretty good, Larry," He replied. "I gleaned a lot of good information from the squadron and Task Force Fourty-three."

"Great," Said Larry. "Lets go into Conference Room 1 and brief the troops."

They proceeded into the room where most of the detachment personnel had already gathered. There were a few stragglers yet to come so they waited a few more minutes.

After a short delay it appeared everyone was present. Larry rose and the room quieted.

"Commander Vernon will give us an update on what he has gleaned from the squadron and Task Force Fourty-three today. After his briefing is completed we will decide where to go from there. Pete, you're up." Larry said.

Pete began. He detailed how he had sent an email to the Commanding Officer outlining the status of the detachment.

Larry and Chief Randall had decided early on that they would need a main wheel/tire assembly. Pete had ordered one from the CO. In his return email the CO had indicated that an assembly had been shipped via DHL and should arrive the next day. The CO included all the details of the situation at Palmer, which he had received from Task Force Forty-three. Pete then began describing what had happened on the ice off Palmer Station and regretfully stated that five lives had been lost in the ensuing ice breakup. He reported that the pararescue team had once again performed in the highest traditions of the Naval Service by rescuing one man and attempting the rescue of Lieutenant MacKay. It put a damper on those assembled but everyone understood that it was beyond their control. Pete continued with his briefing, indicating that an airdrop mission was a distinct possibility before they would be heading for home. If it came to fruition they could not possibly carry it out for at least two, possibly three days. With that Pete ended his briefing and opened the floor for any questions.

Petty Officer Glennon raised his hand and was recognized.

"Commander, did we lose any members of the pararescue team or are they all safe."

"Glennon, they are all alive although Chief McKenna is suffering from a little bit of frostbite from being in the cold water too long when he was trying to rescue Lieutenant MacKay. All personnel lost were members of Antarctic Support Force. As a result of the loss of Lieutenant MacKay, Lieutenant Koenig, Rescue Team member, has been designated O-in-C Palmer Station until properly relieved."

"Okay," Pete continued. "I know you all are anxious about tomorrow so I will turn things back to Lieutenant Commander Beck."

With that, Larry stood once again and began his briefing.

"It appears that we will have a new wheel and tire assembly tomorrow some time. Crew 319 will be on duty. Chief Randall pick a few more people if you think you will need additional help to change that tire."

Chief Randall looked around the room. "Sir, I would like to have Petty Officer Rosenow and Petty Officer Hazzard."

"Are those all the people you will need?" Larry queried.

"Yes sir," Randall replied.

"Lieutenant Junior Grade Robinson will have the Detachment Duty Officer starting right now and I want Lieutenant Junior Grade Pye to relieve you at 1700 tomorrow," Larry stated. "I want everyone to checkout with the duty officer and let him know what your activities will be tomorrow. In addition, everybody should check-in with the duty officer by noon. That way we can account for everybody without having a formal muster. On Tuesday 917 will have the duty beginning tomorrow night. Report to Lieutenant Junior Grade Pye by 1800. We will have an all hands meeting at 1900 on Tuesday evening here in Conference Room 1. At that time we will know what lies ahead for us and what we will be doing for the rest of the week. In the meantime everybody get out, enjoy the sights and sounds of Punta Arenas as best you can. I know there is not much going on during the winter but I am sure all of you will be able to find something to do. The main thing is to relax and have a great time. If you have to have a beer, drink sensibly. Any questions or comments?"

There were no questions so Larry dismissed all-hands. People started to wander out while discussing the events of the past few days and also trying to figure out what they would do the next day.

Larry, Pete Vernon, Mike Brenner, Bill Grammercy and Bill Springer remained for a few minutes. They discussed what needed to be done the next day and what each of them would take care of. Pete would once again contact the squadron and try to determine their next mission whether it would be the trip home or another attack on the Antarctic. Bill Springer was still the liaison officer with the hospital for Bob Avery and he stated that after they visited Bob tonight he would determine his plan of action for tomorrow. Bill Grammercy determined that he would reconnoiter the Palmer Station forecast for the next few days just in case of a new mission and also check out weather enroute to home base, Point Mugu, California. Larry also assigned Bill Grammercy as liaison with DHL and told him to monitor delivery of the wheel/tire assembly arriving from the squadron. Larry would work with Chief Randall supervising the repair and rework of aircraft 319.

The five senior officers once again planned to have dinner around 6:00pm then go to the hospital to visit Bob Avery. They assembled in the lobby just before 6:00pm and discussed amongst themselves where they would have dinner. The consensus settled on the elegant Italian Restaurant just a few blocks down the street. It was a Monday night and they felt it wouldn't be very busy. A van waited out front to take them to the restaurant and the hospital. Things went well at the restaurant with a lot of typical naval aviation banter as to who was the best pilot, navigator, etc. The cute, young waitress caught their attention and of course Bill Springer was kidded a lot that he was trying to make a pass at her just because he was the Spanish speaking person doing the ordering from the menu. Of course Bill told her a few funny lines, which made her laugh and added to his legend. They all finished dinner, paid the bill and moved out to the street to go to the hospital. The weather was miserable. Temperature was about 36°F with a slight drizzle and winds 8 to 10 mph. They all bundled up and climbed into the van from the hotel waiting to take them to the hospital. The driver Julio Estavez had been driving them for a couple of days now and he knew their routine so it was a relaxed atmosphere.

Bill greeted him in his usual Spanish. "Buenas noches Julio, vamos a estar fuera al hospital."

Julio responded with, "Sí señor, lo antes posible.

Julio took off in a smooth start and quickly drove them the 6 or 7 blocks to the hospital.

When they arrived in Bob's room they found him sitting up in a chair reading one of the books they had brought him a couple of days earlier.

Greetings were made all around and they all sat wherever they could find a place. Pete Vernon briefed Bob on the news from the squadron and Task Force Fourty-three while Larry filled him in on the status of Herc 319. Bob expressed his concern about the morale of the troops and all-hands assured him that morale was high and that they had all recovered from the events of the past few days. Bob laughed and said it served Ken Koenig right for volunteering for the pararescue team that he now had to be O-in-C of Palmer for a few more weeks. Bob then asked if anyone knew when a ship would be at Palmer to bring them back to Punta

Arenas for the trip home. Pete said he hadn't heard but would ask the skipper tomorrow when he communicated with the squadron. Bill Grammercy, being the old hand, stated that he thought the earliest a ship had previously visited Palmer was about the middle of June. They all laughed, as the consensus was that the pararescue team would probably end up being deployed for some eleven months before it was all over. All agreed that they were glad it wasn't them. Five months in the Antarctic was enough for most of them they thought one could endure. Larry shared that he had been deployed ten months on the Kitty Hawk back during the Viet Nam War when he was an Ensign flying spads. Bob too indicated he had spent some eight months on board USS Hancock as a young JG flying Skyhawks. Before Bill Grammercy had his eyes go bad and was forced to become a Naval Flight Officer instead of a pilot, he had spent 8 months flying the S-3B Viking off the USS Independence. Bill Springer shared that he too had flown off Independence as a Bombardier-Navigator in the A-5 Vigilante. Mike Brenner was the new guy on the block and was fresh out of flight training and VXE-6 was his first operational squadron.

Bob Avery had been holding out on the group and smiled at them. He announced, "They said I would be released tomorrow but that I should not do any flying for a week or so. Looks like I can ride along but not actually pilot anything for awhile."

"That's great, Bob," replied Larry. He turned to Bill Springer, "You have your assignment for tomorrow I guess, Bill."

"I figured it would be coming soon. I will be here early in the morning and we can get you back to the hotel whenever the hospital releases you, Bob," Bill said.

"The doctor usually comes in around 10:00am and he has to sign the release before I can be processed," Bob replied.

They continued their conversation for another ½ hour and then Larry announced they should head back to the hotel for a good nights rest. They said their goodbyes, left the hospital and piled into the van for their return to the hotel.

10

"Change in Plans"

Punta Arenas: Tuesday Morning.

Morning dawned early on the gray streets of Punta Arenas but most of the crews were up and ready for breakfast before 7:00am. Once again the weather was a low overcast with rain and drizzle with the temperature hovering around the mid-thirties. It was going to be a miserable day for the crews working on Aircraft 319 but also a crummy day for seeing the sights and sounds of Punta Arenas. Some of the detachment personnel were already in the dining room when some of the officers entered. Those who were taking the day off were obviously still getting in a few zzzs. Larry and Pete discussed some of the problems they would have to solve today while also communicating with the squadron and possibly Task Force Forty-three. Larry reminded Bill Grammercy that the first thing he needed to do was contact DHL and tell them where they needed to deliver the wheel assembly for Aircraft 319. Bill Springer chimed in that he would be at the hospital before 10:00am to pick up Bob Avery. Future plans would be the goal of Pete Vernon in his communications with the squadron.

Breakfast being finished, the personnel going to the airport assembled in the lobby and waited for the van to arrive to take them to the airport. The van arrived and the crews piled in and departed. Bill Springer and Pete Vernon walked back into the hotel and sat down for another cup of coffee. Pete knew it was a little early and that the squadron would not yet be at work.

Larry and his crew arrived at the FBO. He reminded them they would break for lunch about 12:20pm. Bill Grammercy immediately grabbed one of the FBO's phones and called DHL. Everything that day depended on when the DHL flight arrived from Rio de Janeiro. Bill couldn't get through on the phone so he decided to travel over to the cargo hangar and talk directly with the cargo manager of DHL. A couple of the navigators decided to go with him as they could easily get to the weather office by walking from there. Larry and his crew remained at the FBO for a donut and coffee awaiting word from Bill. The van was soon loaded and off to the cargo hangar. They arrived at DHL, unloaded and sent the van back to the FBO. Bill went in and introduced himself to the manager. Edwardo Cortez was the manager and spoke fairly good English. Bill explained who he was and that they were expecting a wheel assembly for a C-130 today. Bill was informed that the DHL flight from Rio would be on the ground about 9:30am. Bill gave Edwardo instructions on where to deliver the wheel assembly. Edwardo acknowledged and indicated he would deliver it as soon as it was offloaded and put on the delivery truck. Bill thanked Edwardo for his help and cooperation and left the office with the other navigators. They walked over to the main terminal where the weather office was located. Paul Eskew was already there waiting for them. He had the weather staff working on gathering the forecasts for Palmer station and Point Mugu for the next 5 days.

Meanwhile Bill called back over to the FBO to tell Larry that the DHL should arrive about 9:30am. It was already 9:05am and therefore it would probably be a short wait. Chief Randall and his enlisted crew got a tug and went over to American Airlines to borrow the same wing jack they had previously used. American's maintenance chief, Al Moody, who was from Wichita, Kansas, was more than glad to help out the U.S. Navy. Chief Randall discussed what he had to do with the wheel assembly and Al told Randalls that he had portable equipment to pump up and check the tire pressure if necessary. They gathered the tools necessary to put the wheel assembly on the aircraft and Al had the jack towed over to the aircraft. The only thing the Herc crew couldn't do was cycle the gear. They would probably need to test fly the aircraft to do that. Al also provided a ramp vehicle so they could transport all their tools and equipment over to the aircraft.

Almost on cue the DHL 757 appeared out of the murk on short final for Runway 25. After run out he taxied to the ramp and shut down in front of the DHL hangar. In short order cargo began flowing from the aircraft and being sorted and loaded on cargo trucks. Soon the C-130 wheel assembly appeared, was loaded on a truck, and after clearing the paperwork was on its way over to the navy C-130s parked on the ramp. Chief Randall signed for the delivery and the crews began off-loading it onto the ramp under the aircraft. The starboard wing of the aircraft was jacked-up, raising the starboard wheel off the tarmac. The tire pressure was stabilized at the proper pressure utilizing the equipment borrowed from Al at American Airlines and was ready for installation. At this point Larry Beck showed up at the aircraft and told the crew it was time to knock off for lunch. Most of them were ready to do so as it was hard work and extremely cold damp working conditions.

Larry had a ramp vehicle available where they all climbed in and proceeded over to the terminal for lunch. All the other detachment personnel who were at the airport met them there. Larry spotted Paul Eskew as he entered the restaurant and invited him to join him.

"Hey Paul," he started. "What did you find in your roaming this morning?"

"Not much new Larry," he replied. "No significant weather for Palmer the next few days. It looks good if we have to make an air drop there."

"I expect the Pt. Mugu weather is reasonable," Larry responded.

"Yeah, Larry, it is typical May conditions. A little fog early but scattered to broken after 10:00am."

"Looks good no matter which way we have to go," said Larry.

They continued their not-to-do-about-much conversation and finished their lunch.

Chief Randall gathered his men and told Larry they would get back to work. He said they should be finished in a couple of hours.

Back in Punta Arenas Bill Springer had taken a taxi to the hospital. He arrived around 10:15am and proceeded to Bob Avery's room. Bob was in the process of putting on his street clothes in anticipation of being released.

About 10:35am Bob's doctor entered the room and through Bill once again acting as interpreter the doctor after checking Bob's vital signs and asking a few questions, declared him fit and ready to be released. He gave the nurse the release order and told Bill the release would take about 30 minutes.

Thirty minutes passed and sure enough the nurse returned with Bob's release orders. She also had a wheel chair to take Bob out to the front entrance of the hospital. Bob resisted at first getting into the wheel chair but she insisted it was hospital policy. Bill had an animated conversation in Spanish with her but she prevailed in the end and Bob sat down in the chair.

The nurse wheeled Bob, accompanied by Bill, to the front entrance where they awaited arrival of the taxi which the discharge office had ordered for them.

Bill thanked the nurse and they boarded the taxi when it arrived.

Bill instructed the taxi driver to take them to the Best Western. On arrival at the hotel they went into the dining room and had lunch. Bob told Bill he was famished as he had not had a good meal since he had been admitted to the hotel.

Washington, D.C.

Jack Forester had been at his desk for most of the morning putting the final touches on the Antarctic plan for the coming year. He still had to make a final decision on the proposed scientific research project in the Transantarctic Mountains to begin in October. If he approved it the helos from VXE-6 would be stretched to the limit and he wasn't sure yet what effect it might have on previously approved helo supported projects.

Mary McGuire, his secretary, broke the silence ringing his phone and telling him Admiral Boland would like to talk with him.

He punched the button on the line, "John, Jack here what's up?" he asked.

"Jack, I just hung up with Jere Perriman and he has been in touch with the detachment at Punta Arenas. He reports that Herc 319 will be repaired today and ready for flight later in the day. I believe that since we have the assets already in Punta Arenas and Palmer Station is already operating on a bad roller bearing in their electrical generator that now would be a good time to fly a mission and airdrop supplies and equipment to ease the situation. What's your take on things?"

"I think you are right, John. We should make use of the assets already in place and remedy the situation that exists. If we don't do it now Palmer may end up without electrical power for a while until we could get a new bearing to them."

"Is the squadron ready to move forward on an airdrop mission at this time?" Jack asked.

"Jack, it appears so," John replied.

"Okay, let's recycle all the necessary assets and agencies necessary to get this thing done. I will authorize the appropriate funds and have them transferred to your account with us. Is there anything else we can do over here to help?" Jack said.

"No, Jack, we can handle things from here. I will keep you informed. Take care." With that Admiral Boland hung up the phone.

Admiral Boland quickly notified his staff to proceed with the necessary planning for an airdrop mission to Palmer station and get back to him by 8:00am the next morning.

Washington, D.C.: Next Morning

The staff was quite efficient. They had the plan together and well organized by the time the Admiral took his seat in the briefing room.

The Operations Officer opened the proceedings with his air operations plan. They would direct VXE-6 to execute an airdrop at Palmer Station ASAP, weather conditions permitting and operational readiness of aircraft.

Next the Logistics Officer presented his requirements and expectations. They would notify the U.S. Embassy in Santiago and put on the requirement of delivering the latest mail for Palmer and supply the detachment in Punta Arenas with enough fresh eggs and veggies for the personnel at Palmer.

Communications Officer was next at the podium. He had already prepared the appropriate message to start the ball rolling on the mission. He stated that a live communications conference with Palmer before the Airdrop would be in order to give them first hand information of what to expect. The Admiral nodded in agreement that it should be done although he added that Lieutenant Koenig, now O-in-C, was a VXE-6 pararescue member and was probably well aware of the capabilities of the LC-130 aircraft and knew what to expect.

The Chief-of-Staff wrapped up the briefing by summarizing the operations plan and indicated only the Admiral's approval was needed to proceed. He asked the staff if there was anymore input before the Admiral finished the conference.

There was none and Admiral Boland rose to speak. He complimented the staff on the great job they had done and stated he was pleased with their efficiency in bringing this thing to a rapid conclusion so the mission could be executed as soon as the detachment was ready to do so. He turned to the Chief-of-Staff and told him to execute the plan. With that the Chief-of-Staff called the room to attention and the Admiral departed for his office.

The communications officer passed the message, to be sent to all concerned parties, to the Operations Officer for official release.

Pt. Mugu, California

Commander Perriman received his copy of the message through the normal communications channel. He immediately had the Communications Officer transcribe the contents of the message and put it into an email addressed to Commander Pete Vernon. He added his best wishes and good luck on the mission.

Punta Arenas later that day

It was late in the day when Pete checked his email and received the message from the squadron. All hands had returned from the airport while some stragglers who had been out to see the sights had yet to return. Pete contacted Larry Beck, Bob Avery, Bill Grammercy, Mike Brenner and Bill Springer. They agreed to meet about 6:00pm in the lobby for a trip out for supper. This would give them a chance to discuss the upcoming airdrop mission, which was outlined in the email Pete had just received.

They all arrived in the lobby about the pre-arranged time, exchanged some pleasantries and departed for a local restaurant. They had agreed Chilian food would be the order of the day. Bob Avery interjected "no Italian food tonight." Everybody laughed. They soon settled down in "La Familia Casa." It appeared the special for the day was beef stew and they all ordered. Some of them had a bowl of leek soup as an appetizer. During dinner they discussed the upcoming mission. Bob Avery began by stating that he thought he should remain in Punta Arenas and coordinate and monitor the mission and not participate directly as a pilot or mission commander. They all agreed that since he had not been cleared for flight by a certified flight surgeon he shouldn't take that chance. The aircraft commanders remained the same with basically the same assignments as with the previous mission. Mike would be search and rescue as well as communications relay while Larry and Pete would make the airdrop. They would fly the mission as soon as they could coordinate with the U.S. Embassy in Santiago and receive the new mail, provisions and veggies. They finished dinner and proceeded back to the hotel for a good nights rest. Larry talked with the duty officer and coordinated an all-hands briefing in the dining room for the next morning. The duty officer passed the word to each room in the hotel where crew were staying.

The next morning was routine as all-hands gathered in the dining room after breakfast for the briefing. Bob Avery stood to speak. He indicated he was once again assuming position as mission commander. He detailed his non-flying position and then called on Larry to brief the flight portion of the airdrop mission. After completing the details he called on Paul Eskew to give the weather briefing. Paul indicated that the weather was mostly VFR with broken cloud layers starting at 3500'. Temperatures forecast to be highs of 35°F to lows of 15°F. Winds would be generally north to northeast at 5 to 15 mph. The barometric pressure was falling slowly but Paul expected it to remain high enough to prevent a winter storm from moving into the area before Saturday. The detachment expected to fly on Friday so the weather was not expected to be a problem.

Pete took the podium and told the detachment that Task Force Forty-Three was scheduling a communications conference with Palmer Station and they had been invited to participate which meant they would need to use the aircraft HF radios. Pete said it was scheduled for 1500 hours this afternoon. Bob decided Herc 917 would be the best aircraft radios to use for the conference so that enlisted crew was alerted they should be ready to go to the airport by 1300 hours.

Bob and Larry had a long discussion as to whether Larry should test fly Herc 319. They came to the conclusion that the only parts which were disconnected in changing the tire were the rocker arms for the ski and since they would not be lowering the skis it would be unnecessary.

Bob, Pete, Larry, Bill G., Bill S., and Mike all gathered with the crew of 917 in the lobby about 12:50pm for departure to the airport. The bus arrived and they were soon on their way. This trip was becoming routine, as they had now done it many times. They arrived at the FBO and the enlisted crew made their way to the aircraft to get it ready for the communications conference. The officers gathered in the pilot's ready room to have a cup of coffee and wait until it was time to proceed to the aircraft. Bob directed the discussion on the upcoming mission and assigned responsibilities for the tasks in preparation for the flight. They scheduled the flight to depart at 8:00am Friday, to give them the best light over the base on arrival for the airdrop. Paul Eskew would handle the weather briefings. Mike was once again assigned to acquire the in-flight lunches. Pete would coordinate the mail, eggs and veggies delivery from the embassy on Thursday. Larry was charged with delivery of any additional heavy supplies and equipment from town and the aircraft loading and airdrop rigging. Bill G. was responsible for the flight plans and coordination with Punta Arenas Control. Finally Bill S. would schedule the hotel breakfast and transportation. Bob Avery indicated that he would monitor the flight in the Flight Information Region Control room, which would be receiving position and status reports from Mike in Herc 917.

Time rolled around to 1440 and the officers proceeded to Herc 917. They occupied all available seats in the cockpit. Bill G. was in the navigator's seat so he tuned both HF transceivers to 4595khz, which was the primary frequency of the conference. AD2 Glennon put the signal through on the public address system in the aircraft. At 1455 Ken Nichols came on the radio and radio checked all stations. Lieutenant Koenig at Palmer was loud and clear. Jere Perrigan at Pt. Mugu was also loud and clear. Bob chimed in for 917 and reported slightly weak but clear.

At 1500 Admiral Boland came up on the radio and welcomed all-hands. He queried Lieutenant Koenig on the situation and conditions at Palmer Station. Ken reported that morale was at low ebb because of the loss of Lieutenant MacKay and the four enlisted men. He was upbeat about the readiness of the station however and credited all-hands with their dedication and effort in getting everything there in great working order. He reported that he had reports from the civilian-in-charge that the electrical generator would probably only last another week because the bearing in the motor was showing more and more signs of failure. The Task Force Forty-Three Supply Officer came on and stated that the new bearings were in Punta Arenas and should be in the airdrop package. Ken Koenig then came back on and concluded his report stating they were ready for the airdrop mission.

Admiral Boland next asked Bob Avery what was the status of the detachment. Bob reported that all aircraft were in an up status, Pete Vernon was coordinating deliver of the goods from Santiago, that all-hands were ready to fly except for himself being grounded, not having been cleared by a flight surgeon. He further reported that the mission would depart at 0800 Friday morning and be overhead Palmer at 1230 for the airdrop. He inquired of Ken Koenig as to the best spot for the airdrop in relation to the station. Ken came back on and indicated that the glacier directly behind the station would be a good position but that the drop should be made as close as possible to the base. Larry chimed in and said that would be exactly where he would put the three pallets from his aircraft and Pete flying on his right wing would be put his pallets another fifty feet to the east. Bob asked Ken if they had any smoke flares to mark the wind for the drop. Ken said they would make some sort of smoke but at this point he did not know if they had any smoke flares. They decided this frequency would be primary with 6555mhz as secondary. Bill G. made a little note in his logbook of the frequencies. The last item Bob related was the crew assignments. Larry leading the flight in 319, Pete in 321 and Mike communications coordinator and search and rescue in 917. The Admiral inquired as to the weather expected for the mission. Ken reported weather forecast for Friday was VFR with wind light out of the northeast.

The Admiral finally asked Commander Perriman if he had any questions or anything to add to the conversation. Commander Perriman answered in the negative. All-hands were then asked if they had anything to add to the conversation. All stations reported in the negative. Task Force Forty-Three Chief-of-Staff came up on the frequency and indicated that the conference was concluded. Each station in turn signed off.

With that having been done, Bob Avery indicated to all-hands that they should have a detachment meeting in the morning, at the hotel and discuss the details with all detachment personnel. Pete chimed in that he would contact the embassy in Santaigo and check on the delivery of mail and foodstuffs for delivery tomorrow, Thursday. Everyone gathered at the FBO and boarded the vans for transport back to the hotel.

Once at the hotel Larry contacted the duty officer and told him to notify all hands about a 7:30am briefing in the dining room on Thursday morning.

11

"A Second Try"

Punta Arenas, Chile: Thursday Morning

Hardly anyone was stirring in the hotel as most of the detachment personnel made their way to the dining room for breakfast and eventually the mission briefing. Breakfast was routine and eventually all-hands made their way into the dining room. At 7:36am Bob Avery stood and began to speak.

"Men, tomorrow we will fly an air-drop mission to Palmer Station, Antarctica. I would say we have flown there before and this is a routine mission but all of you know the Antarctic can jump up and bite you in the ass at anytime. So we must all be diligent and pay attention to every detail so that we can be successful and complete the mission as planned. Lieutenant Commander Larry Beck will lead the in-flight portion of the mission. I am still grounded so I will direct and monitor the mission from the Flight Information Region communications facility at the Airport. Commander Pete Vernon will accompany Lieutenant Commander Beck and they will airdrop 6 pallets at Palmer Station. Lieutenant Mike Brenner will fly Herc 917 and act as communications relay and Search and Rescue. We have many tasks to perform today and each crew will be briefed on their work for the day. Commander Vernon has contacted the embassy in Santiago and they will be delivering mail and foodstuffs destined for Palmer this afternoon sometime. Lieutenant Commander Beck will make arrangements with the holding company to deliver the equipment, replacement parts and mail previously assigned to us for delivery to Palmer. We may need a forklift to off-load the trucks and transfer the cargo to the aircraft. I will check on that item at the airport. Other items necessary for the mission will be acquired as necessary today and tomorrow and those officers assigned that responsibility are aware of their tasks. Are there any questions? Oh yes, one other thing, transportation will be available in front of the hotel at approximately 0930 for departure for the airport."

Chief Randall raised his hand and began to speak. "Sir, we have been working with Mr. Al Moody at American Airlines and he may have a lead for a forklift. I can contact him when we get to the airport."

"Sounds good, Chief." Bob responded. "Let's work that lead together when we get there."

"Mr Avery, when can we expect to get out of here and head for home?" Petty Officer Glennon asked.

"If everything gets completed tomorrow we can expect to start back for Pt. Mugu on Sunday morning," Bob said. "We'll take Saturday to ensure the planes and all-hands are ready for departure. That will also give the navigators a chance to plan the flight home."

With that Chief Jim O'Connell, Flight Engineer on Herc 917 piped up. "Sir, I'd like to make a suggestion if I could?"

Bob stated, "Go ahead, chief."

"Well sir, since we have been here we have been operating on JP1. As you know it has limited our flight altitude severely. Since we are going to have to fly over some pretty high mountains on our way home, especially the first leg, I would suggest we take a light load of fuel out of here and fly to Argentina for some good old JP4 or 5. I know the Argentines are flying their C-130s out of El Palomar, Argentina. It is a military base just west of Buenos Aries and is only about 60 feet above sea level."

What a great idea Bob thought. "Great idea, Chief we will try to incorporate that into our planning." Turning to Commander Vernon. "Pete, do you think we could request that through the Embassy in Santiago"

"I'll be talking with them mid-morning and will discuss it with the aviation liaison officer," said Pete

"Any more questions?" asked Bob. "Seeing none, everyone is dismissed. We will have transportation in front of the hotel shortly."

All-hands were prompt, loaded the vans and departed for the airport. There was much discussion amongst the crews about tasks to be performed. Most crews decided they would all pitch in and assist the loadmaster in readying the aircraft to receive the cargo. The aircraft commanders briefed the flight engineers on the fuel load and by the time the aircraft was ready to receive cargo the fuel trucks would be there to refuel the aircraft.

The vans arrived at the FBO on the airport. Enlisted crews headed for the aircraft after ordering the fuel trucks. A couple of the officers grabbed the available phones and called the appropriate numbers to make contact with people who would assist them in their required tasks. Bob Avery and Chief Randall headed over to American Airlines maintenance to talk with Al Moody about a forklift. Navigators and Paul Eskew had one of the vans drop them off at the weather office in the terminal for flight planning. Mike Brenner headed for Macaria Alercon's office to order the in-flight rations. If this schedule kept up Mike and Macaria would soon be close friends.

Pete Vernon made phone contact with the embassy in Santiago. He asked to speak with Commander Ralph Touch as he was the Aircraft Commander of the embassy's twin Otter and was the Aviation Liaison Officer. They discussed the estimated arrival time of the Otter in Punta Arenas that day and Ralph indicated they would arrive by 1:00p.m. Pete then discussed with Ralph the plan to possibly fly to El Palomar, Argentina, for a refueling stop on Sunday on the way to Lima, Peru. Ralph acknowledged Pete's request and told him he would try to get that clearance by Saturday and would let him know for sure by then.

Likewise Larry Beck was successful and managed to have the company holding the mail and machinery a promise to deliver these items to the airport by 2:30pm that afternoon.

In the meantime Bob Avery and Chief Randall talked with Al Moody who said he could get a cargo loader from the American Airlines cargo boss, which would do the job of a forklift and would be easier. The cargo boss also said he would furnish an operator of the equipment to protect the company from liability and save the flight crew from having to learn how to operate the equipment. They agreed that it would probably not be needed until after noon.

The enlisted crews worked hard and had the planes ready to receive cargo within and hour. Pallets were locked into the rail system, tie-downs were laid out and the ramp was in the down position. Shortly, the fuel trucks arrived and the flight engineers filled the tanks to the required fuel load.

Lunchtime was rapidly approaching and the crews all wandered over to the terminal restaurant for lunch. During lunch Mike Brenner reported he had taken care of the in-flight lunches. Paul Eskew had the weather packets on order and the navigators had completed all the flight planning. Bob Avery stated he had even had time to visit with the Flight Information Region controllers and they welcomed his presence in their control center during the mission.

With lunch completed the detachment personnel went back to their duties awaiting the cargo from town and Santiago.

Time was approaching 1:00pm on cue the U.S. Embassy's twin Otter appeared out of the crud on short final for runway 25. After a normal landing the plane taxied over to the parked LC-130s and shut down its engines. Larry Beck greeted the pilots. Ralph Touch and Bill Marsh were once again the pilots and they greeted Larry as the long lost friends they were. The mail and foodstuffs were loaded onto the first pallet on Herc 319. The pallet was fitted into the rail system and rolled forward in the aircraft and locked down. That was all the loadmaster needed to do at that point since he would not rig the pallet for airdrop until all three pallets were loaded and locked into the rail system.

Meanwhile Larry had taken the Otter pilots over to the FBO where they had filed their flight plan for their return flight to Santiago. They returned to their aircraft, said their goodbyes to Larry and wished him and the detachment good luck in the upcoming mission.

Larry, Pete, Mike and Bob Avery drove back over to the FBO and awaited arrival of the cargo from town. Pretty soon a large moving van drove up and stopped outside the FBO. The driver ran into the Herc pilots just as he entered the building and asked whether they were the people to whom he had to deliver the cargo. They in turn stated they were and had received permission for him to drive his truck out onto the ramp for offloading. All he would need to get was a ramp flag, which they picked up in the line shack just outside the FBO. As they started out toward the Hercs they espied the cargo-loading vehicle from American Airlines proceeding in the same direction. The crew of Herc 319 directed him to stop just aft of their aircraft and Larry also directed the cargo van to stop alongside the cargo loader. Dave Hazard, loadmaster of 319, directed the driver on the van to back up to the cargo loader. The cargo loader operator raised the bed of his vehicle even with the truck tailgate so there was a level surface on which to move the cargo. Dave then went over to 319, brought the aircraft ramp to the level position and motioned the cargo loader to move his vehicle over in line with the ramp. When he was in position Dave and his crew moved a pallet down the rails and pushed it off onto the cargo loader. The skate wheels on that vehicle made it easy to do so. When the pallet was locked into position on the loader the operator moved back over to the tailgate of the van and raised his bed level with the truck tailgate. A couple of the crews helped move some of the mail and light cargo onto the pallet. When ready the operator moved the cargo loader back to the aircraft ramp and the pallet was rolled back onto the aircraft sliding into the rails and guided to the front of the cargo compartment. This exercise was repeated some five times with the heavy machinery being the last cargo loaded onto both aircraft. Now all three pallets were loaded on each of the aircraft, locked into the rail system with the cargo being strapped and chained down to each pallet. The pallets were then connected together with airdrop connectors and parachutes attached to each pallet. Two chutes would be used per pallet for this airdrop. The chute used to drag the pallet off the aircraft was left secured at the rear of the aircraft. During the flight to Palmer the loadmaster would rig that chute and static line in readiness for the airdrop. All this intense work took about three hours. All crews reported they were ready for the mission at almost the same time. The senior Loadmaster, Chief

Rosenow, who was the quality control inspector, reviewed each aircraft's pallets and parachutes rigging. He reported everything in order and signed off on the aircraft loading. During pre-flight the next morning all loadmasters would calculate the weight and balance for their own aircraft and file them with Lieutenant Commander Avery.

With all the work being accomplished for the day all-hands once again boarded the vans at the FBO for the trip back to the hotel.

Punta Arenas, Chile: Friday morning

Reveille was early. Pete had made arrangements for the crews to have breakfast by 6:00am. With breakfast complete officers and men loaded the vans for the trip to the airport. Everything was all business. You could almost cut the tension with a knife. Professionalism was oozing from all-hands and everyone wanted to make sure things were done right today. Officers were dropped off at the terminal and the vans continued on to the FBO to drop off the enlisted crews. Everyone knew his job and so no one needed to be directed what to do. Power was applied to each aircraft and both flight engineers on each aircraft began their pre-flight checks. It was another dull winter day in Punta Arenas but with no rain at least. Clouds were about 1200' overcast with temperatures in the mid-thirties and winds west at 5 to 10 mph. All systems on all three aircraft checked out perfectly and soon the planes were judged ready for flight. Soon the copilots reported to the aircraft and each began his visual pre-flight external check of the aircraft. Next to arrive were the navigators who checked out the navigation station and the HF radios. They all checked frequencies with the FIR communications center then switched to Palmer Station frequency and gave Palmer a call. Palmer read 321 and 319 loud and clear while 917 was broken. The navigators next switched on the UHF transceivers and radio checked them with each other on squadron common. The loadmasters on 321 and 319 doubled checked their cargo and each completed their weight and balance. 917 didn't have any cargo but had plenty of survival gear for their responsibility as the search and rescue aircraft. Herc 917 also had 1000-gallon external wing tanks, which were filled for their loitering mission. Soon the pilots arrived along with Paul Eskew and Bob Avery. Paul had asked and received permission from Bob to fly with Larry. Good wishes and handshakes were exchanged all around and the aircraft manned. On the ramp were four lonely figures. They were three ground aircraft handling personnel and Bob Avery. All doors and hatches were secured and checklists completed. Soon the sound of turboprop engines was breaking the crisp winter silence of the airport. It was about 8:15am. With scheduled takeoff time of 8:30am. 917 and 321 checked in with 319 on squadron common and all planes switched to ground control. Charlie Black, copilot on 319, called ground control with three Hercs for taxi. They were cleared to runway 25 with a left turn out of the chocks. Winds were reported out of the west at 5 to 10 mph, altimeter 29.75"hg. While they were taxiing Larry told Charlie to contact ground and ask to switch to Approach Control for clearance. Ground indicated they could remain on this frequency since there was no traffic in the area and receive their clearance. 321 and 917 rogered the transmission.

Herc 319 asked for clearance for take-off for all three aircraft and was granted permission by the tower. Each aircraft in turn took the duty runway and engines roared. Take-offs were smooth and normal with Herc 917 as tail end Charlie. After take-off each aircraft in turn switched to departure control. They were all cleared to climb on course and so they turned their aircraft towards the Antarctic. Larry Beck in Herc 319 reached his assigned altitude first and leveled at 9,500'. Pete was next in Herc 321 and leveled at 10,000'. Mike was last and he finally reached his assigned altitude 75 miles out of Punta Arenas at 10,500'. The aircraft were now positioned 1 mile in trail and separated by 500'. A radio check was made on squadron frequency and when that was completed Larry gave the command to accelerate to a cruise speed of 250 knots. Upon reaching 100 miles out of Punta Arenas Bill Grammercy reported to departure control that they were leaving his control and switching over to the Flight Information Region. Bill directed all three aircraft to reset their altimeters to 29.92"hg and adjust their altitude accordingly to maintain the proper clearance.

The planes were approximately two hours out of Punta Arenas when they reached 60°S latitude where Mike set himself up in a 10-mile racetrack holding pattern. He reported his action to Larry on squadron common frequency and wished both aircraft success in their airdrop mission. Tom Harger, Mike's navigator, then made his position report to Punta Arenas Flight Information Region on the number two HF radio. He had no sooner released his keyed mike when the number one HF transceiver, which was on Palmer Station frequency, crackled to life.

A voice speaking in English but with a heavy Spanish accent began, "Navy 152917, this is Argentine Base Marambio on Seymour Island. Do you read me? Over."

Tom Harger responded, "Roger Marambio Base, we read you loud and clear. What do you need? Over."

"Navy 152917, Marambio Base, we have an emergency and need assistance. Please stand by for our base commander, Colonel Sanchez, he will brief you."

With that statement echoing through the aircraft headsets, everyone on the circuit in the aircraft began to have the hair on the back of their neck stand up.

Marambio came back, "Navy 917 this is Colonel Sanchez, one of our station personnel has fallen and has incurred a severe brain injury. Our medical personnel cannot operate and relieve the pressure on the brain. The man will die unless he receives proper medical treatment as soon as possible. Our Air Force cannot get a C-130 here for about 10 hours that may be to late. Can you help us?" he asked.

Mike looked at Tom, "Tell him to stand by, Tom."

Tom passed that message to Marambio.

Mike immediately switched his radio selector to the UHF radio and keyed the mike.

"319 this is 917 do you read? over."

Bill Grammercy, who was monitoring the UHF responded, "Roger 917 this is 319 go ahead."

"319 this is 917 we just had and emergency call on Palmer's HF frequency from the Argentines' Marambio Base over on Seymour Island requesting assistance."

Larry interrupted, "Mike this is Larry. We monitored all communications from Marambio Base. I approve that you should divert and make the pickup. Just give Lieutenant

Commander Avery a call at Punta Arenas. Advise him of the situation and our conversation and recommend to him that we get this in motion. I know he will approve."

"Roger, Larry," Mike said. "I am turning toward Marambio right now and will talk with Lieutenant Commander Avery. Will keep you advised."

With that Mike only had to look over to Tom Harger and nod in a positive manner. Tom was in the process of plotting the course change and figuring the ETA for Marambio.

Mike then switched to number two HF radio and keyed the mike. "Punta Arenas Radio this is Navy 2917."

"Navy 2917 roger go head."

Mike continued, "We are requesting to speak with Lieutenant Commander Avery."

"Roger Navy 2917. Lieutenant Commander Avery is listening."

"Commander Avery," Mike responded, "The Argentine Base Marambio on Seymour Island has reported to us that they have a medical emergency. One of the base personnel has fallen and sustained a brain injury requiring immediate medical attention beyond their medical personnels' capability. Indications are that he will die without immediate medical treatment. They are asking us to evacuate this individual as soon as practical. I have discussed the situation with Navy 8319 and he concurs that we should assist and make the pickup and evacuation. Requesting your approval and input."

Bob Avery came up on the frequency. "Navy 2917 you are directed to divert to Marambio and make the pickup. Keep everyone advised of your progress."

Mike rogered the transmission. Tom immediately gave Mike a heading to Marambio and announced an arrival of 90 minutes. Mike then directed Tom to make a report to Punta Arenas and advise them of an ETA for Marambio. While Tom worked with Punta Arenas Mike once again spoke to Larry.

"319 this is 917." Larry spoke, "917 go ahead."

"319 this is 917 we have discussed the situation with Lieutenant Commander Avery and he has directed us to proceed with the plan. We will arrive at Marambio in approximately 80 minutes. What is your ETA Palmer?

Please pass your position and ETA and we will relay to Punta Arenas."

Mike then spoke to Ensign Jackle, the 2nd navigator. He directed him to monitor the UHF and handle the communication with 319 while Tom was busy with Punta Arenas. He then turned to Art Herr his co-pilot and told him to break out the briefing sheet they had researched on Seymour Island and Marambio Base. They determined that it had one runway-oriented 060°/250° and was 115' wide by 4134' long and was a grass strip. Their electronic navigational aids were operational and Mike directed Art to tune them to the appropriate radios. They discussed the fact that there was no approved instrument approach but that the weather was VFR and would pose no problem in approach and landing. Field elevation was determined to be 760'.

The navigators were very efficient and all positions were relayed to Punta Arenas and Palmer station and navigation was progressing normally. They had about 1 hour before arrival at Marambio Base so they settled down and discussed short field take-off and landing procedures.

12

"A Hero is Born"

Thursday afternoon

Hercs 319 and 321 were approaching Palmer Station. They had checked the weather and Palmer was reporting 3,500' broken clouds, wind out of the northeast at 5 to 10 mph and the barometer at 29.83"hg. Bill Grammercy was in contact with Lieutenant Ken Koenig at Palmer Station on their primary HF frequency. Ken had advised that the best area for the airdrop would be just slightly southeast of the station on the glacial ice and that he would make smoke as soon as the planes were less than ten minutes out. Larry's plan was to make a low pass, scout out the drop zone then set up a downwind racetrack while configuring the planes for the drop and the come straight in from the southwest with about a ten mile run-in at about 1500'. Bill passed that info to Ken who rogered over the comm link and advised they were ready and standing by.

Bill reported to Larry that they were 100 miles out. Larry in turn signaled to Pete to begin his descent and join up on his starboard wing for a formation airdrop. Both planes began their descent and soon Pete had Larry in sight and was moving into position on his starboard wing at 20' nose to tail, 20' wing tip to wing tip and 20' step-up of his altitude. Larry leveled the formation at 1500', both planes having set their altimeters to 29.83hg. Bill Grammercy directed them to a point ten miles Southwest of Palmer Station. As they approached a magnetic bearing of 240° from Palmer, Bill ordered a left turn to a heading of 060°. The pilots reported a visual on the buildings at Palmer Station and Larry adjusted his heading slightly to put them on a course which would take then about 1000 yards to the right of the station buildings. Bill reported their position to Ken Koenig who acknowledged the information and relayed that he was lighting the smoke pots. Kens' people at the station had taken 2 old scrap truck tires, cut them into small pieces and doused them in diesel fuel. Two members of the pararescue team struck a couple of road flares and dropped them into the 55-gallon drums holding the tire pieces and fuel. They immediately burst into flame and, as soon as the tire pieces caught fire, black smoke billowed from the drums. Bill reported that they had the smoke pots in sight and that they were approximately 3 miles out for a low pass over the drop-zone. The smoke indicated that they were approaching the drop-zone directly into the wind. As they passed over the drop-zone the crews quickly surveyed the drop-zone. It appeared that Ken and his team had selected a great spot, crevasse free and relatively flat for about ½ mile long and some 600 yards wide as the drop-zone which had been marked with bright orange reflective panels. Larry ordered a left 180° turn for about a 10-mile downwind leg. The loadmasters had rigged their parachutes on the pallets and for extraction. All hands were poised for the drop. As soon as Larry leveled out on the downwind leg he called for the airdrop checklist. The checklist was read and each item completed. The copilots airdrop panel on his right side was armed. The loadmasters had donned their winter survival gear and balaclavas because as soon as the ramp was lowered for the airdrop the temperature in the aft of the aircraft would drop well below the freezing mark. The loadmasters made a last minute check of the precious cargo and chutes and then positioned themselves in the forward end of the cabin, well clear of the pallets.

At 10 miles downwind Bill called for a left 180° turn to a final heading of 060°. As soon as the wings were once again level, both Aircraft Commanders slowed the aircraft to 150 knots and called for the ramp and door to be to opened respectively to the airdrop position. The panel lights confirmed that position which was also confirmed by the loadmaster. Pete was holding a good position on Larry's starboard wing and reported ready for drop. The last mile and a half Larry once again adjusted his position to put his aircraft about 50' right of Ken's ground party. When Larry was ¼ mile from directly abeam Kens' position he ordered "Stand-by" followed immediately by "Drop." Both co-pilots hit the drop switch simultaneously and the overhead extraction chute released attached to the static cord. At 20' from the aircraft, the extraction chute blossomed and like a freight train, the three pallets exited the aircraft, fell about 10' and the chutes attached to the pallets then released and blossomed to full canopies. "Bullseye" shouted Chief Rosenow as his chutes made a beautiful sight. "Likewise" retorted Dave Hazzard from Pete's aircraft.

Lieutenant Koenig communicated, "Perfect drop you guys, looks like an easy recovery. Appreciate the mail, veggies and parts. All-hands send their thanks for bringing a little home to this God-forsaken place."

Bill replied, "You guys deserved a break what with all you have been through and what has happened. Enjoy the goodies and mail from home. We're looking forward to seeing you in a month or two."

Bill signed off and indicated they would be monitoring their frequency on the way back to Punta Arenas.

Bob Avery came up on the frequency and asked for a brief report on the mission. Larry responded that it was a complete success and Lieutenant Koenig was in the process of recovering of all pallets.

Down on the glacier Ken Koenig and his troops were beginning to recover everything that was airdropped. The first thing they did was to pull their pickup truck over to the first pallet Herc 321 had dropped. It contained a new 4X4 truck equipped already with huge wide oversize tires and winterized for the Antarctic. Lieutenant Koenig had his team rig a 55-gallon drum of diesel fuel with a handy-billie on that back of the pickup so he in effect had a portable fuel station. The crew began fueling the 4X4 and when they completed their task, Chief McKenna jumped into the cab and started to crank the engine. It suddenly roared to life and they were quickly in the business of loading the bed of the truck with the most valuable cargo from the other pallets.

First on were the two pallets of mail followed by the fresh eggs, veggies and fruit. Chief McKenna became the designated driver by default and made his first trip down the glacier to the station where some of the station personnel came out and quickly helped to unload the precious cargo. Once off-loaded he made his way back up to the field party where they loaded more precious cargo which included the bearings for the electrical power generator. There were other replacement parts for station equipment and some new lab equipment for the scientists to use in their new experiments.

By the time Ken Koenig returned to the station and had the men unload and store the items from the pallets, he already found the cook making a beautiful salad from the fresh veggies. He told the cook to put out fresh fruit on the tables so everyone could have some with their dinner. Meanwhile Lieutenant Koenig and the diesel mechanic were already studying on how long it will take to install the new bearings on the power generator. They were trying to decide when would be the best time to do the job. After evening reveille appeared to be a good time since everyone would be in a warm sleeping bag and not need lights.

The main activity that could be observed throughout the station were people reading their mail and opening packages they received from their loved ones. The postal clerk had done a great job in sorting the mail quickly and getting it to the proper recipients. One thing was certain, morale was improving with this resupply mission and things were looking better for the remainder of the Antarctic winter.

Seymour Island

Meantime, while all this was occurring at Palmer Station, Mike Brenner, in Herc 917 had been proceeding to Marambio Base on Seymour Island. At 100 miles out of Marambio his navigator Tom Harger had contacted Comodoro Rivadavia Flight Information Region on 13,315 khz and informed them of their position. Marambio was still on Palmer Station's frequency so they passed to Marambio that they were be unable to communicate with the tower but would listen on their VOR frequency of 117.1 MHZ. Marambio acknowledged and indicated they would act as go-between for the tower.

They reported no air traffic and told them to report downwind for Runway 06.

Herc 917 began descent and all appropriate checklists were completed down to the before landing checklist. Approach and landing speeds were checked for a short-field landing. The flight engineer had calculated the fuel required for the return flight to Punta Arenas and briefed Mike on the amount of fuel, which needed to be dumped. They wanted as light a load as possible for landing and especially for takeoff. They both determined that they would dump the externals until they were empty and then dump the main tanks for an additional twenty seconds. Mike slowed the plane and ordered fuel dumping commence. Shortly the external low fuel lights illuminated and Tom Harger punched his stopwatch. At 20sec he called out "Mark" and Petty Officer Glennon closed all fuel dump valves. Fuel dumping was successful and they were ready for approach and landing at Marambio. During the flight Mike and his co-pilot had poured over the flight manual and determined separately using current temperature, relative humidity and density altitude that for the calculated weight the takeoff roll would be 3965'. That would leave them a margin of 169' remaining of runway. It appeared that once the brakes were released they were committed for takeoff. No abort would be allowed. Here was a young Lieutenant, with little Antarctic flight experience, being called upon to perform a mission that would bring a pucker factor of ten to a more experienced pilot. This had to be done right with no margin for error and he was the one who was there and required to perform.

Approaching fifty miles out of Marambio they reported the weather almost the same as Larry and Pete had at Palmer. 3,200' broken clouds, winds out of the northeast at 5 to 10 mph, altimeter 29.78"hg. Mike made the observation that at least this was a grass strip and not ice so the braking would be a little better but not as good as concrete. They passed just off the north end of Seymour Island and Mike turned to heading 240° to set up a long downwind for runway 06. They completed the Before Landing Checklist. At a mile abeam the island the copilot called out a visual on the runway. Mike called for the Landing Checklist. He slowed below 150 knots called for the landing gear down, skis up. Flaps were set at 10%. He stabilized the speed of the aircraft at 135 knots. Upon passing the downwind end of the runway he proceeded another two miles so as to give himself a long 2-mile straight-in final. It was a right hand approach in order to keep clear of the hills to the west of the runway. He stopped his turn heading 060°. He was at 2000', reduced power and started his descent to the runway. Passing 1200' he called for flaps 20%, slowed to 125 knots. All-hands were just about now holding their breath. This was going to be a cliff-hangar and going to take all the skill Mike could muster to get the plane on the end of the runway and stop before running out of runway. The copilot reminded him field elevation was 760' and had set his radar altimeter at 30' as an indicator. At 1 mile from the runway Mike called for flaps 30% and slowed to threshold speed of 106 knots. Touchdown speed was calculated as 96 knots. At ½ mile Mike began slowing to 96 knots carrying plenty of power to arrest the sink-rate. At that point the warning light on the radar altimeter blinked. Touchdown was at 97 knots and 30' past the end of the runway. Mike immediately pushed over the nose until the nose wheel contacted the runway with the copilot grasping the yoke and also pushing forward while simultaneously bringing the power levers back and up into the ground range further pulling them all the way back into the reverse detent. The props roared in reverse pitch and Mike switched his left hand to the nose-wheel steering to keep the plane straight on the runway.

Mike had made a beautiful short-field landing and had managed to get it stopped in about 2600'. What an accomplishment for a rookie. They taxied over to a spot, which had be cleared and smoothed as a turn-around and where they had observed a number of trucks and an ambulance. While doing so they completed the After Landing Checklist. Mike had decided to shut down the engines to make the situation safer for all-hands who would be working around the aircraft during this stop. Petty Officer Glennon started the Gas Turbine Compressor to have warm air to heat the cargo compartment while on the ground and also for electrical power for any necessities. Mike set the brakes and called for engine shutdown. Shutdown was completed, and the forward crew entrance door was opened and Colonel Sanchez climbed aboard. He climbed the steps into the cockpit and Mike greeted him. They introduced themselves to each other and Colonel Sanchez couldn't thank them enough for making this rescue flight. Mike indicated that it was their duty to do this, as that was the unwritten code of the Antarctic.

Chief Rosenow had lowered the ramp and opened the rear door to the ground loading position. He supervised the loading of the stretcher from the ambulance and securing it properly in the stanchions which were specifically designed to hold stretchers. Colonel Sanchez and his personnel provided some fresh sandwiches and hot coffee as a snack for the crew while they were on the ground. The loading of the medevac took only about twenty-two minutes. Along with the patient the Colonel sent one medical person to attend the injured man.

Mike said his goodbyes. The Colonel responded with his undying thanks. The crew door, loading ramp and rear door were closed and all-hands manned their flight stations. The colonel had indicated that his people in Buenos Aires would pass all medical information to the hospital in Punta Arenas and ensure that an ambulance and medical personnel would meet the aircraft on arrival.

Mike and his crew cranked up the aircraft and began taxing to the takeoff point at the beginning of runway 06. At the end of the runway he turned the aircraft into the wind and then backed up the some 50' he had used up in turning the aircraft around. The crew went through their aircraft and engine checks. They were now ready for departure. Mike briefed the cockpit crew and placed the power levers down into the flight position. He added power to about 80% of takeoff power and before releasing the brakes scanned all the engine instruments. As Mike released the brakes the copilot pushed the power levers to maximum allowed torque, which was well below the maximum allowed turbine inlet temperature. The aircraft leapt forward while the propellers were at maximum pitch angle and were biting the air as if to devour a raw steak it had longed for over an extended period of time. Acceleration appeared to be normal. Mike lifted the nose wheel at 85 knots. The copilot reported passing 2000'. Mike thought lift off you bastard but then thought better not insult the old girl but coax her into performing like she never did before. He had set the exact correct angle for takeoff and

sure enough the Hercules vaulted into the air at the 4000'
mark. He remarked to the copilot, "Never a doubt. We still
had 134' left." Then called for gear up, accelerated to climb
airspeed and brought up the flaps and completed the after
takeoff/climb check list. Tom Harger had let the 2nd navigator
do the chart and log work while he decided to handle the
communications. The pilots took up the recommended
heading of 320° and the navigator estimated time enroute
at 3 hours, 12 minutes, putting them in Punta Arenas at
4:02p.m. local time. Tom Harger was busy first contacting
Comodoro Rivadavia Flight Information Region advising that
they were airborne in their region, cruising at flight level 120
(12,000') and giving them an ETA for departing their region
and entering Punta Arenas FIR. Next he called Herc 319 on
Palmer's frequency and advised them that they had made the
pickup of the medevac patient and their ETA Punta Arenas.
On the other HF transceiver he contacted Punta Arenas with
their ETA for entering their airspace and asked them to pass
the message on to Lieutenant Commander Avery. He also
advised Punta Arenas about Colonel Sanchez' information
that he would pass the medical information to the local
hospital but asked that Lieutenant Commander Avery check
with the local hospital to ensure medical personnel and an
ambulance would meet Herc 917 on arrival. Bob Avery came
up on the frequency and advised he had copied all requested
and would coordinate with all concerned. Bob asked for 917's
ETA Punta Arenas. Tom responded and passed the ETA of
4:02pm

Bill Grammercy called in on the Punta Arenas frequency
and reported their ETA at Punta Arenas as 3:26pm Pete was
cruising at flight level 10.5(10,500') and Larry was at flight
level 11.0(11,000').

With that last report things in all the Hercs settled
down to a routine flight. With the pressure of each mission
behind them the crews were now very loose and relaxed and
chatter in the airplanes was fast and free.

13

"A Job Well Done"

Thursday Afternoon

The flight back from Palmer had thus far been routine for the Hercs 319 and 321. They were approaching 100 miles out of Punta Arenas. Bill Springer, Navigator in 321, called Bill Grammercy in 319. "How about we switch to Punta Arenas Approach Control, Bill?" he asked. "Commander Vernon would like to get the latest weather at the airport."

"Roger that," Bill G. replied. "Lets switch to 257.5 now."

"Roger switching," Bill S. answered.

"Punta Arenas approach control this is Navy 8321 over."

Punta Arenas approach acknowledged and Bill Springer reported 100 miles out at 11,000' and requested the latest weather.

Punta Arenas reported the current weather as 1500' overcast, winds West at 3 to 5 mph, altimeter 29.80"hg.

Charlie Black in 319 rogered the weather and reported 100 miles out of Punta Arenas at 10,500'. Punta Arenas cleared Navy 8319 to the Punta arenas Airport to descend to and maintain 5000'. He next cleared Navy 8321 to the Punta Arenas Airport to descend to and maintain 6000'.

At about 50 miles from the airport radar contact was established with both aircraft and they were eventually directed to a ten-mile final for runway 25. Both aircraft landed safely and taxied to their assigned parking space, which they had previously occupied.

Upon deplaning both crews had hugs and hardy handshakes all around for a job well done. Bob Avery was there to meet them and he joined in the congratulations. Larry praised Lieutenant Koenig for an outstanding job of marking the drop zone and providing plenty of black smoke, which made the airdrop easy and successful. The talk then turned to Mike Brenner who obviously was thrust into the toughest job they had yet. Having to make that emergency flight into Marambio and then land and takeoff on their short runway. Obviously he had done both successfully and was now only twenty minutes from touchdown at Punta Arenas.

The crews of 321 and 319 were conducting a post-flight of their aircraft but all eyes were glued to the skies at the approach to Runway 25.

Nobody noticed the two police cars and an ambulance coming through the gate at the FBO and headed toward the aircraft. Bob Avery saw them first and asked Bill Springer to be the interpreter for those approaching as he knew that English would be hard to decipher. The vehicles came to a stop in front of the aircraft and one of the policemen who appeared to be an officer in the highway patrol stepped out and addressed Bill, as he was approaching, in very broken English. Bill quickly responded in his fluent Spanish dialect, which brought a wide grin to the face of the policeman. They quickly established some rapport and Bill told him they expected the medevac to arrive shortly. The ambulance crew consisted of two EMTs and a Doctor who had been assigned to accompany the patient to the hospital. Bill introduced the policeman to Bob Avery and told him he was the commanding officer of the detachment.

It wasn't more than a couple of minutes when 917 broke through the overcast layer and was a ½ mile from touchdown. Mike made a beautiful landing and after turning off the duty runway taxied quickly to his parking place next to the other Hercs parked on the ramp. As he turned into the parking space Chief Rosenow was already lowering the ramp and opening the rear door. Engines were shutdown and a sense of urgency swept over those waiting to retrieve the patient. Chief Rosenow lowered the ramp to the ground loading position and the ambulance was directed to a position directly under the tail of the aircraft, to receive the patient. Other flight crewmembers went aboard 917 and assisted lowering the stretcher and began carrying it towards the ramp. They were extremely careful because of the IV's and fragility of the patient. They quickly loaded the stretcher aboard the ambulance and closed the door. Upon seeing that movement, the police cars turned on their emergency lights and led the ambulance off the airport and headed toward the hospital.

Airport customs and immigration drove up in their vehicle. Bob Avery intercepted them and asked if he could assist them. They wanted to speak to the Aircraft Commander of Herc 917. Mike Brenner stepped forward and the inspectors indicated to Mike that he would have to come over to their office and sign some paperwork.

Mike accompanied the officials. He was asked a few questions and eventually signed a series of papers indicating the emergency situation, which required him to land at Marambio. He also certified that the same crewmembers that departed Punta Arenas earlier that morning were in fact the same ones who returned on the aircraft with no additions or subtractions. They indicated to Mike that they would take care of the additional paperwork required for his unexpected passenger but would do that separately and would not need his presence. Having completed their paperwork they gave Mike a ride back to his aircraft where all detachment personnel were awaiting his return.

There was still backslapping and congratulations being offered all around. When they spotted Mike, all-hands broke out in a stirring round of cheers and applause.

It was the first time in weeks that there was so much enthusiasm and joy openly expressed by the personnel. It had been a tough three weeks and had brought little reason for this kind of expression until today. The Antarctic had jumped up and tried to bite them once again in the ass but they had beat her at everything that was thrown at them. They all boarded the busses and headed for the hotel. Bob Avery told all-hands they would have a banquet that night and to check with the duty officer for time and place. There was plenty of laughter and chatter on the bus going to the hotel.

When they had arrived Bob found the concierge at the hotel and asked her to help him find a restaurant and make arrangements to feed 31 people. She suggested the "La Familia" restaurant.

The detachment arrived at the restaurant around 7:00pm and was directed to an area in the rear. It was the non-smoking area, which was mostly unused since almost all resident patrons were usually smokers. Drinks were ordered all around with the most popular being the local cerveza. Some people ordered the local red wine, which was somewhat near a burgundy. Bill Springer's language skills were used many times in ordering dinner as some men of the detachment had difficulty understanding items listed on the menu. The staff was patient and attentive to the Navymen and dinner was well prepared, served and eaten. The concensus was that the food was great and the staff cared that they all were pleased with the dinner. Flan was the preferred dessert and as the men were in the final stages of dinner, Bob Avery rose to speak.

He quickly had their attention and began, "Men, I just wanted to say a few words before we start back to the hotel. First I want to ask Bill to thank the staff for the great dinner."

Bill Springer stood and asked the manager to assemble all the staff in the dining room. The wait staff and the cooks came out of the kitchen and stood on one side of the dining room facing the crew assembled. In his best Spanish Bill said, "Ladies and Gentlemen, the people gathered here tonight would like to thank you for the wonderful food, for the service provided and for your friendship. We appreciate the special attention provided and wish you all well."

He especially thanked the manager for accommodating them on such short notice and for his great staff. At that point in the proceedings a huge round of applause was given and received with a lot of smiles from the staff. When things quieted down and the staff filtered out, Bob once again took center stage and said, "Thanks, Bill," he continued, "This time in Punta Arenas has not been easy for all of us. You have worked hard and overcome many obstacles. Some roadblocks we encountered we were unable to bridge but in the long run we have had a successful time. My special recognition to Mike Brenner and his crew for a job well done. Stepping up and being thrust into the unknown is a credit to how well I had trained you." All-hands laughed and burst into applause. "In all seriousness, your performance in the face of adversity is a great credit to all of you." Turning to Mike, Bob said, "Mike, I have one question, how much runway did you have remaining on your takeoff from Marambio?"

Mike stood and responded. "Hell Bob, we had at least 67' left so who needed it. Short runways are always welcome." He sat down and was thinking to himself, don't need any more of those for a while.

Once more Bob continued. "I know this has been a long day and everyone is unwinding so let's continue and we can plan on leaving here for the hotel in about two hours. We will have transportation out front about then so enjoy." With that, Bob sat down and ordered another round of drinks for his tablemates.

Before dinner Bob had recommended that the officers sit with their respective crews. Now that everyone had relaxed a bit there was a lot of visiting between tables and the social atmosphere was great. There was a lot of kidding between crews as to which one had done the best job and the typical "my pilots are better than yours." Between pilots, no matter how good you were, no naval aviator worth his salt would ever admit that somebody else was a better pilot. The same was true about naval flight officers and also enlisted crews. Deep down however there was great respect for each other but to admit it was seen as a sign of weakness. It was truly a great sight to observe and Bob was enjoying every minute of it. He had great pride in Mike Brenner for his high degree of professionalism but would never admit it publicly.

At the designated time, all-hands finished their drinks, put on their jackets and moved out to the street to board the transportation for the hotel. Each in turn shook hands and thanked the staff of the restaurant. There was a language barrier but not recognition of the friendship and appreciation exhibited between the cultures.

Tomorrow was a day of rest and recuperation, which all hands were looking forward to.

Punta Arenas: Saturday Morning

Commander Pete Vernon awoke early after a good night's sleep. While showering he went over the things he had to do today. It was after 7:00am but the sun had not broken over the horizon yet. He thought, winter could surely be depressing with late sunrises and early sunsets. After dressing he went down to the main level and went into the dining room for breakfast. Bob Avery was already having coffee so he joined him. They discussed the tasks which needed to be accomplished today. Pete told Bob he would take care of the travel itinerary with the squadron and the Embassy in Santiago. They agreed they should depart Sunday morning as early as practical since it would be 12 hours of flying to La Paz, Bolivia, with a stop at Buenos Aires for fuel. They would remain overnight (RON) in La Paz and then fly to Howard AFB, Panama, on Monday where they would RON before making the final flight to Point Mugu on Tuesday.

As breakfast progressed more of the detachment officers began wandering into the dining room and soon the main table of senior officers became a giant caffee clatch. Conversation now settled on getting home and seeing the wife and playing with the kids. It was a very relaxed atmosphere as there were no pressing problems or deadlines. Today would be as enjoyable as the men of this detachment could make it.

After breakfast Pete went back to his room, as that would be the best spot to contact Ralph Touch in Santiago. He dialed the phone and after a couple of rings a voice came on the line, "United States Embassy, how may I direct your call?" the operator said.

Pete responded, "Could you connect me with Commander Touch, please?"

The operator then said, "One moment please and may I say who is calling?"

"This is Commander Pete Vernon calling from Punta Arenas."

"Thank you sir. I will put you through," she said.

In a few seconds Ralph Touch came on the phone. "Hey Pete great too hear from you, I was planning on calling you later today. How was your flight to Palmer Station?"

"The air drops went smoothly and everything arrived safely and intact. I don't know if you remember meeting

Lieutenant Mike Brenner but anyway he made and emergency medevac in and out of the Argentine base on Seymour Island. He did a beautiful job on their 4,134' grass runway. What a great accomplishment for a young kid. We are real proud of him," Pete said.

"That's great to hear. By the way I have good news for you," Ralph said.

"Well give it to me old friend I need some good news right now," Pete said.

"I was in contact with the Argentinians and we have permission for you to refuel at El Palomar Military Air Base tomorrow. Have you decided on your flight times yet, Pete?" He asked.

"Yeah, Ralph, get your pencil handy. I will give you our itinerary and would like you to send out a message for us as we don't have that capability down here," Pete said.

"Okay Pete, we can do that for you. Give me your times and stops and I will get out a message for you. I have my pencil in hand so go ahead," Ralph said.

"Sounds great Ralph. Here are the times and places. We will depart Punta Arenas at 1100 zulu arriving El Palomar at 1720 zulu. Two hours on the ground and then departing EL Palomar 1930 zulu arriving La Paz, Bolivia, at 0130 zulu. We are going to RON in La Paz and depart Monday morning at 1300 zulu arriving Howard AFB, Panama, at 2200 zulu. On Tuesday we will depart Howard AFB at 1100 zulu with a refueling stop at Guadalajara, Mexico, arriving 1700 zulu, departing at 1900 zulu and arriving Point Mugu, California at 0100 zulu. You copy all that Ralph?" Pete asked.

Ralph replied that he had copied all, and then asked to whom he should copy the message.

Pete continued. "We need to info Antarctic Development Squadron Six, Commander, Task Force Forty-Three and Office Polar Programs at the National Science Foundation."

"I got all that, Pete. We will of course notify all airports and countries you will be transiting on your flight back to Mugu. Have you any other things we might be able to help you with?" Ralph inquired.

"You guys have been absolutely flawless in your support of us while we have been here and we sincerely appreciate all the help you have provided us. Thanks, Ralph, I don't think we have any other needs right now. Give my love to Margie and tell her we miss her Mai Tais and Hors d' oeuvres. My best to you and Bill Marsh. Hope we see you next time around."

"Happy to serve you guys, Pete. Have a good flight and will pass your message on to Margie. Give us a call when you are in the area. Take care."

With that Pete hung up the phone. His next task would be to email the squadron.

Pete went down to the Business Center in the hotel, sat down at one of their computers and sent off an email to the CO. He included their itinerary and a short message stating that he would see him late Tuesday evening.

The detachment personnel had completed all other preparations for the flight and they all spent the day relaxing just reading, writing and hoisting a few brews.

Late in the day the officers did their usual thing. They strolled down the street to the little Mexican restaurant for dinner. It was a quiet gathering and soon they were walking back to the hotel to get settled down for the evening.

Punta Arenas: Sunday Morning

Morning arrived early for all-hands as they had scheduled a 0700 departure. They followed their normal routine and departed the hotel around 5:00am. The vans all stopped at the terminal at the airport to drop off the pilots and navigators. The enlisted crews proceeded to the airport FBO and preflighted each aircraft. They had previously fueled the aircraft on Saturday. In short order they completed their assigned tasks and proceeded back over to the terminal for breakfast. The pilots and navigators had in turn completed their flight planning, filed their flight plans and were already sitting down in the restaurant for breakfast. The enlisted crews joined them and soon they were enjoying their last meal in Punta Arenas. It was a happy group as they were all a little tired of being away and were looking forward to getting home.

After breakfast the crews went down onto the ramp and strode over to their aircraft.

All aircraft were quickly manned and were soon airborne for El Palomar in Buenos Aires, Argentina.

In Flight over Southern California

The flight back home had thus far gone off without a hitch. They had stopped overnight in Panama and refueled in Guadalajara, Mexico.

Herc 319 was leading the way and cruising north at 30,000'. Los Angeles Center had them in radar contact and was routing them directly to Point Mugu. Herc 321 soon checked in 6 miles astern at 32,000' and Herc 917 was 10 miles back at 34,000'. Larry Beck requested descent to 3000'. The other two aircraft were also cleared to descend and Larry cancelled his IFR flight plan passing through 5000'. Pete Vernon on 321 also cancelled, as did Mike Brenner in 917. Larry instructed the other two aircraft to join in a right echelon formation at 3000'. He was now twenty miles from Point Mugu and reported he was circling left at 3000'. Pete soon joined on Larry's wing followed closely by Mike. It was just after 5:00pm and the sun would not set for another hour or so. Larry's copilot, Charlie Black, switched the formation over to Point Mugu Tower frequency.

He keyed the mike, "Point Mugu Tower this is Navy 48319, 20 miles south with three birds for the break for landing, over."

Point Mugu responded, "Roger Navy 48319. Cleared to break Runway 03, sky clear, winds light and variable, altimeter 30.02"hg."

Charlie knew what Larry had in mind so he responded to the tower, "Roger tower, copied all and your altimeter 30.02"hg, request 500 foot break, over."

"Navy 48321 you're cleared for a low pass and 500' break, over."

Larry began a left turn followed by a right to line up on Runway 03 all the while descending to 500' and increasing his speed to 250 knots. As he approached the threshold of the runway he eased to the right so as to pass almost over VXE-6's hangar. He had accelerated to 250 knots and as he passed over the hangar he saw the large crowd of people awaiting their arrival. It was a classy formation with 20' nose to tail, 20' wingtip to wingtip and a 20' step-up. As he passed the upwind end of the runway he broke left, began a slight climb to 1500' pattern altitude and reduced the power levers to flight idle. Pete followed and broke at 10 seconds later with

Mike another 10 seconds behind. They were now level at 1500' parallel to Runway 03. As each slowed below 155 knots they lowered the landing gear, flaps 10%. As Larry passed abeam of the end of the runway Charlie called the tower, "Mugu Tower, 319 base, gear down for landing."

Tower responded, "319 You're cleared for landing."

Charlie responded, "319 roger."

In turn 321 and 917 reported base with gear down and were cleared to land.

As Larry turned off the runway Pete touched down followed by Mike. Larry taxied slowly and soon the three aircraft were nose to tail and were directed by ground control to the VXE-6 hangar. As they approached the fight line each picked up their taxi director who directed them into their parking space. It was beautiful as if it had been a dance choreographed by the best Hollywood director. They all came to a stop almost instantaneously and given the signal to cut engines. The crews went through the shutdown checklist and soon the Commanding Officer was out front of Pete's aircraft awaiting the crews to deplane. He greeted Pete followed by Bob Avery, Larry and Mike. Soon all crewmen were swarming over the ramp and running quickly into the arms of their wives, sweethearts and children. It was a happy time but not an unusual event for the men of VXE-6. As quickly as the ramp had filled with the men of the detachment it just as quickly emptied as each family made their way to their vehicles for the ride home where they would continue their family reunion. The bachelors in the crews made their way to their respective clubs for a quick drink and dinner before retiring to their quarters.

Before they had departed the hangar the CO had passed the word that the crews would have a week off before reporting back for work.

14

"The Decision"

Point Mugu, California: Next day

The phone in the CO's office rang twice when he picked up it was Jack Forester. He began," Jeri, I heard the detachment all made it home safely last night,"

"Yeah, Jack they got in around 5pm last night. They were all beat from the long flight back home so I gave them all the week off. What's going on?" he asked.

"I just wanted to check-in and see how they were feeling after that long detachment and also wanted to fill you in on what we are planning," Jack said.

"I was kind of wondering what you had in store," Jeri offered.

"The RN Laurence M. Gould is scheduled to sail for Antarctica in late August but we are going to move that up to late June, early July, to pick up the pararescue team and send a new O-in-C to Palmer Station. Their first port-of-call will be Punta Arenas where the team can off-load and catch a flight for the states. That should put them home some time about the middle of July. We want to get them home as soon as possible as they have been in Antarctica long enough and I know we will need that capability next season starting in October," Jack said.

"Hey, that sounds great, may I pass that word on to the families?" Jeri asked.

"Yeah, we're firm enough on the schedule, so that would be okay," Jack said.

"Okay Jack will do. By the way Pete and I haven't discussed an exact date but in the next week we will decide when he will relieve me of the command and assume duties as Commanding Officer."

"Keep us posted here, Jeri. We will want to attend as will Admiral Boland. Are you going to recommend some awards for the crew of 917?" Jack asked.

"I expect we will, probably as soon as I get a chance to talk with Bob Avery. That young man, Mike Brenner, sure did a fine job as did his crew. We will work out the details as quickly as possible," Jeri offered.

"Also, Jeri, talk with Pete and pick your team for the upcoming planning conference. We will need your attendees in about two weeks. We are going to host it at the Natural Bridge Conference Center this year," Jack added.

"Roger, copied that Jack. Pete and I will decide in about a week or so. Will keep you advised," said Jeri.

"Okay, Jeri. Will be in touch soon. Take care and my best to the detachment."

"Great, Jack. Talk to you soon"

With the call complete Jeri hung up the phone and returned to more mundane routine squadron business.

The week passed very quickly and on Tuesday all detachment personnel returned to work after a week's rest and relaxation. After squadron muster on the hangar deck Pete walked into Jeri's office.

"Welcome back officially, Pete!" Jeri proffered.

"Thanks, Jeri. It's great to be back in civilization. Not to say that Punta Arenas is bad but it's not like home," Pete said. "I don't know where to start so I guess an informal report on the detachment would be in order."

"Yeah, I'd like to hear all the details, Pete." Jeri said.

"Well, the flight down to Punta Arenas went well until we got within 100 miles of Punta Arenas." At this point Pete told the story of how the crews had made blind approaches to the airport because of the power failure and the great flying skill and professionalism demonstrated by all-hands.

"Wow, Pete." Jeri exclaimed. "Being a helicopter pilot I didn't know just how skilled these guys were. I knew they had talent but that's some great accomplishment. Not many guys could have pulled that one off."

Pete began, "They certainly were amazing. Anyway things went smoothly until we lost Bob for the mission with his appendicitis. Mike Brenner certainly stepped up, as did Larry during the rest of the mission. The first flight to Palmer turned out to be the disaster. I couldn't even begin to describe to you what the ice break-up looked like except to say it resembled a 2000 pound bomb going off. There was debris everywhere and pieces as big as houses were flying every direction. Larry was lucky to sustain only the little damage to the airplane that he had. His reaction to the whole situation was instantaneous and professional. Anyway the loss of life on the ice was regretful and is something etched in my mind forever. The next flight was pretty much routine and went smoothly. The rescue of the Argentinian by Mike was commendable and his landing and takeoff from that short unimproved airstrip should be recognized. I will take care of that and will have my recommendations for awards on your desk later this week. As far as support, the embassy in Santiago was outstanding as well as from all others concerned. They helped us with anything we needed and were very timely in their contribution to our success. Perhaps a letter of appreciation to the embassy would be in order."

Jeri then turned the conversation to the change of command. "When would you like to have the change of command?" he asked Pete.

"How about the 21st of June? That will give us about 6 weeks to clear up any items we have hanging. When do your orders say you have to report to USS Independence, Jeri?" Pete asked.

"I have to relieve the navigator in July so that date sounds great. It will give me time to take two weeks leave along the way so Rebekah and I can take a little vacation."

"Okay, Jeri. Let's plan on doing it then. I will take care of the necessary notifications."

Having completed their meeting Pete stepped over to his office and began to review his paperwork, which had come to a complete standstill while he was gone.

The other officers and men resumed their normal routine at the squadron.

H.J. "Walt" Walter

Washington, DC: Present Time

Jack was jolted from his daydreaming by the sound of the intercom. "Jack, this is Ken. Are you busy or can I come up and give you a briefing?"

"Come on up from your dungeon," Jack responded. He realized that Ken must have a report from Jack Shepard concerning the space shuttle. It was standard practice not to discuss AFV activity on any communications equipment.

Ken had indeed received a coded message from Jack. Jack had now been operations director at the new AFV base in Utah for one year and was quite adept in his operation.

Ken gathered his papers and left his office. He had taken over Arsene's old cubbyhole when he left which was located in the building one level below the street. He quickly moved to the stairs, emerging on the second level and proceeding directly to Jack's outer office. Mary McGuire had secured for the day so he knocked on Jack's door and entered. They both exchanged greetings and Jack asked, "Well, what do you have for me, Ken?"

Ken responded and began his report, "Jack debriefed Bruce Fleming, AFV pilot, who had been assigned to reconnoiter the space shuttle Enterprise. In Bruce's words, "I approached the shuttle from rear port quarter. As I approached within two miles and since the shuttle's cargo bay was facing earthward, I went inverted, slowed to a closing speed of approximately 200 miles per hour and passed over the shuttle at ½ mile. I had all my cameras turned on, infrared, standard color digital as well as my radar camera. When I was directly over the shuttle I veered off toward the starboard aft quarter and accelerated too 800 mph differential speed so as to get some distance between it and me in a hurry. When passing over inverted, my systems analyst and I were able to visually check her out for any anomalies. She was venting a little water vapor from her scrubber unit, which appeared to be normal. I guess the crew is sweating a bit more than normal given the situation. We observed no other gasses venting, nor any visible damage to the shuttle. We were also monitoring their communications frequencies and during our pass their discussion with mission control remained normal so we were unseen and our radar image was undetected. Our visual contact with the shuttle was just before sunset over the Indian

Ocean. Our approach was from west to east and breakaway direction was southwesterly. We had a good look at her and she appears normal except for loss of fuel."

"That was the complete report from Jack. I have nothing further to report. Have you made any decision on a rescue yet?" Ken asked.

"No." Jack replied. "I need to have a meeting with Bill Reynolds before we decide what to do. Your report will help us along with Bill's report from NASA. Bill will also have the pictures analyzed from the pass by Bruce Fleming. Thanks, Ken, Keep me up to date on anything you hear."

"Will do, Jack." With his meeting complete Ken left Jack's office and returned to his cubbyhole in the basement. Ken immediately shredded his written notes and placed the shreds in his burn bag. He never left the building without burning. Jack had instilled in him the necessity for complete secrecy on the AFV program and his years as a communications officer had made it a habit also.

Jack picked up his phone and placed a call to Bill Reynolds. It was approaching 4:30pm and they made plans to have dinner around 7:00pm that evening in Bill Reynolds' office. Bill told Jack he had invited Don Ransford, SecDef, for dinner also. Jack didn't question that. He knew Don Ransford was a member of MJ-12 and should probably be in on the decision as to whether to make a rescue with the AFV's since it might expose the AFV program to the public.

Jack left his office around 6:00pm so as to arrive in plenty of time for the 7:00pm meeting and dinner. The drive through Arlington and then onto the George Washington Memorial Parkway was fairly normal for that time of day on a Wednesday. He drove at the speed of the traffic and finally took the Mclean exit for the CIA. He was cleared through security at the gate and parked in the underground garage. He made his way over to the elevator and pushed the button for the director's office floor. When he arrived in the director's outer office the director's assistant ushered him in as the director was expecting him.

"Hey, Jack, good to see you. Hope you had a good trip out here," Bill asked.

"Yeah, traffic was starting to thin out so it wasn't too bad. I see Don hasn't arrived yet," he noticed.

"Oh, Don called and he will be a couple of minutes late. He had a briefing from his staff on something related to Afghanistan. Have a seat and give me the details from Utah if you have any."

Jack began, "I had a briefing secondhand by Ken Nichols from one of our AFV pilots Bruce Fleming." Jack repeated practically word for word what Ken had told him about the shuttle.

"Sounds like the shuttles in good shape except for no damn fuel," Bill responded. "We are currently analyzing the pictures from the flight."

About that time Don Ransford entered Bill's office. "Glad you could make it Don," Bill offered.

"Thanks, Bill. Hey Jack good to see you once again." Don said as he extended his hand. Jack shook his hand and said he was also glad to see him. Both men then took seats on the couches and were joined by Bill.

Bill opened the conversation. "Don, Jack has just given me a briefing from one of our AFV pilots who was monitoring the space shuttle. All appears physically normal except of course the loss of all maneuvering fuel and engine thruster fuel for reentry. I was about to tell Jack about my discussion with Ed Grimes at NASA and his report and assessment of the shuttle crew and their rescue efforts. Let me begin by saying NASA has no rescue capability. They have mothballed all the other shuttles in their process of getting ready to shutdown the shuttle program. It would take them nine days working twenty-four hours a day to get a shuttle up to Enterprise for a rescue. They have inquired to the Chinese and Russians to see if they could mount a rescue. Both have indicated they cannot within the window available. Ed indicated to me, the mental state of the crew and it is deteriorating as might be expected. The closer they get to oxygen running out the worse it will get. Which brings us down to the main reason we are all here tonight. I believe we have the capability within our AFV program to rescue the crew so let's discuss it. Jack what do you think?" Bill asked.

Jack began. "I have reviewed the emergency contingency plan previously approved by MJ-12 about 5 years ago and it gives us a step by step action on how to make a space rescue and remain secret. One of the missions of the AFV program from the beginning has been a possible space rescue of astronauts who are determined to be in need."

"Bill, I have thought hard and long on this issue. The three of us are all former naval aviators. There are at least two naval aviators on the shuttle crew. Over the years there has always been camaraderie between naval aviators no matter when we served. I personally feel a bond with those crewmembers trapped in the shuttle and maybe I am leading with my feelings and not logic but I say we should rescue the crew regardless of the consequences to the AFV program. I am ready to take the heat if it is exposed to the world. If we follow the MJ-12 plan we have better than a 50-50 chance of the AFV program remaining secret. I figure the crew of the shuttle has less than sixty-six hours of oxygen remaining and we should get them down as soon as possible so they don't have to much time to think about their fate if we were to leave them up there. Don, I know Bill invited you as a member of MJ-12 and it is your sworn duty to protect the AFV program no matter what happens. So let's hear your feelings on this thing." Having said his peace Jack looked to Don as did Bill for his response.

Don took a couple of slow deep breaths and began, "Jack thanks for your candor. I too have had long and thoughtful considerations on what should we do if ever faced with this type of situation. If we don't save these people we protect the AFV program. If we save them we could possibly expose the whole program. However let me use a sea story to make my point. Toward the end of WWII the USS Indianapolis was cruising towards Guam. Our intelligence people had broken the Japanese code and we knew they were waiting with submarines to sink the Indianapolis. We did not warn them because if we did the Japanese would know we had broken their code so we did nothing. We lost the ship and many lives. We could have prevented all that but we didn't. After the war the stories came out and the truth was revealed. Let me put it to you this way, I don't want this same story to be repeated and go down in history as one who could have prevented the loss of the shuttle crew because I did nothing. Therefore you can guess how I vote. Let's do it and as soon as possible. If you can figure a way to get it done and keep the program secret then that will be great. If not I too am ready to take the heat. I guess that's two votes to do it Bill. How do you feel about it?"

Bill smiled at his two friends. "You guys know how I feel. Let's do it and the sooner the better. Jack, Don and I will work with you to help with a cover-up if it's necessary. Don and I will review the MJ-12 plan so we know what needs to be done to keep the program secret. So, since we're all in agreement let's have a drink and order dinner."

The three friends had a drink and they all felt better that they had made the decision to make the rescue. Bill called down to the kitchen and ordered dinner from the cook, Willie Sutton. Soon they were munching down on the prime Rib and joking about things in general.

15

"A Change in Direction"

Arlington, Virginia: Next day

Kate had already been in bed when Jack got home last night. He had kissed her when he got in bed but didn't wake her. This morning he arose early and again tried not to wake Kate but as he started to shower she stirred and soon greeted him.

"Hey, sailor. You ignoring me or something?" She said as she stepped into the shower with him.

"Nah, it was late last night and this morning I knew I had to get to the office early so I didn't want to disturb you," he said as he cuddled her in his arms. They just stood there with the water pouring down on them as each enjoyed the few minutes they had together.

Jack let Kate step out of the shower first.

"Whatcha want for breakfast?" she yelled.

"How about a couple of waffles, some orange juice and coffee," Jack responded.

"You got it fella," Kate remarked.

She didn't say any more to Jack since she knew this would be a stressful day. Jack had made her aware of the full extent of the problem and what he needed to consider and put in motion. He knew this would take some exceptional planning and execution. He couldn't help but be wary of the situation.

He was soon dressed and came down for breakfast. He told Kate he didn't even want to read the morning paper or watch the television since his dilemma would be all over the TV as it had been for the past day 24/7.

He quickly finished breakfast, grabbed his briefcase, kissed Kate goodbye and headed out the door. He was soon on I-66 bogged down in all the traffic. As he hit the stop and go traffic his mind once again wandered.

Pt. Mugu: Four years earlier

The squadron was preparing for the change of command where Commander Pete Vernon was relieving Commander Jeri Perriman. Jack had travelled with Admiral Boland to Point Mugu, California for the ceremony. The squadron was in parade formation with the Operations Officer in charge of the formation. Commander Williams had been on board for about 6 months and he would relieve Commander Vernon, as Executive Officer after the change of command was complete. The squadron was brought to attention as each VIP arrived. The first to arrive was Captain Joe Rogers, Commanding Officer, of Naval Air Station Point Mugu. Next on scene was Captain Wesley Russell, Commander, Fleet Air Wing 10, then Jack and Admiral Boland followed closely by Vice Admiral Bob Fitzsimmons, ComNavAirPac. All VIPs were greeted by The CO and XO and soon took their seats on the dais.

Commander Perriman approached the microphone and asked the ops officer if the squadron was ready for inspection. Commander Williams reported ready for inspection. Commander Perriman asked Admiral Fitzsimmons if he would like to accompany him on the inspection tour. He nodded in the affirmative and they stepped down off the dais. As they approached Commander Williams he saluted with his sword, which was returned by Admiral Fitzsimmons and Commander Perriman. Commander Williams sheathed his sword and turned to accompany the inspection party. They quickly inspected all-hands, saluted then returned to the dais. Commander Williams once again took his position in front of the formation. Commander Perriman directed Commander Williams to bring the squadron to parade rest. He then introduced Admiral Fitzsimmons as the guest speaker. Admiral Fitzsimmons delivered an inspiring speech praising the squadron for their accomplishments during the past year under the command of Commander Perriman. As he finished Commander Perriman once again stepped up to the podium and then thanked the Admiral for his kind words.

He next spoke of the recent detachment of the three Hercs to Punta Arenas, their accomplishments under severe conditions, and their attempt to return the pararescue team and Lieutenant Mike Brenner's medivac flight into Mirambio Field on Seymour Island. At the completion of his remarks he asked the Senior Chief Yeoman John Carey to approach the mike. He then called Lieutenant Brenner front and center. As he did so he turned the mike over to Carey and stepped down where he stopped directly in front of Lieutenant Brenner. Chief Carey began reading the paper he had in front of him.

> *"The Commander-in-Chief Pacific Fleet takes great pleasure in awarding Lieutenant Michael Brenner the Air Medal for heroism in the performance of his duties while assigned to Antarctic Development Squadron Six. His actions on April 10th, in the year of our lord one thousand nine hundred ninety-five while on routine search and rescue mission were in keeping with the highest traditions of the naval service. During his flight he was alerted to an injured man at the Argentine Base on Seymour Island, Antarctica, in need of evacuation to a medical facility without which he would surely die. Lieutenant Brenner diverted his aircraft as quickly as possible to that base and with great skill placed his aircraft down on a short, unimproved runway without damage to his aircraft. After loading his precious cargo, he launched his aircraft from that field with little or no runway to spare and returned this patient to Punta Arenas, Chile, thus saving his life. The aviation skills exhibited that day were more than could be expected from a naval aviator of his rank. His actions that day were in the highest traditions of naval aviation and in keeping with those of the naval service. Well done Lieutenant Brenner."*

Commander Perriman opened the medal case he held and took out the air medal and pinned it on the left breast of Mike's shiny blue uniform. Commander Perriman stepped back, saluted him and shook his hand.

He then asked Mike to join him. Mike took a position alongside Commander Perriman.

Once again Senior Chief Carey began; "The remainder of the flight crew is directed to report front and center." The two copilots, navigators, flight engineers, loadmaster and scanner came forward and lined up in a line in front of Commander Perriman.

Chief Carey continued,

> *"The Commander-in-Chief, Pacific Fleet takes great pleasure in presenting the Navy and Marine Corp Medal to the crew of LC-130 Aircraft 152917 for heroic service in the rescue of the Argentine national from the Marambio Base, Seymour Island, Antarctica. Their support of their aircraft commander in performing this medevac was in keeping with the highest standards of naval aviation and the naval service. Well done."*

Commander Perriman stepped forward along with Lieutenant Brenner. Senior Chief Carey brought down eight medals and handed one in turn to Commander Perriman who pinned it on each of the 917 crew. Mike Brenner followed and shook each man's hand.

At the completion of the pinning Commander Perriman directed all hands to return to their posts. He then returned to the dais. He took his place behind the podium and delivered a short inspiring farewell speech. Next he read his orders stating, "When relieved." Commander Vernon then stepped up to the podium and read his orders. His orders directed him to take command of Antarctic Development Squadron Six. Upon completion of reading his orders he turned to Commander Perriman. Both men snapped to attention and Commander Vernon saluted and stated in a loud clear voice, "I relieve you, sir." Commander Perriman returned the salute and stated, "I stand relieved." They shook hands and Commander Perriman took his seat on the dais. Commander Vernon turned to the microphone and delivered an inspiring speech urging the squadron to continue on the path Commander Perriman had led them for the past 18 months. He then called the squadron to attention and turned to the visiting dignitaries. He escorted them off the dais and across the hangar where each departed in reverse order of arrival. After the last VIP departed he returned to the dais where he directed Commander Williams to take charge and dismiss the squadron. Commander Williams acknowledged with a sword salute, turned to the squadron and directed company commanders to take charge and dismiss their troops. With that command all-hands were soon on their way out the hangar door and headed home. They had been given the day off and were taking advantage of that directive. The duty section assumed their required positions and the squadron duty officer was relieved. Commanders Perriman and Vernon proceeded to the CO's office where they signed the required paperwork for the change of command and had a cup of coffee. They sat and chatted for a short time and soon Commander Perriman indicated he needed to get home and help Rebekah with the movers. They rose; shook hands and Commander Perriman departed the hangar. Members of the duty section stood by and soon Chief Carey directed them to move all of Commander Vernon's belongings from the XO's office into the CO's office. In the next few days Commander Williams would occupy the XO's office and Commander Newman would assume duties as Operations Officer.

Pete Vernon was about to wrap things up for the day when Admiral Boland and Jack Forester appeared in his door.

"Pete," Jack started, "Do you have a few minutes? We need to discuss a few things and make a few decisions."

"Sure," Pete replied. "Come on in and have a seat. How about a cup of coffee?"

The Admiral nodded in the affirmative and Jack indicated he also would like a cup.

Pete keyed the intercom and asked the SDO to have the duty steward bring three cups of coffee to his office. The SDO acknowledged and soon three hot cups of coffee appeared carried by the duty steward.

Jack began the discussion. "Pete, this will be a major revelation to you. After the season next year the squadron will be decommissioned and the New York Air National Guard will assume the Antarctic mission. This upcoming season we will have to shut-down Siple Station as part of the mission." The three of them knew what Jack was taking about but because of the secrecy protocols the could only speak in coded terms.

Pete asked, "I suppose you will lay out the timetable and required missions in the Operations Order, Admiral?"

"Pete, we will set the priority of that shut-down and fit it in with all the other flights which will be required. Jack and I have discussed what we need to remove and that will be the subject of a classified message in the next few weeks. I believe the only things we can retrieve are the special tools we have out there and some other items, which we will identify later. We will have to transport the Petersnowmillers out there to do some cosmetic work upon shut-down."

"What about the personnel problems?" Pete asked.

"We will lay that out over the next few months and you will have to have a one on one with each of those men involved because of the decommissioning," Jack responded.

"You will have to bring Commander Newman into the (AFV) program if he agrees to the terms. Otherwise we will transfer him and make Bob Avery Ops Boss. We still need to restrict C-130 crews going to Siple Station to those already in the program," Admiral Boland said.

"We will have him take a flight to Nellis AFB where we can openly discuss this whole thing," Pete responded.

"This whole thing will take a great deal of coordination so we need to keep the lines of communication fluid and open," Jack added.

After they finished their conversation Jack and Admiral Boland departed the hangar leaving Commander Vernon in his office to ponder. The conversation they just had was devastating. The fact that the squadron was being decommissioned after all these years was hard to fathom. It had been in commission since 1954 and had produced many hero's and legends. He thought of all those who preceded him in service to science and exploration.

The squadron was the first to land a plane at the South Pole. Had made many landings in places where no one had even set foot before. Made a rescue during the Antarctic night of a Brit at Halley Bay who would have died had he not been returned to civilization. Not to mention the first flight to land in Antarctica having taken off from outside the continent.

That was not to mention helicopter pilot Lieutenant Commander Jim Brandies who rescued numerous people only to have his hand severely burned trying to rescue two scientists trapped in his helicopter after it lost power, crashed and caught fire.

The rescue of the crew of a downed LC-130 after four days on the Polar Plateau was no mean feat. This brought to mind the LC-130, which made an emergency landing on the Ross Ice Shelf after losing three engines due to contaminated fuel.

There were a thousand stories of heroism some of which would never come to light.

He remembered the plight of the loss of the first LC-130. It had happened right at Williams Field. As the story was told to him it had started the day before on a flight returning from the South Pole. While cruising at 31,000' the loadmaster had called attention to the pilot of two loud bangs in the cargo compartment. The loadmaster then asked the pilot to come back in the cargo compartment and look at something strange and unusual with the aircraft. When the pilot went back he saw the wing spars on each side of the cargo compartment to be cracked and separated. He immediately instructed the co-pilot to descend and depressurize the aircraft. As he did the cracks came back together but were still visible.

The next day, after the Lockheed Engineers, who declared it safe for one flight to overhaul in New Zealand, had inspected the aircraft the starboard wing fell off while taxing around the tower in a whiteout. The fuel exploded around the aircraft but the crew by exiting the paratroop door managed to escape unhurt. The aircraft was a complete loss.

He wondered how these famous exploits would ever be captured and remembered by future generations.

16

"Deployment Ended"

West Coast: Four Years Earlier

The RN Laurence M. Gould was scheduled to depart Port Hueneme, California around June 7th for Punta Arenas and points south. She would be loading cargo destined for Palmer Station from the Naval Construction Battalion Base there. The squadron had been advised of this and needed to send necessary items for the pararescue team. They had packed the pararescue team's personal gear, which the team had taken to McMurdo Station, Antarctica, when they deployed the previous year. They had left it there before setting out on their rescue on Anvers Island. The squadron was aware they would need ID cards, passports and especially money for the return trip to Pt. Mugu.

The personnel officer was assigned that task. He contacted each family to whom the gear had been returned and directed them to pack a small suitcase with the necessary items for their loved ones return trip. He had them in his possession and inspected them to ensure that ID's and passports were present. He contacted the base Disbursing Officer, who was the keeper of the pay records, and had him transfer money in each man's name to the Finance Officer at the American Embassy in Santiago, Chile. The embassy would send a representative to meet the Gould on its return from Palmer Station and handle the team's transit from Chile back to Pt. Mugu. He in turn contacted the squadron Supply Officer and had the suitcases crated and transported to Port

Hueneme to be loaded on the RN Laurence M. Gould. This way they would be delivered to the team when the ship arrived at Palmer and the men would have the proper clothes to travel in. Task Force Forty-Three also directed the SeaBees at Port Hueneme to ship cold weather gear for the team to wear on the transit across the Antarctic Ocean back to Punta Arenas.

With all preparations being completed RN Laurence M. Gould departed Port Hueneme on the 8th of June headed for Punta Arenas. They made one stop in Guayaquil, Ecuador, before transiting the Straits of Magellan and arriving in Punta Arenas, Chile, on June 30th. Upon arrival they tied up to the pier at the foot of Independence Street and Cost Street. Gurdura Ship Chandlers serviced the ship, supplies and cargo were loaded and within two days they were ready to depart for Palmer Station. Lieutenant Al Cromwell had arrived by air from the states and boarded the ship. He would relieve Lieutenant Koenig as O-in-C of the station. Normal personnel rotation of navymen and scientists would wait until a later trip in August so he was the only one traveling at this time. Al Cromwell was a graduate of the NROTC program at Purdue University and had recently served aboard the USS Mustin, an Arleigh Burke-class guided missile destroyer in the United States Navy. He had been operations officer and they had just finished a 6 months cruise deployed to the Indian Ocean where they had been hunting down Somalian Pirates. He had been reassigned on an emergency basis due to the death of Lieutenant MacKay.

On July 2nd the Gould weighed anchor and set sail for Anvers Island. It would be approximately a day and a half to Palmer Station.

All concerned had been advised of the departure and when word reached Palmer Station there was some celebrating by the pararescue team. They had now been there since early January and had been away from their families since the past September. They were all anxious to get underway towards Pt. Mugu.

Finally the Gould arrived and tied up against the shore right next to the station. The crew was greeted with huge smiles and enthusiasm. All-hands began helping unload the ship while Lieutenants Cromwell and Koenig found an unoccupied corner of the dining hall where they discussed the station's status, personnel morale and scientific project progress. Ken reported that he and the chief engineer had replaced the bearing on the electrical generator and they were in good condition. Fuel storage tanks were at ½ but would be okay after taking on a couple thousand gallons from the Gould and would be filled to the brim when the Gould returned later in August. Ken then took Al Cromwell on a walking tour of the station. They had to button up their parkas as the mid-winter temperature had taken a dip down to 0°F and the wind chill was—15°F. This temperature didn't deter those off-loading the ship however but they did take more breaks than normal in the dining hall to absorb the warmth and drink a hot cup of coffee. The pararescue team had pitched right in and helped with the off-loading. Soon they found the crate, which had been packed especially for them but they deferred from opening it until the ship had been completely off-loaded. That occurred some eight hours after they started. Everyone at the station was exhausted and most lay down for a short rest. The ship's skipper, Captain Horton, indicated he would like to get underway at first light the next morning. Russ Parker passed that word to the team and they all acknowledged they would be ready to board the ship at sunup.

It was a fitful night of sleep and most were up early, had breakfast and were all in the dining hall chatting over a cup of coffee when Lieutenant Parker walked in. He picked up his breakfast and joined them at their table. Ken Koenig and Al Cromwell were the last to arrive and pick up their breakfast. They had been up through the late hours discussing the station and where things stood in that regard. After breakfast and with almost all-hands present Ken stood and asked for quiet. When the room had settled down Ken began.

"It has been a pleasure serving with all of you. It is unfortunate how our team came to be here but I hope we have added to the efficiency of this station and now leave you in better shape than when we came. I would ask now for a moment of silence honoring those who were lost in the ice breakup disaster and who we shall always remember."

After about 30 seconds Ken continued, "Our team will be departing on the Gould at 9:00 o'clock and I wish all of you good luck and good health for the remainder of your tour."

He turned to Lieutenant Cromwell and said, "I am ready to be relieved."

Lieutenant Cromwell stood and spoke. "I relieve you, sir." And saluted.

Ken faced him and said, "I stand relieved," and returned his salute. They shook hands.

Ken then turned to Russ Parker and stated, "I think its time for us to gather our belongings and depart."

Russ acknowledged and all-hands stood and crowded around the team. There were many hugs, handshakes and best wishes for a good trip home. The team filtered out and went to their quarters, gathered their gear and headed for the ship. There were many people gathered on the pier to see them off and to help the ship get underway.

Captain Horton was on the right wing of the bridge of the ship and called for all lines to be cast off. The twin engines were humming below decks and he ordered the helmsman 1/3 ahead, steer 325°. The team waved final goodbyes and went below decks to settle down in their bunks. After stowing their gear they found their way to the galley and the cook offered them fresh coffee. This trip was going to be a snap after the last six months they had spent at Palmer.

A mid-winter crossing of the Antarctic Ocean was no easy task. The waves were sometimes 30'-40' high and the surface wind averaged 12-21 mph. There was ice all over the superstructure. The ship however took it in stride as she was designed for Antarctic travel. The pararescue team spent most of their time below decks drinking coffee, eating and snoozing in their bunks.

The ship entered the Straights of Magellan and would soon dock at Punta Arenas. About 3:00pm the city was in sight and by 3:30pm the ship was docked. After tying up, the gangway attached, two well-dressed Americans boarded the ship along with Chilean customs and immigration. The Captain and the pararescue team invited them down to the galley where they were met. Captain Horton was engaged with customs and immigration while the two Americans introduced themselves to the team as representatives of the American embassy who had been assigned as liaison officers while the team was in Chile. The immigration officers finished with Captain Horton and turned to the team. One of the embassy reps, Ralph Esposito, spoke to the immigration officer in Spanish. He explained where the team had been and how they came to be at Palmer Station. He mentioned that they had parachuted onto a glacier and rescued two American scientists. The immigration officers smiled widely at the team and said, "bravo, bueno." Ralph presented the team's passports, which he had previously collected from them, to the immigration officer who stamped them and returned them to Ralph. The team had filled out a Chilean customs form prior to arrival and Captain Horton had presented them when he dealt with the customs officer.

With all paperwork taken care of, the team bid Captain Horton adieu and started down the gangway accompanied by the embassy officials. They were really loaded down carrying their rescue gear, parachutes and personal things. They had changed their clothes prior to arrival and shed their Seabee greens for civilian clothes. They were still wearing their Antarctic parkas, as the weather in Punta Arenas was still very cold and damp. After all, it was wintertime in southern Chile and below freezing temperatures were still prevalent. They had been booked at the Best Western Hotel for one night and the hotel had sent their mini-bus down to the wharves to transport them to the hotel. It was the same hotel the VXE-6 detachment had stayed in during their time in Punta Arenas. Upon arrival at the hotel they were greeted like long lost family. The staff had already been alerted that these men were from VXE-6 as the previous Americans had been. They had come to admire and appreciate the men of VXE-6 and were determined to make their stay memorable. They knew of the team's exploits in the Antarctic and when Lieutenant Parker checked in at the front desk he was given the VIP treatment. There were fruit baskets in each room and free drink chits for the bar. The manager also told Russ he had alerted "Casa Familia Restaurant" of their arrival and to plan a dinner for them about 6:30pm. He said the mini-bus would be available out front at 6:15pm to take them to the restaurant. Russ and the team thanked him and made their way to their rooms. Russ had invited Ralph Esposito and his assistant to his room for a drink and to brief him on the travel plans. They were assigned adjacent rooms, which made it convenient so Ralph and his assistant stopped off in their rooms, dropped off their outer jackets and then stepped next door to Russ' room. Russ had already ordered drinks. They all sat in Russ' sitting area and starting sipping their drinks. Ralph started the conversation by telling Russ the team would be departing on LAN airlines, flight 2606 to Santiago, changing to AerMexico with a stop in Mexico City then on to Los Angeles arriving the following day at 4:15pm. The squadron had been advised of their itinerary and would have transportation waiting for them at LAX. That was the main subject after which was some small talk. Ralph knew Russ would like to shower before going to dinner so he and his assistant excused themselves after finishing their drinks and said they would meet the team out front at 6:15pm for dinner.

The team gathered around the 6:15 hour in lobby of the hotel refreshed from hot showers. Many of them looked slightly red from having been in the shower for most of a half hour. Some of them had taken a hot bath and soaked for some 45 minutes while sipping a drink. For some it was their first regular hot shower in almost 10 months and it was the first time they had been able to relax in a long long time. Russ noticed a distinct increase in morale and a lot more laughing and joking than he had seen in many months.

The mini-bus pulled up in front and they piled on, took their seats and off they went for an evening at La Casa Familia. On arrival they were greeted at the door by the manager and heartily welcomed. Once again they were given the VIP treatment as the staff remembered what a great group the VXE-6 detachment had been. Ralph served as interpreter and soon drinks and dinner had been ordered all around. The restaurant was for all practical purposes empty this time of year so the staff hovered over the team like a den mother. The only memorable quote from Russ Parker was "That's what you get for volunteering for the pararescue team." Everyone knew to what he was referring to but deep down they all knew they would do it again because that's who they were. Doc Kealey paid close attention to ensure that nobody overindulged after having been away from booze for such a long time. Nobody did and his concerns were unfounded. This was a solid group of men who knew how and when to act. They finished their gathering around 10:00pm and the mini-bus was waiting at the curb to transport them back to the hotel. During the evening Russ had passed the word that they would depart the hotel the next day at 2:30pm with aircraft departure at 4:00pm.

Ralph Esposito paid the restaurant bill leaving a generous tip since the manager and staff had been so nice to them. It took them only fifteen minutes to return to the hotel where they each went their separate ways to their rooms after Russ told them the dining room would close for breakfast at 10:00am if they wanted to indulge themselves.

They would all enjoy the clean, soft sheets and the relaxing mattress after navy bunks for so many months.

Five of them met for breakfast around 8:00am. Doc Kealey chose to remain in bed taking advantage of all the comforts of home. They all lounged around the hotel lobby and around 11:30am Russ called the Doc and invited him to lunch with the rest of the team at 12:30pm. With few guests in the hotel this time of year the restaurant had only a few entrees for lunch. Most chose the basil tomato soup and a BLT sandwich with coffee. They sat and chatted about the trip home and broke up about 1:45pm so they could pack and checkout by 2:15pm.

The team once again assembled in the lobby at 2:15pm, checked-out and walked out front to the waiting mini-bus. Ralph and his assistant were also scheduled on the same flight to Santiago so they too boarded the bus. Once underway Ralph distributed their one-way ticket to Los Angeles, California.

Arrival at the airport was about 2:50pm. They disembarked and carried their personal gear into the airport and over to the LAN check-in desk. Check-in was simple as they did not have to show their passports but only their tickets and photo ID. They all checked in their bags through to LAX so they needn't be bothered with them. After a short wait their flight was called and they boarded. They occupied the two front rows of the Canadair Regional Jet as the embassy had obtained VIP seating for them the whole way to LAX.

It was a short flight to Santiago with a short wait for their next plane. Mexico city was also a short time between planes and soon they were on descent to LAX. It had been almost twenty-four hours since they departed Punta Arenas but they were so pumped up about finally getting home they didn't seem to mind.

At LAX they practically ran to the baggage pick-up. Approaching they espied this large crowd of people and quickly they recognized their wives and kids waving to them. It was a sight to behold. Hugs, kisses and tears all around. They couldn't stop touching each other. What a great sight and feeling seeing loved ones reunited after such a long separation.

The odd man out was the skipper, Commander Vernon. He had accompanied the dependents to LAX and was now just an observer of the joy and love now being expressed. After a few minutes the members of the team saw the skipper and he greeted them and welcomed them home.

Finally the team gathered their bags from the baggage carousel and started towards the bus waiting for them in the arrivals area.

With all-hands aboard the bus began its short trip back to NAS Pt. Mugu. It took about an hour and a half and soon the bus pulled up alongside the VXE-6 hangar. To their surprise many of the officers and men of the squadron had remained in the area after normal working hours just to welcome home the pararescue team. Before the team left the bus the skipper informed them that they had the next thirty days off and to plan on returning to duty in mid-August. They thanked the skipper and as they departed the bus there was a rousing cheer and applause for these heroes of the Antarctic. Once again there were many hugs and handshakes welcoming them home and telling them how much they had been missed.

The team gathered their gear and now loaded their vehicles for the drive home to some welcome peace, quiet and reconnection to their family.

17

"The Last Frontier"

Point Mugu, California: Four years earlier

September 12th arrived much too early. The squadron had been preparing all summer for deployment to Antarctica and this was D-day. It was still early but the LC-130 crews and the Point Mugu detachment personnel were all that remained of the squadron at the base. The flight crews and their dependents had gathered slowly since 0700 and were in the hangar visiting and exchanging last minute hugs and kisses in preparation for the Hercs' departures. Flight plans for the first leg to Hawaii had been filed and the planes loaded with personal gear. The time approached for departure and last minute moments together were finished with lingering hugs of wives, kids, girlfriends and other relatives.

The crews boarded, turboprop engines lit off and the adventure started. Departure was normal and soon they were winging their way to Hawaii. Overnight was spent at NAS Barbers Point with an early flight to Pago Pago, refueling, and a shorter flight onward to Christchurch, New Zealand. Arrival was early in the afternoon and soon all hands were on their way to whatever quarters they had secured in the Christchurch area. The flight crews were given 4 days off before they had to check-in with the SDO. In the meantime the squadrons' Christchurch detachment went about winterizing the LC-130s for the upcoming deployment to Antarctica.

Bill Grammercy and Larry Beck took the opportunity to take the train to the west coast. Before boarding the train they had taken the time to purchase a flagon of ale. During the trip they befriended the conductor and had been invited up into the cab of the engine. The engineer had decided to imbibe in the flagon and before they reached the Greymouth Station the engineer was so drunk Larry had to drive the train into the station. Needless-to-say it was an exciting trip.

Meanwhile Bill Springer and a couple of young navigators chose to take a ski trip to Mt. Cook. It was early spring in New Zealand and spring skiing was a kick. To get to the top of the 12,000' peak they took a Cessna 172 on skis, which flew them there in about twenty-four minutes. The trip down usually took forty-five to fifty minutes with another trip back to the top in the Cessna. As in the States there were plenty of snow bunnies in the lodge at the base of the mountain to while away the time and a bar added to the pleasure.

After a couple of days the wanderers rendezvoused at the Yaldhurst hotel, just six miles off the southwest corner of the Christchurch airport. The McTavish family operated the hotel and all family members worked there to make it profitable. The old folks had passed away some years ago but Colin and Noel still catered to the men of VXE-6 with whom they had a special relationship. They still raced their horses and owned three pacers, which they entered in the Christchurch meeting. The guys were also invited to dine in the dining room with the staff, which made for a friendlier stay. The bar was the favorite watering hole and many ales where hoisted with their cobbers.

Pete Vernon, Derek Williams and Ray Newman had taken only two days off and soon were meeting in their hangar office planning for the flight to McMurdo Station, Antarctica, to begin support of the United States Antarctic Program's science projects for the season. The weather was checked daily and departure dates were being formulated based on the week's forecast.

Ray Newman had taken the required flight to Nellis AFB with Bob Avery and had accepted the terms of entering the AFV program; he was a young, virile naval officer at age 35 and was chomping at the bit to get his hands on an AFV. Unfortunately his flights would be limited since evacuation of the AFVs would be one of the first tasks in shutting down Siple Station.

The squadron had been made aware that they would be decommissioned upon return to Point Mugu at the end of the season. Six AFV pilots and six crewmen had remained with the Point Mugu Detachment with the bulk of the ferrying of AFVs to Area 51 on their shoulders. Many questions remained to be answered with the AFV crews before the season ended.

Pete Vernon and Ray Newman finally made the decision to attempt the flights to McMurdo. The weather forecast beginning on Sunday was favorable for the flights. That would give all-hands another four days to get them and the planes ready for the flight.

The crews had a great four days off to renew old acquaintances and adjust to the deployment. They began checking in and finally were told to report personally to the squadron on Wednesday morning to begin preparation for departure to Antarctica. When they reported on Wednesday the duty officer mustered the officers while the flight crews all mustered on the hangar deck by the leading Flight Engineer of each Herc. Three of the six planes were ready for test flights while the other three still required maintenance. Bob Avery and Larry Beck were the designated test pilots so that task fell on them to complete. Enlisted flight crews assigned to the aircraft would assist in the test flight for their particular aircraft. Copilots, where available, would also fly with their aircraft as would the assigned aircraft commander but the test flight would be performed by the designated test pilots.

Navigators were assigned to inventory the aircraft's survival gear and ensure that it was safely stowed in its designated space on the aircraft. Personal survival gear was the responsibility of the individual.

Departure from Christchurch for McMurdo was always like a zoo. There were many base Navy personnel, squadron personnel and scientists scheduled on the first flights to the ice. Adding to the crowd were girl friends and other guests seeing Antarctic personnel off. The airport restaurant was doing a land office business and they loved it. Every seat and piece of floor space was occupied especially young Navymen saying goodbye to his or her newfound friends. This resulted in a crowded airport terminal and a hectic departure desk administered by the squadron-leading chief. Cargo for the Hercs was generally loaded in the hangar then the plane pulled up to the terminal for passenger boarding. First up was the Commanding Officer, Commander Vernon. Flight plans were filed at Deep Freeze Control before walking over to the terminal. Deep Freeze Control would monitor the flight to 60°S then they would be shifted over to McMurdo Control for the final hours of flight. After loading, the skipper taxied out and departed. At half hour intervals each Herc in turn was loaded and departed. This time, tail end Charlie was a U.S. Air Force C-141, flown by Antarctic veteran, Major Howard Gordon. He would depart some five hours after the first Herc so as to arrive about the same time as the skipper. His flight time was about half of what it was for the C-130s.

The weather enroute was typical for this time of year. Layered clouds up to 26,000', winds at altitude westerly varying from 20 to 60 knots. The navigators switched over to grid navigation passing Campbell Island. The arrival weather was 3500' overcast, fifty miles visibility and temperature— 35°F. The skipper arrived after 10.2 hours of flight time and put his Herc down gently on the skiway. He parked in front of VXE-6 maintenance control. Most of his passengers were squadron maintenance personnel. After stowing their gear in their quarters they set about opening the maintenance shops and maintenance control. By the time the third Herc was on final for skiway 27, maintenance control was up and operating. The terminal and galley were manned by base wintering over personnel and they were ready for business. Antarctic designed busses were available to take the senior officers up to the hill, the main base at McMurdo. It was some twelve miles from the skiway complex. At this time of year the busses drove down off the glacial ice onto the sea ice covering McMurdo sound, past the off-load area for the ice runway and then on up the hill to the main base. When the C-141 arrived he would land on the ice runway established purposely for wheeled aircraft. The runway was designated 27 and was perfectly aligned with the skiway on the ice shelf. There were no buildings in the off-loading area, only a refueling capability. The fuel hoses had been run out from the main base some eight miles to the wheeled refueling pits and then on out to Williams field skiway complex another four miles. 3000-gallon fuel bladders were laid out on platforms off the ice and were a reservoir for JP4.

About the same time as the third LC-130 touched down on the skiway the C-141 arrived on the wheeled runway. Major Gordon was a great pilot and set his bird down gently on the iceway. It was 8000' long but he only needed 4500' to get it stopped. Once again the busses were available to transport passengers to the hill. Many VXE-6 helo pilots and crewman were on this flight along with some of the squadron admin personnel. They all made their way to the hill where the squadron headquarters and helo pad were located. After the helo crew got settled they made their way to the helo hangar and began to take the three UH-1Ns out of winter storage, getting them ready for the summer season. The other three UH-1Ns, just out of overhaul, would be flown in the next day by the C-141s. Arrival of the last three Hercs was uneventful.

Soon McMurdo base and Williams Field were humming with activity. Obviously the summer season in Antarctica had begun with great precision.

The officers in Bob Avery's quarters began their annual shopping tour of the base supply facilities. Food was needed for their kitchen. Every set of quarters required that plenty of food and water be available when Antarctic storms decided to blow. This sometimes restricted everyone to quarters allowing no outside travel because of zero visibility and whiteout conditions due to blowing snow. Ralph Gonzalez found his usual supply of Mexican food in one supply building. Canned tortillas, refried beans, and jalapenos were the main fare. Meanwhile Bob and friends found number ten cans of freeze dried shrimp, frozen beef tenderloins, ground beef and African lobster tails. There was also canned bacon, powdered eggs as well as packaged cheese. It was a good start to their larder and they carried it back to their quarters. They dug a hole in the ice outside their quarters and stored the frozen food in their newfound freezer. Now all that was left to do was get some beer and mix for the booze. That they would have to pay for as the Navy did not furnish that free. They managed an ample supply of Budweiser, Coors, bitter lemon, Pepsi and diet coke. As the season progressed they would accumulate fruitcakes and other pastries from the in-flight C rations.

Things at McMurdo were settling down to a normal routine when the expected happened. Snow began blowing over Minna Bluff, which was the first indication that storm conditions at McMurdo were imminent within four hours. All planes were secure at Williams Field and the C-141 due in that day had been turned around before reaching 60° south. Condition one was set at McMurdo/Williams field complexes and all outside activity ceased. Winds picked up to 45-50mph and blowing snow filled the atmosphere. Whiteout conditions were in full effect and zero visibility ensued. Bob Avery's quarters had obtained some freshly baked bread and cold cuts from the galley before conditions at McMurdo worsened so they now had all the necessary ingredients to survive for as long as they were prisoners in their own quarters. A few of them started a game of Bridge, while drinking a few beers and snacking on some treats, which Ralph Gonzalez had prepared for them. Ralph loved to cook and putter around the kitchen so the others in quarters with him didn't interfere with his activities.

The storm lasted only a couple of days and as it subsided outside activities resumed. The squadron became responsive and organized while USARP director, Phil Moulder, was beginning his daily meeting with all organizations and laying out the plan for the next week.

There were so many activities it was difficult to keep up with their progress. The last three UH-1Ns arrived and were delivered to the helo hangar where they were readied for flight. Test flights were performed and in short order reported ready for their assigned missions.

Busses were constantly running from the Hill to the Ice Runway and Williams Field. LC-130 flights were flown to checkout VXE-6s new pilots on ski landings. NATOPS officer, Bob Avery, rode a UH-1N and checked out the emergency whiteout landing area south and east of the Willliams Field Skiway. It was an area some fifty miles wide by fifty miles long, where a Herc, which might be caught out when weather conditions deteriorated at Williams field, could make a zero zero landing. It was glacial ice and needed to be checked for obvious crevasses. This situation had occurred many times in the past. Hercs would be making routine flights to Byrd or Pole Station and would have insufficient fuel to proceed back to a prepared skiway or landing field from Williams because of a fast moving, unforeseen weather system catching McMurdo complex by surprise. This had happened to Lieutenant Commander Hap Rocketto who got caught in just that situation. He made four Ground Control radar approaches and could not see Skiway 36. The fifth time he reached minimums at 100' and ¼ mile then transitioned to grid heading 330° and 200' per minute rate of descent. He finally touched down at fourteen miles from the skiway. After a complete stop he reversed his direction to grid heading 150° and began taxiing back to Williams Field. The visibility was so restricted that he had a crewman lie down on the flight deck and look out the lower window next to the pilots seat to relay to him when he was moving. They were still in radio contact with GCA and at three miles radar picked them up and directed them back onto Skiway 18. After some thirty minutes they arrived back in front of Maintenance Control but still couldn't see the building. They shutdown the engines still 50' from the building. Someone in Maintenance Control attached a lifeline to a pickup truck, which slowly inched its way out towards the parked Herc. After some fifteen minutes and within 10' of the Herc they finally espied it and came to a stop next to the forward crew entry door. The crew secured the aircraft and, after donning their winter Parkas, departed the aircraft and attaching themselves to the lifeline with carabineers and bungee cords previously attached around their waists. They all stayed within a pace of each other and made their way back to Maintenance Control. The pickup then reeled in the lifeline as they made their way back to Maintenance Control. This is what the men of VXE-6 described as the Antarctic jumping up and trying to bite you in the ass. In this case they beat the Antarctic.

The next item on the agenda for the squadron was to open Brocton Station. Brocton Station was a weather observation post manned by two weathermen. It was located on the Ross Ice Shelf, some two hundred forty miles from McMurdo and was critical to forecasting storms moving into the McMurdo area. The station had originally been built on the surface but over the years it had been covered by storms and was now located 14'-20' below the surface of the snow. Since it was manned only during the summer season no help would be available to find it. Also the ice shelf moved at the rate of about one mile per year so it would not be exactly in the same position as the previously year. Larry Beck was assigned the mission with Ray Newman as his copilot. Tom Harger was the first navigator and finding the station would be on his shoulders. The USARP glacial scientists gave the navigator their best estimate as to the direction and distance the station had moved since the previous year. Tom plotted both positions on his chart and drew a line connecting them extending the line for a short distance in the direction of movement. They knew the station was located somewhere along that line.

The crew manned the aircraft and was quickly airborne winging their way towards Brocton. Fifteen minutes before landing Tom shot a sun line with his sextant. He advanced it to intersect last year's position of Brocton. Next he directed Larry on a grid heading to position him on the sun line upon landing. Larry was precise in his airmanship and soon landed. After stopping Tom again shot a sun line and plotted it on his chart. He directed Larry to a new grid heading and he taxied until Tom indicated he was now on the line previously plotted for the direction of movement of the station. Larry directed crewmembers not occupied in aircraft movement plus the weathermen, who would man the station, to form a line out in front of the aircraft spread 20' apart and heading down the line of movement of the station. They were tied together with a safety line and each man was also equipped with an ice axe and a 10' bamboo pole. They began poking the snow with the poles and moving forward. Fortunately the weather had a clear sky, temperature in the range of 3°-5°F and winds calm. After twenty-eight minutes of searching one of the weathermen poked through the snow. After more poking it was determined to be a snow bridge over a crevasse so movement continued forward. After another fifteen minutes they discovered the entrance to the station. A signal was sent to the aircraft and Larry taxied forward until he was within 30' of their position. The ramp was lowered and shovels were removed and digging commenced to reach the entrance of the station. They quickly reached the cover to the vertical shaft down to the station, removed the cover and the second flight engineer plus a weatherman descended the ladder to the station. Petty Officer Glennon was a seasoned engineer and old Antarctic hand who had opened many a station so he knew exactly what to do. The electrical generating unit had been dug out of the snow so he primed the motor for the electrical generator and within minutes had the generator up and running, producing electricity for the station. After clearing the exhaust pipe, Glennon next opened the fuel line to the furnace, primed the line with the attached pump and struck the lighter. The furnace roared to life and soon heat was exhausting from the furnace providing heat to all the station. The weathermen were in the process of unpacking their instruments. Glennon asked them if they were ready for the aircraft to depart. They said they were but Glennon knew he had one more task to accomplish. He turned on the HF radio, checked the primary McMurdo frequency and keyed the mike, "McMurdo Control this is Brocton Station, how do you read, over?"

McMurdo came back, "Loud and clear Brocton, how do you read, over?"

Glennon replied, "Read you 5 by 5 McMurdo."

"Roger that," McMurdo replied.

With that Glennon told the weathermen he was going topside and the plane would depart immediately. They shook hands, thanked him for the help and he disappeared up the ladder onto the ice surface.

The plane was buttoned up already except for the forward crew entrance hatch. Glennon boarded, closed the hatch and gave Larry thumbs up. Larry pushed the power levers forward and began his takeoff slide. He knew without asking that the two basic safety regs for the Antarctic had been met. You never left anyone out in the Antarctic with out first being assured they had heat and radio contact with someone. They had accomplished their mission despite all the difficulties. Old Antarctic hands were efficient and knew just what to do in most circumstances. He was proud of all of them. The flight back to McMurdo was uneventful.

18

"The Last Missions"

McMurdo Station, Antarctica

One of the missions the squadron was tasked with was the possible recovery of two de Havilland Canada DHC-3 Otter from Eights Station.

Eights Station coordinates were 75 degrees 10'S 77 degrees 10'W.

Eights was 200 kilometers east-northeast of Siple Station. It operated from January 1963 to January 1965, mainly in support of upper atmosphere physics. Station population during winter was 10-11. The station was named for James Eights, who in 1830 was the earliest American scientist in the Antarctic.

During the summer of 1965 a scientific project to study ice cores near the Sentinel Mountains was established. To support this project, USARP had acquired two brand new Otters to carry the ice cores back to Eights Station on a daily basis for further transfer by LC-130 to McMurdo where they could be preserved. They would then be packaged and shipped by boat to the United States bound for the University of Buffalo where they would be studied by yearly deposits.

The Otters were transported by ship to McMurdo and late in the year were loaded, still in their crates, onto LC-130s and transported to Eights Station.

They were placed on the surface near the station awaiting personnel from VXE-6 to remove them from the crates and assemble them. Before this could occur Eights

Station suffered a 6.4 earthquake on the Richter scale, which did minor damage.

It was determined by the scientists present at Eights Station that it was located on an earthquake prone fault and further occupancy of the station was unsuitable and dangerous to all personnel. This was later named Bentley Sub glacial Trench or Trough, a deep bedrock chasm between MBL and the Transantarctic Mountains of East Antarctica. An LC-130 was dispatched, post haste, and the crew ordered to extract all personnel as quickly as possible. While enroute they notified Eights Station team leader that they were enroute and when they arrived they would remain on deck only fifteen minutes. When this message was passed the LC-130 was only thirty minutes from touchdown.

The station personnel grabbed only their valuables and anything personal they could pack in thirty minutes. When the aircraft arrived they climbed out of the station and in the process shutdown the station.

It had now been some thirty years since shutdown of the station and the men from VXE-6 were expected to find it and recover the two single engine Otters.

A mission was scheduled and an LC-130 sent out with extra personnel to try to find Eights Station and thereby make preparations to complete this impossible mission.

The crew manned their aircraft early one morning and after an uneventful takeoff headed down the coast for the previously known position of Eights Station. They were cruising along at 26,000' and the visibility was about two hundred miles. Roosevelt Island came into view as well of the Bay of Whales. Next in sight were the Rockefeller Mountains and the Edsel Ford Ranges farther to the east. It was a great day for sightseeing. Bruce Fleming who was the aircraft commander suddenly spotted what he thought was aircraft wreckage. He began circling and alerted the other crewmembers to what he saw. It was on the upslope of the mountain just above the snow and ice line located on what appeared to be solid rock. He reduced the power on the aircraft and told the crew they needed to take a closer look, as this may be an Antarctic artifact. As he got lower one of the navigators who was an old aircraft buff said,

"That looks like the wreckage of an autogiro."

"How could that be," someone else replied, "anybody know of an autogiro ever being flown in Antarctica?"

One of the co-pilots chimed in, "Yeah, Admiral Byrd had one on one of his expeditions."

"Navigator, record its geographic position on you chart and make a note in your navigation log. That's probably a valuable artifact and we should report its location when we get back to base." Bruce noted.

With that entity having been identified he began his climb back to 26,000'. They cruised on for another forty minutes and the navigator reported they were about sixty miles from the previously known position of Eights Station. The crew had talked with some of the geologists and they had reported to them that the station should still be in its same location since it was built over a rock formation even though there was a couple of hundred feet of snow on top of the rock.

The navigator observed the sun through his sextant and plotted the sun line on his chart. He advanced it through the last known stations position and gave Bruce a new grid heading to fly to intersect the sun line. Bruce began his descent and prepared for landing. He leveled the aircraft at five hundred feet above the surface and told the loadmaster to prepare to drop a smoke flare to detect the wind direction on the surface. Bruce slowed to below 150 knots and the loadmaster opened the port paratroop door. The co-pilot in turn extended the air deflector doors to protect the loadmaster from windblast. When the navigator reported they were over the probable stations position he called out "Mark" on the intercom and the loadmaster ignited the smoke flare and threw it out the paratroop door. He reported flare away and told all-hands on the circuit it was orange smoke. Bruce made a 360° turn while all-hands strained to see the direction of the smoke. They determined it to be a wind blowing out of Grid 040°. Bruce stopped his turn on heading 220°, which would set him up down wind for a landing. He called for the checklists to be completed and lowered the skis for landing. Flaps were set for approach and Bruce began a descending right turn. He stopped his turn heading 040° and continued his descent. Touchdown was smooth on the powdery snow. The aircraft slid to a stop and the navigator once again observed the sun through his sextant. Within five minutes he had it plotted on his chart and told Bruce they needed to taxi about ¼ mile southwest to correct their position for the stations location. Bruce turned the aircraft around and moved the distance advised by the navigator. When he stopped he ordered the search crew out of the aircraft.

The search crew were attached to each other by a safety rope about ten feet apart and provided with a ten foot pole of bamboo. They were instructed by the navigator to search from the aircraft in an easterly direction. The seven search crewmembers spread out in a straight line and when they were set began probing the snow in an easterly direction. They were covering a swath of sixty feet in their search. They were all experienced in this type of search and they moved rather quickly. After an hour they had covered about ½ mile. They then turned and swung around headed west and searched another sixty-foot swath south of the first swath they had just searched. When they reached a point abeam the aircraft the moved north one hundred twenty feet and started east once again.

Halfway through the search on this leg one of the searchers fell through the snow. At first everyone thought it was a crevasse but it turned out to be the Plexiglas observation dome of the station. He didn't fall too far since he was still roped to his search-mates. Shovels were taken out of the cargo compartment and digging began to expose the roof of the station. Once the end walls of the station were located the searchers dug down to expose the west wall where it had been determined from inside the station by the searcher who had fallen into the dome, that the entrance existed. This digging and searching had taken up the best part of three hours. The entrance door was reached about twelve feet below the surface. Flashlights were obtained and the flight crew opened the door and entered the station. One of the pilots reported it was like entering a ghost house. There were still half eaten meals on the table, books and papers spread out on tables. Unmade beds. Shoes under the beds. Pictures and maps still on the walls.

The station personnel had left in such a hurry that they even took and axe and chopped the power cable to the station to cut the power. One of the crew was charged with making notes on what needed to be done to make the station livable because everyone knew it was going to take more than one day to find those buried planes.

After inventorying all the rooms in the station a list was compiled of needed repairs, equipment and supplies for reoccupying the station. When they felt they could do no more Bruce gathered up all-hands, closed the door and marked the location with a series of flags so they could find the station when they returned. Everyone boarded the aircraft and soon they were winging their way back to McMurdo.

Bruce reported back to the McMurdo USARP rep that determined they would have a meeting the next day to discuss reoccupying the station, searching for the lost aircraft and returning them to McMurdo.

Within a week another LC-130 was heading to Eights Station. Four people had been tapped to search for the lost aircraft. All necessary supplies and equipment were aboard as well as an electrician who would be needed to splice the power cable back together. Bruce's crew had dug out the smokestack for the diesel-powered unit, which powered the electrical generator. They were carrying enough diesel fuel to power the station for two weeks and after that new supplies of fifty-five galleon drums would need to be carried out to Eights.

Eights was easily found by the LC-130 crew and upon arrival the electrician went about his task while the supplies and equipment were off-loaded. Within an hour everything was in place, power had been restored to the station and the heater was working fine. The radio room was restored and contact with McMurdo Control had been established. The Herc crew wished the station personnel well and success in their quest and departed for McMurdo.

It took about six days and low and behold a message was received from Eights that they had indeed found two crates with the aircraft. It took another week and a half to dig the crates out of the snow. When they were ready two Hercs were dispatched to Eights. Each one loaded one of the crates and returned them to McMurdo. They were reclaimed by the National Science Foundation and eventually it was decided they could not be used so one was donated to the

Smithsonian and the other to the National Museum of Naval Aviation.

Next on the USARP list of missions was the first flight to Hallett Station. Now this was a horse of a different color. A complete switch of operating procedures. Lieutenant Mike Brenner was assigned this mission.

Hallett Station was located due north of McMurdo towards New Zealand on Seabee Hook at Cape Hallett. It was approximately 2-1/2 hour flight from McMurdo. There was a wintering over party there and they had been charged with making a runway on the bay ice for wheeled landings. At 2 hours 10 minutes into the flight Mike began his descent into his approach for Hallett Station. The weather was high overcast clouds breaking into scattered to broken layers at the lower altitudes. His navigator vectored him so as to keep him clear of the mountainous terrain to his west until he was VFR below the cloud layers. They broke out of the clouds at 5000' and continued to descend to 3500'. They finally reached the opening to the bay and Mike made a wide left turn into the bay. Seabee Hook was a short distance down the bay and up against the mountains on the left, which ran up to over 8000' in places. The crew spotted the runway just south and slightly west of Seabee Hook. Mike called for checklists and soon they were on short final for the ice runway. The copilot looked at the runway and commented "Damn Mike that baby sure looks short!"

Mike replied, "Yeah it does. It's supposed to be 5000'."

He set up for a short field landing, dragged it over the small snow berm on the end of the runway and touched down fifty feet from the end. He quickly placed all power levers in ground detent and immediately went into full reverse. His landing roll was no more than 2500' and still he went through the small snow berm at the end. He turned around and taxied back north towards the station. He stopped, set the brakes and shutdown for off-loading. They were met by the senior petty officer who was O-in-C of the station with his pickup truck.

He greeted Mike, whose first words were, "Damn Hudson, that sure is a short runway you gave us. How long is it?"

Petty officer Hudson responded, "Supposed to be 5000' sir. I laid it our with the odometer on my pickup truck."

Mike took one quick glance at the pickup, smiled and said, "Do you suppose they forgot to recalibrate the odometer when they put those huge oversized tires on her?"

Petty officer blushed sheepishly and admitted that no, they probably didn't and that the runway was only about 3000' as a result.

Mike quickly added, "I guess you ought to make it another 2000' just for safety reasons."

"Roger that sir will do," Hudson responded.

Mike and his crew took a tour of the base, had a cup of coffee and relaxed while the plane was being unloaded. Petty Officer Hazzard appeared in the galley and told Mike they were off-loaded and ready for departure. They said their goodbyes and were soon on their way back to McMurdo.

Planning had been underway for some time on the shutdown of Siple Station and transfer of the AFVs to Area 51. It had been decided that only essential AFV tools and related test equipment and a few items from operations control would be flown out of Siple. The remainder would be buried with the station deep in the ice. Since all LC-130 crews were now involved with the AFVs, scheduling of crews out to Siple was an easy task. First out was Lieutenant Bruce Fleming. His copilots were Lieutenants Terry Richardson and Jerry Elliott. They carried cargo and fresh food out to Byrd Station then flew to Siple where they off-loaded a couple of wooden crates to be packed for future shipment to Area 51. The hangar bay doors were slid back and the crates were lowered into the hangar bay. Jerry Elliott was selected to fly the first AFV to Area 51 and within a half hour he was lifting up out of the hangar bay and was on his way. The remainder of the crew settled down in the station lounge and chatted with Choyce Proulx and drank coffee. Choyce had on his headset so he could monitor the AFV frequency and listen for the return Flight. After 2 hours 46 minutes the radio crackled to life. Charlie Black from the Pt. Mugu detachment was flying the bird. "Whisper control this is "Stretch" 100 out for recovery, over."

Choyce responded, "Stretch you are number one for recovery weather VFR visibility 200 miles. Pad one is available, over."

Charlie acknowledged and Choyce turned to Bruce and told him, "Charlie is cleared for touchdown on pad one so we won't have to open the hanger doors. He will set it down next to your bird and you can be on your way ASAP. Charlie was bringing Jerry back after taking the bird north to Area 51. This is how the other 2 AFVs would be moved out. A pilot from Antarctica would fly to Area 51 and then PT Mugu AFV pilots would take the bird and return the delivery pilot back to Antarctica. This was possible by leaving the crew chief of the AFV seat empty for the returning pilot. It was not desirable but was not dangerous.

Charlie landed. Jerry disembarked and walked quickly over to the Herc. He was in his regular flight suit as he had undressed just prior to landing and stowed his pressure suit in a special locker in the AFV. Charlie and his crew would off-load it at AREA 51 and have it available when Jerry needed it there.

Bruce and Terry started the Herc and after a beautiful slide down the skiway they were winging their way back to McMurdo. Weather on the continent was gorgeous and visibility was 200 miles. After passing over Byrd Station they were listening to UHF squadron frequency and heard Bud Hageman talking with three of the UH-1Ns. They were making their way to the Amundsen Glacier located in the Transantarctic Mountains. They were to establish a field camp for a geologic expedition, which was searching for the Lystrosaurus amphibian fossil proving Antarctica was part of Gondwanaland. They had just taken off from the site of the former Beardmore Station where Bud and his crew had fed the helo pilots and crewman and refueled the helos for the final leg of the trip. A couple of previous Herc flights to Amundsen Glacier had already established the field camp, erecting a couple of Jameways and putting in a fuel bladder, which held 3000 gallons of JP4. A few scientists were already there and heat, food and radio contact had been established.

Bruce Fleming and his crew arrived safely at McMurdo while Bud Hageman and the helos arrived at Amundsen Camp. A skiway was beginning to form with Bud being the third aircraft to land there. It had been established on the south side of the camp close to the mountains, which ran east/west along the glacier.

Bud returned to McMurdo in record time.

This camp would now become almost a daily routine in the flight pattern for Antarctica as food, fuel and scientists were needed there and were constantly being shuffled in and out of camp.

As the temperature climbed slightly at the pole, the squadron opened contact with pole station and began to shuttle personnel, fuel, food and cargo. 200,000 gallons of diesel fuel were needed to replenish the fuel tanks at pole. This would take almost all season to accomplish and required almost daily flights to the pole. To the tanker pilots this was sometimes boring so they made up sayings and substitutes for the radio communications. One example was the air traffic control clearance from McMurdo center. It was broadcast as "Navy 48321 is cleared to McMurdo via the pole. Maintain Flight Level 260 to the pole and 310 on return to McMurdo." The pilots changed the read back as follows: "321 cleared Rickety rack to the pole and back, 26 out 31 back." It just added a little levity to the day. Wintering personnel also had to be exchanged and there were always plenty of visitors who just needed to get to the pole for photo ops. This included Congressmen, Admirals and foreign visitors.

The season was moving along swiftly and after four weeks Siple cargo had been returned to McMurdo for further transfer to Nellis AFB, Las Vegas, Nevada. This included all pilots and crewmen's pressure suits, which had each been individually repacked in their original shipping containers. They were fiberglass, green in color, and marked scientific test equipment. The AFVs were all safely at Area 51 and Choyce Proulx and his assistant were all who remained at Siple. Three heavy equipment operators were flown in from the states to take over operation of the Petersnowmillers and one D8 cat now required at Siple. No one was sure where they came from and no one asked. Burying the station was a classified operation because of the AFVs and only a few people were privy to this whole operation. Three Hercs were loaded with the Petersnowmillers and the D8 cat and flown out to Siple. The Hercs would remain until the job was complete and the machines once again loaded and returned to McMurdo. The D8 cat pushed the hangar doors down into the hangar bay and also moved some snow. The millers, who blew snow from

30'-50' away from the hangar bay into it filling it to the brim, moved the bulk of the snow. The D8 cat was instrumental in moving snow on the surface toward the hangar bay so the millers could then do their job of filling the huge cavity. This evolution took approximately three hours without a break. The operators knew exactly what needed to be done and accomplished their task quickly and efficiently. When the cavity was filled, the D8 packed it down and the millers touched it up with a little more snow.

No effort had been made to save the long wire antenna so the ten miles of wire remained buried just south of the station under a foot of snow. It would remain as a reminder of what once was.

Choyce Proulx was up on the bench in the rear of the cockpit enjoying the heat and eating a steak prepared by the crew just for him. He was ready to return to civilization as this had been a long winter and he had been there for almost ten months.

After four hours on deck the Hercs loaded the Petersnowillers, D8 cat and were once again making their way back to McMurdo.

During this long season of scientific support, Commander Vernon or Bob Avery interviewed AFV crews. They were all asked if they wished to continue flying the AFV after the squadron was decommissioned. To the man every one of them answered in the affirmative. Plans moved forward to keep them flying.

The summer season was now winding down in the Antarctic and plans for moving men and equipment north and closing off all contact with Antarctica were proceeding. The last 3000 gallons of diesel fuel was delivered and exchange of personnel at South Pole station completed. The flight departed and the station was considered closed for the season. The station was now isolated from the world.

The field party on Amundsen glacier and three UH-1Ns were successfully redeployed to McMurdo and the field camp closed.

Three Hercs were repositioned to Christchurch, New Zealand, and would begin round-trip flights to McMurdo withdrawing mostly summer personnel and some cargo. After the remaining Hercs at McMurdo completed all flights within

Antarctica they too redeployed to Christchurch to assist in the withdrawal of McMurdo personnel. The skipper, Bob Avery, and Larry Beck were the last crews to leave McMurdo. The skipper flying the last flight of the season out of Williams Field took off and made the traditional low pass over Scott Base and McMurdo then climbed on course and headed for New Zealand.

With Antarctica now successfully closed the squadron prepared for redeployment to Pt. Mugu. Planes were reconfigured for normal flying. Cold weather prop seals were replaced with warm weather seals; aircraft survival gear was removed and stored as well as personnel survival gear. These procedures only took a few days and soon the squadron was ready to depart to home. An early Friday morning was the scheduled departure time and all commands within Task Force Forty-Three were geared up for this day. The hustle and bustle at the airport was about the same as it had been for the departure to Antarctica earlier in the season. The terminal was buzzing with girlfriends, guests, Navy personnel and some dependents. The bank of New Zealand was doing a land office business exchanging Kiwi money for U.S. dollars since it was illegal to remove more than six Kiwi dollars from New Zealand. The food court was full of people and humming like a beehive. Most of the flight crews however avoided this zoo by dining at the White Heron's dining room just across the street from the VXE-6 hangar.

Flight plans were filed and one by one the Hercs were positioned at the terminal loaded and soon were on their way to Pago Pago. After successful refueling they were once again winging their way to NAS Barbers Point on the island of Oahu in Hawaii. Landing was on Thursday as they had crossed the International Date Line during their flight. Friday was relived with a direct flight to Pt. Mugu taking just over 10 hours.

The reuniting of families was a sight to behold. Wives were more beautiful than ever and the kids had grown unbelievably. It seems it took only seconds before all necessary paperwork was completed and the ramp deserted. These Navymen were quickly making their way to their homes and resuming a normal life.

19

"From Old to New"

Pt. Mugu, California: Four years earlier

After thirty days off from duty, the squadron personnel resumed a normal working day routine. Commander Pete Vernon received orders from the Chief of Naval Operations via the chain of command to decommission the squadron by June 1st. Pete called a meeting of all department heads and they began to plan the decommissioning. It would take place on the 31st of May with an officers dining-in on the evening of the 29th and a parade and picnic on the 31st. All-hands were informed and preparations were begun to make it happen.

Lieutenant Commander Bob Avery had previously decided to put in his papers for retirement but with developments within the AFV community and the new organization which was forming he decided to do what was required to remain in the AFV community.

A new company was formed called Omega Aviation. It would be based at Salt Lake City International Airport. Six brand new Gulfstream G-4's were on order and a new hangar being built to house this organization. Jack Forester at the National Science Foundation would be the sponsoring organization but Bill Reynolds at the CIA was the real brains and money behind this operation. Bob Avery was asked to be the CEO of the corporation and all AFV personnel would work for him. A housing complex and corporate headquarters was being built just east of the town of Kamas, Utah, some twenty-five miles east of Salt Lake City. The AFV base was established on the east side of Hoyts Peak at about the 6000' level. John Walker was hired as Vice President of operations and Larry Beck would be chief pilot for Omega Aviation. Four Bell 412 Helicopters would be required so eight VXE-6 helicopter pilots were recruited for the company. They were all vetted and agreed to the secrecy requirement to protect the AFV program. As the 31st of May approached resignations from the navy of all officer AFV personnel were accepted and all enlisted personnel would be discharged. The resignations were forwarded to Jack Forester were he placed them in his emergency safe behind his desk in his office. The public perception was that these personnel were civilians but realistically they were all still in the Navy and were earning time towards retirement. Should there be a death in the AFV program their status would be immediately changed to civilian and papers forwarded to the Navy department verifying that status. However all would be promoted under normal procedures and when ready for retirement would be returned to the Navy for processing.

Construction of all sites in Utah were incomplete so AFV operations would need to continue out of Area 51 temporarily.

May 29th rolled around very quickly and that evening the officers gathered in the Pt. Mugu officers club for their final Dining-in. A dining-in was a tradition carried over from ancient times where the warriors returned from the war with their plunder and divided it up. They all dressed in their finest war dress and had a banquet while celebrating their victories and admiring their achievements. This modern dining-in required mess dress uniforms which consisted of blue trousers, white dress jacket with shoulder boards, indicating rank, plus miniature medals and badges or awards. Aviators and Naval Flight Officers wore their gold wings as well as a gold cummerbund with black socks and shoes. Officers were seated at tables by rank from highest to lowest. The officer furthest from the Commanding Officer was the newest Ensign also known as Mr. Vice while the commanding officer was known and addressed as Mr. President in his official position as senior officer in charge of the officers' mess. Mr. Vice was charged with recording and collecting fines levied by the skipper for breaches in etiquette committed by junior officers as well as other duties. The evening would normally begin in the bar with a few cocktails. The main entrée, usually roast beef, would then be wheeled into the bar and a slice given to the skipper where he would declare it fit to eat and ask the officers to join him in the dining room for dinner. All officers would then move to the chair they were assigned and stand until the commanding office took his seat. They would then be seated. The table place setting consisted of two forks on the left, one knife on the right along with a teaspoon and soup spoon. At the top of the setting was a fish fork and a desert fork. Three wine glasses were set at the top of the knife with a water glass alongside. On the left at the top of the forks was a coffee cup and saucer. The first course for dinner was the fish followed by the soup and served with white wine. When that was cleared the main course was served, which was usually roast beef with potatoes and vegetables. Along with this was the red burgundy wine. Decanters were set on the table and wine refills were unlimited. The last served was the port wine used for the toasts.

At the completion of dinner, the skipper, Commander Pete Vernon stood and announced, "The smoking lamp is lit." Cigars were furnished at the table and those who desired lit up. Next up was Ensign Donahue, Mr. Vice. He rose and was recognized by the skipper. "Mr. President, I propose a toast to the President of the United States."

All officers stood, raised their wine glasses and toasted, "To the President," then took their seats.

The senior Lieutenant Junior Grade arose and was recognized. "Mr. President, I propose a toast to the Secretary of the Navy."

All officers stood, raised their glasses and toasted, "To the Secretary," then took their seats.

The toasting continued for another 20 minutes ending with a toast to all the girls they had known intimately. After the toast the skipper arose and said, "Gentlemen, the dinner is complete, join me at the bar." With that, all hands stood and moved into the bar for more cocktails. Most of the talk turned to the upcoming decommissioning and what the future held for most of them. Slowly the officers drifted out of the bar and began to depart for their quarters. Lieutenant Mick Preston, the squadron drunk, was the last to leave.

May 31ˢᵗ came early for the men of VXE-6. By 0600 the hangar was humming with people. The west side of the hangar had been adorned with decorations and three hundred chairs had been set up for guests. A dais on the north end was a raised platform with a podium, microphone and eight chairs for VIPs and the commanding officer. All known past members of VXE-6 had been invited and it was expected that over two hundred of those past members would attend. The ceremony was to commence at 0900 and many guests began arriving around 0800. By 0835 almost every chair was filled with stragglers still arriving. The squadron was mustered by the Executive Officer, Commander Derek Williams, and in formation to the right of the chairs on the hangar deck. At 0845 the first of the VIPs began arriving. First to arrive was Commanding Officer NAS Point Mugu, Captain Henry Battistoni, USN, along with Commander, Fleet Air Wing 6, Captain Richard Brunwald, USN. They were greeted by Commander Vernon and took seats on the dais. Next to arrive were Commander, Task Force Forty-Three, Admiral Boland, USN, and Jack Forester, Office of Polar Programs, National Science Foundation. They said their hellos and took seats on the dais. Commander, Naval Air Forces, Pacific, VADM Ward Simpson, USN, was next to arrive. Finally VADM Billie McElroy, USN, Commander-in-Chief Pacific Fleet arrived and was piped aboard by an honor guard. Commander Vernon escorted him to the dais where he took the seat of honor as the senior officer present.

Commander Vernon went to the podium and called for the colors to be posted. Everyone stood while the color guard marched forward to the front of the assembled crowd and stopped front and center. The Pacific Fleet band, which was there for this occasion, struck up the Star Spangled Banner. Honors were rendered to the flag and everyone in uniform saluted while all those in civilian clothes placed their hand over their heart. At the completion of the last note hands were smartly returned to the side while everyone remained at attention. Commander Vernon then called for the colors to be withdrawn and everyone once again saluted as the colors passed. Pete Vernon asked Lieutenant Commander Vince Crowley, USN, navy chaplain, to give the invocation and also asked the crowd to remain standing. Lieutenant

Commander Crowley's prayer was inspiring and he asked the blessing on the men of VXE-6 along with the proceedings which were about to unfold. At the completion of the prayer Pete Vernon asked everyone to take their seats. He introduced the VIP guests on the dais after which he introduced the final VIP, VADM McElroy, and asked him to deliver a few words. Admiral McElroy was eloquent and spoke of the many deeds and missions the squadron had flown in building a legendary legacy never to be equaled in the annals of naval aviation. He likened the squadron to the pathfinders who explored the United States during its beginning and asked that those who gave their lives in the exploration of the white continent forever be remembered as the pioneers of Antarctic aviation. He had special words for Lieutenant Commander Gus Schwin who made the first landing at the South Pole, he recalled specifically the rescue of the crew of the Maverick Explorer and of Swede Larson who had died after rescue from Little America. He spoke of the courage of Lieutenant Commander Brandis after his helicopter crash in the dry valleys and his attempted rescue of the trapped scientists in the burning helicopter. He once again commended the crew of the LC-130 for their daring rescue of the crew of the crashed LC-130 at the French site at Carrefor in whiteout conditions. Strangely enough most of those two crews were in the audience that day and they were proud of what they had done. Admiral McELroy completed his speech with comforting words to all that had contributed to the mission of the squadron throughout the years. He wished all-hands well and indicated that they were a great credit to Naval Aviation and would never be forgotten. He then asked Commander Vernon to approach the podium where he read the citation for a Navy Unit Commendation for the squadron and pinned the ribbon on Commander Vernon's right breast. The admiral then read a citation for the Legion of Merit to be awarded to Commander Vernon. The squadron's chief yeoman came up on the dais, handed the admiral the medal, which he in turn pinned on the left breast of Commander Vernon. Commander Vernon saluted and the Admiral retired to his seat.

Commander Vernon then turned to the audience and began his farewell speech. He praised all-hands for a job well done and expounded on the accomplishments of the squadron.

Finally after what seemed an agonizing thirty minutes where it appeared he did not want to decommission the squadron he read his orders relieving him of duties as commanding officer and decommissioning the squadron. There was hardly a dry eye in the place. Many an old Antarctic explorer of VXE-6 was in tears at the sound of the death knell of the thing they held so near and dear to their hearts. But there it was, the squadron was gone but the camaraderie would last forever. Pete Vernon then dismissed the active duty people still standing in formation and then invited everyone to join him at a picnic in the east side of the hangar which had been set up for that purpose. Beer flowed like water, penguin burgers and seal dogs were available along with cole slaw and beans. All in all it was a great time to renew old acquaintances and say goodbye to old friends. One of the big surprises for those not in the know were the resignations of eighteen Herc pilots and eighteen NFOs who indicated they were going to work for Omega Aviation. Included in those resigning were the eight helo pilots as well as the twenty-six enlisted personnel who were following those officers to Omega Aviation. At the close of the day it was really a sad time.

Las Vegas, Nevada: Four years earlier

Half of the personnel flying the AFVs left Pt. Mugu and moved to Nellis AFB reporting in with Jack Shepard. They would take over the load of flying the AFV missions until the remainder of the personnel who were sent to Savannah, Georgia, for training on the Gulfstream G4 completed their training. They would then exchange places and the second half of personnel would take their G4 training. All dependents would remain at Pt. Mugu until housing was available at the headquarters in Utah.

Bob Avery moved to Salt Lake City where he rendezvoused with John Walker. They met daily at the airport and planned the startup of Omega Aviation. John Walker had been vetted by Admiral Reynolds and was cleared for all operations although he was not scheduled to fly the AFVs. They both monitored hangar construction, which was progressing at a rapid pace. The eight helo pilots completed their training on the Bell 412 and delivery was accepted and the birds flown back across country from Dallas, TX.

As hangar construction was continuing Bob Avery made trips weekly to the headquarters facility east of Kamas where he directed final touches to the housing and headquarters building. The compound at Kamas was located slightly west of the old McCarthy gold mine on the slope of Mt. Hoyt. It was a gated community with restricted entry. The entire compound had been completely fenced in with an 8-foot chain link fence with three strands on razor wire on top and the only entrance was on the west entry road. This was to be a large operation. The housing development consisted of one hundred homes on five separate streets. There would be a motor pool and a helo pad alongside the headquarters building. All personnel involved with AFV flying would be located on the property while other personnel working only for Omega Aviation would live off the property. John Walker and all helo pilots were the exception of who would reside on the property. Omega would provide bus service for the children to attend school in Kamas.

The second group of pilots, observers and maintenance personnel completed their G4 training about the time the hangar construction was complete. Two G4s were ready to be delivered so after graduation the pilots accepted the aircraft and ferried them to the Salt Lake City facility. Offices at the hangar were furnished as well as maintenance equipment delivered and Omega Aviation was officially up and running. Within a week headquarters building was completed as well as all housing. Personnel soon began moving into their offices as well as moving dependents into their new houses. Flight operations began in earnest with pilots acquiring 15-20 hours in the G4. Charter helicopter flights were also being scheduled, which kept everyone busy. Support personnel were hired and operations were beginning to smooth out a little. A few charter flights were being flown as well as charter flights for a few government agencies.

Bob Avery had moved into corporate headquarters, which was located on the eastern end of the compound set against the forest to the east. Pilots and observers were assigned offices in headquarters instead of the hangar. This was to ensure privacy as soon as the AFV operation moved to

Utah. Bob Avery set about to establish a schedule for all flight personnel. It was simple. Two weeks flying G4s, two weeks flying AFVs and two weeks off duty. It would probably vary by a day or two but generally it was a workable solution.

Bob soon received word that the AFV base located up on Mt. Hoyt was ready to receive the birds. He asked Larry Beck to accompany him on the initial trip up to inspect the facility. It was a slightly complicated journey. Inside the rear of headquarters was a security door. Each person entering was required to give visual eye identification and enter a code to open the door. Bob and Larry performed the proper procedure and the door opened. They proceeded in and entered the elevator. Larry pushed the down button and soon they were on their way to a level some one hundred feet below the surface. The door opened and as they stepped out they saw their next mode of transportation. It was a monorail car, built to handle four persons. They stepped in and after the forward switch was activated the monorail car started forward smoothly headed up the mountain. Within a few minutes it came to a stop within the old McCarthy mine complex. Once again they exited the vehicle and were amazed and surprised at the two circular tubes facing them. They had been briefed on what to expect but were still amazed by what greeted them. They entered one of them, which was built to accommodate two people, closed the outer door and then the inner door. It was a pneumatically operated system and as soon as the lever was placed in the up position the vehicle lurched upward from the force of the high-pressure air being applied to the underside of the vehicle. The monorail had brought them up 3000' and the pneumatic tube the final 3000'. The new AFV hangar complex was about 6500' above the valley floor. When the vehicle came to a stop Bob opened the inner and outer doors and stepped out into the new AFV complex. He stood there in awe. The construction crew, which he figured was from the CIA, had carved out two hangar bays, crew quarters and an operations center. The two bays were set up to handle three AFVs each. The hangar bay doors and landing platform were just big enough to accommodate the latest model of AFV. The doors were hinged at the bottom and unfolded out to become a landing platform. The outside of the doors were camouflaged to blend into the sheer cliff they had been cut out from solid rock. The old claxon horn from Siple Station had been reinstalled and sounded whenever the doors were to open or close. This whole complex had been blended into their surroundings and was completely invisible from outside visual observation.

Bob and Larry were greeted by Choyce Proulx who had been there for about a week. "Hey Bob and Larry, how you guys been doing? Haven't seen you for a few months."

As they were shaking hands, Larry responded with "Missed your shining face, Choyce. We've been busy decommissioning the squadron and commissioning this whole new operation."

Bob chimed in, "Yeah, Choyce, this thing is a monster compared to the smooth running operation we had at Siple. It is ten times more difficult and going to be a challenge. How are things progressing here?"

"We have a few problems but nothing we won't be able to solve," he said. "We still have some more testing on equipment but should be up and running in about three days, I think."

"We haven't tested our direct line to operations yet, Choyce," Bob said. "When Larry and I get back down the mountain we will give you a call." Turning to Larry, Bob said, "It's located in my office on the left side of the desk behind the lower door, Larry. I forgot to show you but we can review it when we get back to the office. There's also a direct line to Jack Forester tied into the same communications receiver. We are going to restrict it to emergency use only."

"How about the ten cent tour, Choyce," Larry asked.

"You got it Larry. Follow me," Choyce replied.

Choyce led them across the hangar bay and into the ops center. There was an array of CRT's, some off and some displaying various scenes and information. Choyce moved behind a large desk control panel. Bob and Larry stood alongside and Choyce began, "That top row of TV screens shows us the area to the east of us for 180°. Below that are a few screens showing us the radar presentation for the same area. It can show us air targets, superimposed and infrared targets for 75 miles. We use that information to time the opening and closing of the hangar doors for recovery and launch. The two screens in the lower left are off currently since we are not controlling any AFVs but when we do they will display all the current info and the left one will display its current position. The rest of the displays give us the status of all our equipment. We have added burst capability in our communications equipment. We can send a message compressed to a one second burst and the vehicles can download and decipher it in real time. We have VHF, UHF, HF, microwave and digital capability and will soon have telephone capability. You name it we have it," Choyce concluded. "I can monitor all of our systems and remote equipment from this panel as well as operate the hangar doors and pneumatic tubes from here. There's a master switch for turning off the whole complex under that clear plastic box you see right here." He was pointing to it as he spoke. "That's about it here in ops," Choyce said. "Follow me and I will show you the crew quarters." With that he turned and started toward the back of the hangar bay. He made his way through a doorway and stopped upon entering. To his right was obviously a kitchen with all the trimmings including table and chairs for dining. On his left was a lounge with 54" TV, soft chairs and matching couch and of course the usual acey-deucy game table. Bob wondered but didn't ask how they got all this stuff up on the mountain. The construction crew had done wonders and he wasn't about to search for the answer. He was just pleased that the crews were being taken care of. Choyce continued down a hall where there was a bathroom, shower and bedrooms.

Larry commented that they had done a great job and he was looking forward to trying out the quarters.

Choyce moved back out into the hangar bay and on to the next door at the back of the bay. He stepped in and stated, "This is the flight equipment and dressing area, where the crews will don their pressure suits and test their suit and oxygen equipment prior to flight. There are 75 lockers back here for individual storage of each crewmembers flight equipment. We also have a complete pressure chamber behind this room."

Larry and Bob were pleased with this area.

Choyce moved out and continued further on down the back wall of the hangar bay. "From here on down are the maintenance shops and equipment repair facilities," he said. "We can generally repair any maintenance problem on the AFV and repair any piece of personal flight gear. Without the squadron support, Bob, I think we should consider hiring at least two flight equipment repairmen. A couple of former pararescue team members are available."

"That sounds like a good idea, Choyce. Send me a note to remind me and make a couple of suggestions on personnel," Bob related.

"As part of this complex we have the service tubes. They were designed to bring up our supplies needed daily for our crews to exist here. It is connected to another part of the old McCarthy mine complex. Those are the trucks you see occasionally driving up the mine road," Choice said

Choyce acknowledged and asked Bob and Larry if they had any questions. Each nodded that they did not and they said their goodbyes. Choyce escorted them back to the pneumatic tubes for their descent back down the mountain. They retraced their tracks and soon they were reentering the headquarters complex through the rear security door.

They made their way to Bob's office where Bob's directed Larry's attention to the door panel on the left side of his desk.

"Open the door, Larry, and we will check out the comm with Choyce. When you pickup the handset and push the select button it will automatically ring on his end," Bob directed.

Larry lifted the handset, punched the appropriate button and put the handset to his ear. He heard it ring twice and Choyce was on the line. "Roger headquarters this is ops. How do you read, over?"

"Roger ops, this is HQ reading you loud and clear, I believe we are operational, HQ out," Larry responded.

"Ops out," Choyce said.

"Looks like that system is working fine," Larry said. With that he placed the headset back in its cradle and closed the door panel.

"I guess we are in business with that system," Larry said.

"That's good Larry," Bob responded.

Bob explained to Larry that normal comm with ops would be through coded emails and that hotline would be for emergency use only. They discussed the timetable for moving the AFVs to Hoyt Mountain and activating the new operations center.

20

"The Ultimate Mission"

Kamas, Utah

Over the past couple of days all the AFVs were moved to the new complex in Utah. The remaining flight crews from Area 51 were moving their families to Utah and Jack Shepard was also wrapping things up in Nevada and on his way to Omega headquarters. Choyce and Jack were bachelors so they shared one of the houses in the housing development. They would relieve each other every couple of weeks in AFV ops so they would barely see each other except when changing the watch in ops.

Omega Aviation was now up and running smoothly and even showing a profit. The crews were flying charter flights all over the world and the six G4s were operating to the maximum. Helicopters were also keeping fairly busy. Crews were broken down into three sections. Bob's plan was in effect and seemed to be working without a hitch. six crews were flying the AFVs and six crews had two weeks off with the other six crews operating the G4s.

The AFVs had picked up one of the primary missions in January and were shadowing space shuttle Discovery for mission STS 42. That one was a seven-day mission and was pretty routine.

On April 5, 1992, the AFVs began monitoring the Siege of Sarajevo and the beginning of the Bosnian War. This would continue for some four years.

Washington, DC: Present time

Having made the decision to rescue the space shuttle Enterprise, Jack picked up the emergency headset in his office and pushed the button for Bob Avery at Omega. He could hear it ring and Bob Avery immediately picked up on the other end.

"Bob Avery here," he said as he spoke into the mike.

"Jack here, Bob, we have made the decision here in Washington that the AFVs will attempt to rescue the crew of space shuttle Enterprise as quickly as possible."

"Roger that Jack. We need to get it done ASAP."

"That's correct, Bob. Put Emergency Ops Plan AFVEX-90-126 Code name "Project Enterprise" into effect. I suggest you brief your pilots taking part in this mission on all aspects so we can maybe get out of this without making the AFV project public knowledge. No matter what, however, the rescue comes first, secrecy comes second. Do you have any questions?"

"I got it, Jack. Will keep you up to speed on developments. Do you want emails or direct on this line?" Bob asked.

"I suggest you tie in this line with Jack Shepard in ops and maybe give us a blow by blow of how things are going," Jack said.

"I can do that. I will have to go to ops center to brief the crews Jack," Bob said.

"Okay, Bob. Get moving and I will hear from you soon," Said Jack.

Bob returned the headset to its cradle, got up and went to the wall safe and opened it. He extracted Ops Plan AFVEX-90-126, closed the safe and moved quickly to the security door at the back of the complex.

His trip up the mountain seemed endless although it only took him about twenty minutes. He exited the pneumatic tube, stepped out onto the hangar deck where Jack Shepard met him.

"What's up, Bob?" Jack inquired. "I saw the tube activated and knew someone was on their way up."

"We got the green light to rescue the crew of Enterprise. What's our status?" Bob asked.

"We have two birds in maintenance, two on reccon. Bird 2 is due back in twelve minutes while Bird 6 in twenty-five," Jack said.

"Send both birds an emergency recall message, Jack."

"Where's Larry?" Bob asked.

"He's back in the crew quarters, Bob," Jack said

"I'm going back to the crew quarters to meet with Larry and the other crewmembers and brief them on the mission," Bob stated.

Bob proceeded immediately to the crew quarters where he found Larry and others lounging and relaxing.

Larry smiled as Bob entered. "Must be big," Larry said. "My guess it's the rescue we've been planning for but hoping would never happen."

"You hit the nail on the head," Bob answered. "Looks like you have inherited the task, old buddy," Bob quipped. "Let's gather all crews here in the lounge for a briefing in five minutes. This mission is hot and we need to get it done ASAP."

All personnel were notified and quickly gathered in the lounge.

"Looks like everyone is here, Bob," Said Larry.

Bob stood up in front of the TV, which had been turned off. He began his briefing. "This will be a four vehicle mission. Crews 2 and 6 will be returning shortly and we want to launch as soon as possible after they return. You four crews will fly the mission. We want to get this done. If we can retain our stealth that's great but rescue is primary. Let's try to start our rendezvous with Enterprise over western Russia since there are no tracking stations from there to eastern Asia. We can probably get it done within those parameters. I suggest the first three contacts take two of their crew each. The space shuttle airlock in the cargo bay will allow two crewmembers to exit at the same time. This way we save time. There will be a ten-minute window for them to get aboard your AFV and for you to pressurize. That is the limit of their emergency escape oxygen system. After you get them aboard, make haste and set them down as quickly as possible. Pick a spot where you have some isolation and where they will need to hike awhile to get to civilization. Larry how about taking over and let's review the specifics."

Larry moved to the front of the room. "Pete you take Number 2. Bruce you are assigned 3. Jim you have number 4 and I will fly number 6. I will depart within the next forty-five-minutes and pick up the shuttle in orbit over the central Pacific. I will need to brief the shuttle commander on what's going to happen and what our procedures will be. We will use UHF frequency 414.2 MHZ. Enterprise will be using that frequency on low power so you will probably be able to read them only at one hundred miles or less. Pickup order will be Pete first, followed by Bruce and then Jim. I will pickup the shuttle commander last. Let's try to keep our contact to twenty-minutes each. Standoff at least three hundred miles before you come in for your rescue so we don't present a big radar target. Each of you has read the op plan but remember lower your rear-landing strut and put it up against the tie-down cleat in the aft end of the cargo bay. Then after you depressurize, lower your boarding ladder. That will be the signal for the shuttle crewmembers to exit and board your vehicle. I suggest each of you have one of your crewmembers assist the shuttle personnel strap into the seats located just next to the entry ladder in the lower bay of your bird. Once you are pressurized, get your vehicle out of the way."

During Larry's briefing the claxon had sounded and Jack Shepard activated the hangar doors for recovery. The big doors rotated out and down and very quickly the two AFVs landed on the doors now presented as landing pads. They were quickly rolled into the hangar bay and once again the claxon sounded and the hangar doors closed.

Jack entered and caught Bob's attention. As soon as Larry finished his briefing, Bob stood and asked Jack if he had anything to add to the briefing.

From where he stood Jack added to the conversation, "The two birds are on deck and I will be loading the space shuttle flight and orbit parameters into each birds SPS (Space Positioning System). You flight officers be sure to reset all your navigation equipment on startup. I also suggest a radio check on 414.2 MHZ before you liftoff so we know the transceiver is working properly. When you are on the perch waiting for your turn to conduct the rescue, I will coordinate your approach with Larry and give you a go when it's clear to proceed."

Bob then asked, "Anybody have any questions?"

Geoff Haskins raised his hand and asked, "Are we going to be pushing the shuttle crew with the twenty-minute time interval between pickups?"

Larry answered that question, "Geoff, I don't think so but we don't need to worry about that, we will just let the shuttle crew work as fast as the equipment will allow. Their main delay will be pressurizing the space lock so the next two crewmembers can enter for repositioning for rescue. Whatever time it takes we can live with. We have orbital distance from over Russia until we reach the coast of the western hemisphere. If we are spotted so be it. The lives of the astronauts are most important. Any other questions?"

There were none. "Looks like we are a go. My crew and I will be departing in approximately twenty-five minutes so plan your departures accordingly. I suggest a twenty-minute departure interval."

Larry and his crew proceeded to the equipment room, donned their pressure suits, completed their equipment checkout and walked directly to their AFV. Checklists were complete, the AFV started and departure permission requested from Jack in ops control. The claxon sounded, hangar door extended and Larry soon departed the spaceport. The mission was on.

Larry pointed his AFV skyward and proceeded westward over the Pacific. He made a long sweeping port turn still climbing to one hundred six miles high. He accelerated to 18,000 mph and as he rolled out of his turn he was just two hundred feet from the shuttle Enterprise. Larry engaged his voice distortion software on his UHF and keyed the mike.

He began, "Enterprise do you read, over?"

Inside Enterprise Paul Anderson was shocked and in awe. As he looked out his side window he couldn't believe what he was seeing. His first instinct was to call mission control but his pilot Tori Croft had beat him to it. She was on the HF radio calling mission control but was only hearing static.

Larry once again called Enterprise, "Enterprise do you read, over."

Paul Anderson was now fully aware of the situation and keyed his UHF transceiver, "This is Enterprise, over."

"Enterprise I will only transmit this one time so pay close attention. Within 20 minutes a vehicle will dock with you and be prepared to take aboard two of your crewmembers. When you see the boarding ladder come down that will be your signal to move out of Enterprise and enter the vehicle. You will need to use your emergency escape oxygen system (EEOS) so move quickly. We will repeat this procedure until all your crewmembers are aboard our vehicles. Do you understand?"

Paul responded, "Roger, copy. Will be prepared to debark two crewmembers in twenty minutes."

"Enterprise, do not waste time trying to call mission control as your other communications have been disabled," Larry said.

Inside Enterprise there were many fast beating hearts. Most crewmembers had not heard the exchange of transmissions between Paul Anderson and the AFV and they were all trying to talk at once. They had all seen the AFV but were not aware of what was going to happen. Paul can up on the intercom and addressed the crew.

"Here is the situation. I just talked with that space vehicle but do not know who or what they are but they have put forth a plan to rescue us and we are going to take advantage of it. Apparently each of their vehicles can take only two of us at a time. We need to get our pressure suits on as quickly as possible. In twos, we will proceed to the air lock and be ready to depressurize. They will rendezvous over the cargo bay and extend their boarding ladder. That is our signal to depressurize, activate our EEOS and proceed to board their vehicle. Remember you have only a ten-minute oxygen supply so move quickly. As soon as the air lock door is secured we will pressurize and the next two will move into the air lock and await the next vehicle. Hank and Sally, you will be the first out so get going on donning your space suits."

Tori spoke first, "Paul how do we know they have oxygen and that their system is compatible."

"They seemed to know our requirements and our limitations so we will have to rely on them." Paul responded.

Hank Reitz and Sally Gorkowski were already proceeding to the air lock. They entered and locked the door securely behind them. The red warning light turned green indicating they were positioned and that the Enterprise would be safe from depressurization when they activated the air lock.

Larry backed off about one hundred miles from Enterprise, called ops and directed Pete to begin his approach and rescue.

Jack relayed the message in a burst transmission to Pete. Pete O'Malley was a seasoned AFV pilot and quickly accelerated to intercept Enterprise. He came to a hover over the cargo bay and lowered his rear landing strut then eased the AFV down using his lower TV camera until his strut was firmly against the cargo bay tie-down. When stable, he lowered his boarding ladder.

Inside the air lock Sally hit the depressurization switch and she and Hank pulled the little green apple to activate their emergency escape oxygen system. Both their pulse rates were in the extreme range. Neither knew what to expect and whether they would be meeting the little green men from Mars. They did know that this was their ticket out of a dead end situation as there was no rescue from NASA forthcoming. They had settled in their minds that they were going to die in space and had accepted their fate but this was their reprieve. They were depressurized in two minutes, twenty-five seconds. They opened their outer doors and swiftly moved out into the cargo bay. The boarding ladder of the AFV was only about ten feet away and they quickly floated in zero gravity to the ladder. Hand over had they made their way up the ladder where once inside Flight Engineer Walter Glennon, who to them was just a space traveler in a green suit, met them in the AFV. The AFV pressure suits were still green as that was the only color that would take to the material the suits were made of. The AFV crewmembers had complained for years but the old color still prevailed. Glennon grabbed each of them and sat them onto the emergency seats just inside the vehicle next to the boarding ladder. He got them strapped in and communicated to Pete that they were ready to uncouple from Enterprise. The boarding ladder was retracted and the door closed. Pressurization was quickly restored. It had taken just nine minutes since Sally and Hank had activated their EEOS. Each could now feel the pressurization and the valve in their flight suits opened so they were breathing oxygen from the AFV. Sally became aware of this situation and opened her faceplate. Hank observed that she could breath normally so he did the same. Glennon went back up into the upper deck of the AFV and strapped into his seat at the engineers panel. All this activity had taken place over the former Soviet Republics of Asia so Pete headed for a landing spot as quickly as possible. Pete descended straight down and spotted and open field along side a major highway. Turned out to be sixty miles west of Ulaan Baatar, the capital of Mongolia. Pete came to a hover, lowered his tricycle landing gear and gently set the AFV down on the grass amongst the few trees. He lowered the boarding ladder while Glennon went down in the AFV to the lower bay and unstrapped the bewildered astronauts. Glennon directed them to proceed down the ladder where he followed and got them moving away from under the vehicle. Sally and Hank sat down on the ground, as they were a little shaky trying to adjust to the gravity of earth. Glennon boarded the AFV and they were airborne within a few seconds. Sally and Hank just looked at each other and said nothing. There was no way to describe what had just happened but one thing was sure they were just glad to be back on Mother Earth and alive.

21

"A Job Well Done"

Kamas, Utah

Meanwhile back in ops, Jack and Bob had been monitoring the mission with Jack Forester on the hotline back in Washington, DC. Jack Shepard had piped in Larry's description of what was happening while the monitors on the wall showed the approach and departure of Pete's vehicle from Enterprise. There was not much conversation except Bob who interjected, "Two down five to go."

In space, as soon as Larry viewed Pete's departure, he messaged Jack to release Bruce Fleming for his rescue attempt. Bruce was just as smooth and efficient as Pete and just as quickly moved in and docked with Enterprise. The second pair of Enterprise crewmembers were just as efficient and within eight minutes Bruce was loaded and undocked from Enterprise. He was over Australia and decided that was as good a place as any to drop his passengers. He touched down about sixty miles from Alice Springs. He pointed the Enterprise crewmembers in the right direction so they would be found shortly.

Next up was Jim Huskins. He was vectored in to pick up the next two crewmembers. The pilot, Tori Croft, and Cargo Specialist, Jody West, moved down to the air lock in their space suits. They entered and performed the proper procedures to isolate the air lock from the shuttle. Green light was observed on their panel and they stood ready to depart. They had observed the first two rescue craft pick up the other crewmembers so they were not quite as excited in anticipation of their rescue. They watched through the air lock doors as Jim maneuvered his AFV into position for pickup. He slowly moved down towards the cargo bay and soon lowered his aft landing strut and locked it into the cargo bay tie-down. As soon as he was stable he lowered the boarding ladder and when it was fully extended, Tori pressed the decompression switch and Tori and Jody activated their EEOS. Once depressurized they opened the air lock doors and moved to the boarding ladder. Up the ladder they went and were met by the flight engineer who grabbed them and settled them in the emergency seats in the lower bay. He strapped them in and moved to the upper deck for departure. Jim had reactivated pressurization as soon as he got a green light indicating the boarding door was up and locked. Tori and Jody's pressure suits worked as advertised and as soon as pressure was sensed outside the suit their emergency oxygen cutoff and they began breathing AFV cabin air. Their brains were racing as to what was happening to them. The unknown of who were their rescuers, whether the crafts internal systems were compatible and what was going to happen to them once aboard this strange craft made them very nervous. Jim descended and slowed quickly into the atmosphere. He found himself within fifty miles of Pitcairn Island so he figured that was as good a place as any to set down his two guests.

Larry moved his AFV into position to pickup Mission Commander Paul Anderson. While doing so the UHF crackled to life. It was Paul. "Saucer, this is Enterprise, I am having difficulty pressurizing my space suit, I believe I have a leak in one of the gloves."

Larry responded, "Roger Enterprise, what are your intentions, over?"

"We have some repair material which I can inject into the glove but it will take about fifteen minutes before it will be safe to pressurize," Paul said.

"Roger Enterprise," Larry responded. "Do what you need to do. We will be standing by. Call us when you are ready for transfer."

It was the longest fifteen minutes for both Larry's crew and Paul waiting for the repair to dry. Paul moved to the air lock and plugged into the shuttle's intercom system. He had rigged the cockpit radio so he could activate it from the air lock. He locked the air lock inner door, got a green light and keyed the mike in his helmet. "Enterprise, I'm ready for transfer, over."

Larry answered, "Roger stand by."

Larry maneuvered the AFV into position in Enterprise's cargo bay.

Tom Harger activated the boarding ladder to the down position. Paul observed it lock down and hit the depressurization switch and activated his EEOS. As soon as he was depressurized, he opened the air lock door and moved swiftly to the ladder and in zero gravity moved quickly up the ladder. Flight engineer Randles met him and soon had him strapped into the seat in the lower bay of the AFV. Just as quickly the boarding ladder retracted and the door came up and locked. Larry activated the pressurization and Paul's space suit responded by switching him to cabin air. Larry headed the AFV down through the atmosphere. Because the glove repair had taken so much time the AFV was approaching 57°S in the middle of the South Indian Ocean. Larry headed the AFV directly for McMurdo in the Antarctic. It was winter and 24 hours of darkness. Larry would drop Paul on the ice in McMurdo Sound where he could easily make his way to the base and be found. Paul felt comfortable in this unknown vehicle. His conversations with whom he presumed was the pilot gave him confidence but also made him wonder where these vehicles came from and who was operating them. As much as he strained to see and hear anything going on in the upper cabin of the AFV he could hear nor see nothing.

Larry put the AFV in stealth mode so he would not produce the usual visible green ionized layer of gas on the outside of the vehicle as he passed 100,000'. He came over the Transantarctic Mountains on the west side of McMurdo Sound, slowed the vehicle about a mile off of Ross Island and came to a hover. Tom lowered the landing pads and they touched down on the ice. The boarding ladder was lowered and Randle assisted Paul getting down onto the ice. During this procedure Randle slipped a card into one of the outer pockets on Paul's flight suit without his knowledge. Paul was a little wobbly from the effects of gravity as he had been in zero gravity for about a week and his body functions needed to get used to it again. Randle started him towards the lights of McMurdo and walked with him for a few hundred yards. The temperature was only—36°F and there was no wind so walking wasn't all that bad. He took the flashing strobe light out of Paul's survival kit and activated it. He also ensured Paul's survival radio was on and working and sending a signal on 243.0 MHZ. Once Randle was sure he would be okay he turned him loose by himself and returned to the AFV. The AFV lifted off and streaked across the sky headed back to the base in Utah.

Washington, DC

Jack Forester had been privy to all the conversations and tracking info as the rescues had progressed. He was ecstatic when Paul Anderson was extracted from Enterprise. He picked up the red phone in his office and rang Bill Reynolds. Bill picked up almost immediately, "What's the latest Jack?" he asked.

"I am happy to report that all crewmembers of space shuttle Enterprise have been rescued from space and are on the ground somewhere in the world."

He was slightly kidding of course but Bill took it in stride. "Yeah, Jack, and where are our intrepid astronauts?" he queried.

"That's why I was joking, Bill. We won't know until we get a debriefing of our AFV pilots. They are due back in Utah in about thirty to fifty minutes. Larry had a little delay because of a space suit problem with Paul Anderson. He separated from Enterprise somewhere over the South Indian Ocean and knowing Larry and his being so close to Antarctica I would suspect he dropped Paul in the Antarctic, probably at McMurdo. I will pass that info on to you as soon as I am briefed. I don't know if there were any sightings when the space shuttle passed over North and South America but we won't know until tomorrow morning when the newspapers begin to hit the streets and our military bases begin to report."

"Jack, I have had the Fox News channel on during most of this afternoon and early evening and have had no news alerts so the reports aren't filtering in yet if there are any.

Perhaps we got off easily for right now. When the astronauts are recovered and are back in Huston and after debrief the press will exert great pressure for them to tell their story. That's when we will know if we are still in business," Bill said.

"If anybody takes the initial heat it will be Don Ransford at DOD," Jack mused.

"Yeah Jack he will but I think he is thick skinned enough that he can handle it. I believe we will be okay as long as the astronauts are in the dark about who and what happened. Anyway give me a ring when you finished the debriefing."

"Will do, Bill. Talk to you later," Jack said.

Kamas, Utah

Pete O'Malley was the first to return followed shortly by Jim Huskins and Bruce Fleming. They were just getting out of their flight suits when the claxon sounded announcing hangar door operation. Larry set down his AFV and soon he was clear and the door was returned to the closed position. Bob met Larry as he exited AFV number 6 on the hangar deck. Larry and Bob were all smiles and as they greeted each other hugs and high fives were exchanged. "What a mission that was," Larry quipped.

"You guys sure know how to age the boss," Bob shot back.

"That was not the toughest mission I've ever flown but boy was it tense up there. The guys did a fine job. The ten-minute exchange time was the hairiest part. Lotsa lives depended on us doing it right so let's don't schedule many of those kind of missions again soon," Larry responded.

"Will take that under advisement Larry," Bob said. "Go ahead and get changed and meet me in the crew quarters and we will debrief there."

About that time Jack Shepard came over. "Great job, Larry," Jack said. "You guys did a great job up there today. About time for a drink, don't you think?"

"You're on Jack. I will meet you both in the crew quarters shortly," Jack said.

Larry made his way into the equipment room along with his crew. The other crews were almost finished changing.

There were a lot of smiles, back slaps and high fives still going on. Larry spoke, "I am so proud of you guys. What you did today was beyond belief. Today we saved seven beautiful people and unfortunately they will never be able to thank you for that. I am proud to have served with every one of you. I'll see you in the crew quarters in a minute."

To the man they then thanked Larry for the job he had done that day and they began to wander out a few at a time.

When they entered the living quarter's loud cheers from the other two crews, which had not participated in the mission, greeted them. They shook hands all around and after getting something to drink sat down and waited for Larry's crew to join them. There was a lot of interaction and conversing when Larry's crew stepped through the door. Everybody stopped what they were doing stood and applauded and shouted, "Great job guys."

Larry responded with, "Put a lid on it you guys. You did as much as I did."

Bob took center stage and asked the all to sit down. "Let's get the debriefing over with and then start the party."

All-hands quieted down and took seats in the lounge.

"Okay, Pete. Give us your take on the mission but before you start where did you drop your passengers?" Bob asked.

"We set them down alongside the main highway about sixty miles west of Ulaan Baatar, Mongolia." Pete reported. He continued, "As for my crew we saw our portion go off without a hitch. We couldn't hear any UHF communications from the perch so Jack's relays were very important."

"Anything for us, Pete?" Bob asked.

"The only human contact the passengers had had been with George my engineer and I don't think he even spoke to them. Is that correct George?" Pete quiried.

George nodded in the affirmative. "They were exposed to only the lower bay of our AFV and it was sanitized before the mission so there was nothing which would give away our origin and, no, I didn't speak to them at all. Also I kept my dark shaded visor down at all times so they could not see my face."

"Okay, Pete. That's good." Turning to Bruce Fleming Bob asked, "What's your take on the mission, Bruce?"

"We set our passengers down about fifty-five east of Alice Springs in central Australia. They were on a main east/ west road so I don't think they will have any trouble being found. Everything went good for us, our only heartburn was the passenger exchange. It took ten minutes twelve seconds and we were sweating every second. Fortunately they did not run out of oxygen and we got pressurized very quickly. We got them on and off pretty rapidly and I think they were in shock at what was happening so there was no compromise on our mission or vehicle. The briefings and ops plan were excellent. I don't think we ran into anything that wasn't briefed or that we hadn't read in the ops plan. I would like to thank my crew for the efficient way they handled everything during the mission. Thanks guys," Bruce said.

"Jim, you're next up. How'd the mission go from your aspect?" Bob asked.

"Our position was almost over Pitcairn Island so we thought that was a good enough place so we set them down in a farmers field. They shouldn't be hard to find. We had to go direct to our standoff position since we were running a few minutes late on our intercept but we made it on time and were ready to rendezvous when Jack relayed our go message. I had a little trouble stabilizing our position when we went to hover but I guess the shuttle was in a slight roll due to the two previous rescues. Once we matched up with the shuttle movement we were just fine and our rescue went by the book. There was no interaction or exposure to the passengers so I think we are fine in that respect."

"Thanks, Jim," Bob responded.

"Okay, Larry, you're on deck. What's your take on the mission?" Bob said.

"I think it went pretty much by the numbers, Bob," Said Larry. "Paul Anderson was dropped off about one mile from McMurdo Base. Randle headed him toward the lights at the base, turned on his strobe light and made sure his survival radio was operating. We were delayed getting Paul Anderson off the shuttle in a timely manner because of his leaking glove from his space suit. I was stressed as it was, but those fifteen minutes were the worst in history. We were so damn nervous we were almost chewing the insulation off the bulkhead."

Tom Harger interjected, "We were lit up by a couple of radars on our pass over western United States and South America so I don't know how much rumbling that's going to cause in the media but all in all we didn't have any exposure to the shuttle crew except what they could see visually out their windows. There will be lots of speculation in a few days but I think we are in a great position to do what we do."

Larry continued, "Ops plan and briefings were completely satisfactory and everything went like clockwork. I said it before and I will say it again you guys are the ultimate professionals and this will always be a memorable day in our lives. So, Bob, let's get the party started."

"Before we break up this briefing, Jack have you anything to add?" Bob asked.

"No, Bob. Everything clicked like it was designed to do. Great job guys," Jack said.

Bob stood and said, "We will stand down with no AFV flights for 36 hours so let's bring on the booze and have a party."

Everyone thought this was a great idea and the glasses started to clank and a roaring party that would soon not be forgotten got underway.

22

"Where is Everyone"

Washington, DC

While the party was getting underway, Bob Avery called Jack Forester on the hot line from operations. The phone rang once and Jack picked up.

"Okay, Bob. Give me the rundown on the mission."

"Jack," Bob started. "There is not much to tell you except where the astronauts were dropped off. Hank Reitz and Sally Gorkowski were first rescued and were dropped off on a main highway sixty miles west of Ulaan Baatar, Mongolia. Burt Simmons and Michael Syong were deposited on the road fifty-five miles east of Alice Springs in Australia. Tori Croft and Jodi West landed on Pitcairn Island, and Paul Anderson was set down at McMurdo about one mile offshore on the bay ice."

Jack interjected, "Pitcairn Island, you got to be kidding, Bob. What were your guys thinking."

"I briefed them to disembark their passengers as quickly as possible and that's what they did so I can't fault them for that. Jack, you were in on all the communications so I can't add much there. Tom Harger said they were painted on a couple of radars as they orbited down across the United States and South America. Not sure that will cause us any problem however there may be so home video from that pass down the Americas. Right now there is a celebration going on here and I want to get back to the party."

"Okay, Bob. I am pleased the way the mission went down. Thank all the guys for a job well done. I will probably be talking with you in the next few days. Take care."

"Roger that, Jack." Bob disconnected from the console and went back to the party now in full swing in the lounge.

It was approaching 6:00pm on the east coast but Jack knew Bill Reynolds would still be in his office. He picked up the red phone behind his desk and put it to his ear just as the phone rang on the other end.

"Bill here, What's the report from Utah, Jack?" he asked.

"The rescue was a rousing success Bill. All astronauts are safe and sound and back on earth. The AFV crews were directed to get them off their vehicles as quickly as possible so here are their current positions. The first pair are in Mongolia. Second group in Australia. Third pair in Pitcairn Island and mission commander in McMurdo, Antarctica.

Bill interrupted, "Pitcairn Island Jack? What were your guys thinking? That recovery is going to take a few days, maybe a week."

"Bill, I think it is a good thing. I'm not sure what scenario is going to play out but my take on it is that NASA will be unable to contact the astronauts so they will assume they are dead. They will confirm that at a press conference and the media will report it. NASA will take all the heat about not being able to rescue them. The story will quickly drift off the front pages and nightly newscasts and it will become a local story. In a couple of days information will come to light that they are alive and well at the various places I just ascribed. After the couple of days of doom and gloom there will be rejoicing in the streets and everyone will be so glad that how they returned to earth will be a secondary story. We will then have someone pick them up and return them to Houston. After that no telling where the press will go with the story. The media will bug the astronauts until they have had enough and we will be forgotten just as we planned and like it to be. It all depends on what the astronauts have to say and how they describe their rescue. My guys didn't give them any insight into the AFV or who was operating them so it will all be conjecture on the part of the media. There are no close up pictures and the astronauts only viewed the AFV when Larry

Beck first contacted them before the rescue. I think we will be home free on this one."

"Did we have any problems with the rescue Jack?" Bill asked.

"We only had one glitch Bill. On Larry's rescue Paul Anderson had a leaking glove problem. He put in some of that magic sealer but it apparently took fifteen minutes to harden so they were delayed in making the rescue. The AFV kept in close contact, docked in the cargo bay of the shuttle so they were pretty well shielded from earth visually and radar wise they only appeared as one object on the screen. They reported being painted by a couple of radar sites on their pass down the Americas but I don't think there was any exposure."

"There have been no UFO sightings reported on the ground in the last few hours from the sites you just named Jack but that doesn't mean there won't be later reports once the media starts digging," Bill reported.

"I guess we will deal with it as it unfolds, Bill," Jack said.

"Good job, Jack, Pass my congratulations on to Utah. I will be in touch. Have a good night."

"Okay, Bill. Will be in touch. Talk to you later."

Jack hung up the phone and just sat and pondered what had just occurred over the past two hours. He felt he should do more but his instincts kicked in and he would leave the media frenzy to Bill and Don Ransford over at the Pentagon. Jack packed it in and called it a night.

Houston, TX

Pete Crown had been on duty late in the afternoon and had attempted to contact the space shuttle Enterprise without success. The controllers had been directed to monitor Enterprise but not disturb them unless it was at all necessary. There had been a pall of doom over the Houston space center because they knew that no rescue was possible and the astronauts had also been deeply depressed. NASA had planned to allow the dependents final access to their loved ones with a short teleconference with Enterprise and it had been planned for late the next day. With this new development with no communication contact with Enterprise,

Pete Crown had called a meeting of all the controllers to discuss what they were reading on their monitors. Those who were monitoring the shuttle itself reported everything normal except the fuel problem. Human resources had no telemetry since shortly after orbital insertion as the astronauts had removed the monitors and live monitoring was conducted by medical interview each day with each astronaut. Pete's assistant had continued to call Enterprise on all voice radios without success. Pete had notified his boss, the Director of manned space flight, who had in turn notified NASA Administrator, Charles H. Wilson. They conferred late into the night trying to decide what to say at a news conference they knew had to be held the next day.

Washington, DC

Jack arrived early at the National Science Foundation. He knew today would be a big news day so he turned on his television with the sound off. Ken Nichols was first to knock on his door. He stuck his head in, "You busy, Jack?" he asked.

"No come on in, Ken, I needed to talk with you anyway. Have a seat." Jack directed Ken to his sofa.

"What's up this morning, Jack?' Ken asked.

"We rescued the astronauts from the space shuttle late yesterday with the AFVs. They are all safe and sound on earth but have not been reported as such yet. I think NASA will have a press conference some time this morning reporting them dead or condition unknown. I just thought you needed to know. We used the emergency communication voice net so we didn't have you involved with electronic messages but I am sure we will have a bunch today. The mission commander is at McMurdo so they will probably be reporting him safe there. Just monitor the situation and keep me up to speed on any developments from your end."

"Wow, Jack that is some development. I guess I need to check my messages from McMurdo?" Ken offered.

"Yeah and check your State Department stuff while you're at it too," Jack said.

Ken got up and departed, headed for his office in the basement.

Fox News on Jack's TV suddenly caught his attention. He unmuted the TV. Their news alert said that NASA would have a news conference at 10 o'clock.

Jack had to work on his story of what to tell NASA when he finally got word from McMurdo, which he knew would be forthcoming.

Ken returned from the basement very quickly with a message in his hand.

"I see you got the word from McMurdo, Ken," Jack observed.

'Here it is, Jack," Ken said. "I knew you would be waiting so I brought it as quickly as possible."

He handed it to Jack. It read, "Captain Paul Anderson, USN Space Shuttle Enterprise Commander suddenly appeared at our base yesterday in the early morning. He states that he was rescued and deposited here by a flying saucer, origin unknown, and no description of the crew. He is anxious to speak to NASA, Houston. Will schedule a microwave telephone conference ASAP this afternoon.

Jack placed a call to the Manned Space Flight Center in Houston and asked to speak to Director, Winston Perry. He was put on hold and shortly Director Perry came on the line.

"Win Perry here. I understand I am speaking to Jack Forester of the Office of Polar Programs."

"That's correct, Director. I am in charge of Antarctic scientific research and control all operations for the U.S. in Antarctica. I am in receipt of a message sent this morning by the Senior OPP scientist stating that Captain Paul Anderson is safe and sound at McMurdo Station and wishing to speak to you ASAP." Jack offered.

"Oh my God, Jack. Are you sure of your facts or could this be a hoax?" The director replied. You could hear the excitement in his voice but he was obviously leery of a deception.

"Sir, let me assure you these facts are correct and he is there in McMurdo," Jack responded.

You could now hear the excitement in his voice and sound of joy breaking through the gloom that had been there before. Speaking very quickly now he asked, "How did he get there? Do you have any more information, Jack?" he asked.

"Yes, he states that he was rescued and deposited there by a flying saucer, origin unknown, no description of the crew. In addition he is requesting a telephone conference with you as soon as possible. We can handle that through our microwave phone capability. It will be routed through our communications here at headquarters and then we can patch it into the phone system. During this call let's find out from McMurdo Base how long it will take to groom the ice runway so a flight can be scheduled into Antarctica to pick him up. Also if you wish we could use Omega Aviation, a private company, which operates out of Salt Lake City to make the pickup. The reason I suggest this company is they have some pilots with Antarctic flying experience. They also have Antarctic survival training and know what clothing and equipment they will need from our storage in Christchurch, New Zealand. Should you decide to go this route we can coordinate the Antarctic portion from here at Polar Programs."

"Jack, that sounds great. How soon can we have the phone conference?" Win asked.

"My communications director is working on the call as we speak. As soon as we get things set up I will ring you at this number. Are you still having you news conference at 10:00am?" Jack asked.

"I think we better delay that until I talk with Paul and have better information to pass on to the media. If you think you can get the call through pretty quickly we will reschedule it for 11:00 o'clock," Win said.

"We should be ready in a couple of minutes. I will call you," Jack said.

Jack hung up his phone and waited for Ken to ring. He knew all-hands were working on it so he did some busy work to stay out of the process and let his people do their thing.

Washington, DC

The phone in Jack's office rang and he picked it up. On the other end was Phil Weston, Senior OPP representative at McMurdo.

"Hey, Jack," He started. "How are things in DC."

"They are great here, Phil. What's your status?"

"Captain Anderson is eager to speak to NASA Houston. Do we have that set up yet?" he asked.

"We will connect in a few minutes but first let me pose the questions and, after Captain Anderson speaks to NASA Houston you can come back on the line and we will discuss what will happen next, okay?" Jack said.

"Got it, Jack. What are the questions?" Phil asked.

"How soon can you prepare the ice runway to receive a Gulfstream G4 to pick up the Captain? Also do you have runway lighting capability?" Jack asked. "Ken, ring the NASA Houston number and Phil you can put Captain Anderson on the line."

Ken didn't answer he just switched on the landline and rang the Houston number. The next voice on the line was that of Captain Anderson. "Stand by for Director Perry, captain," Jack said.

"Roger sir," Paul answered.

Director Perry came on the line. "Paul this is Win Perry. Oh my God, I just so glad to hear from you. What's your condition?"

"I'm in great shape, Win. Just glad to be alive. The people here at McMurdo are treating me just fine. I am warm and not lacking anything to eat. I would like to talk to Janelle if that's possible," Paul said.

"Janelle is supposed to be in this afternoon and I am sure Jack Forster can arrange a phone call for you. Thank God you're alive. How in the Hell did you get to McMurdo and where is the rest of your crew, Paul?" Win asked.

"First thanks for arranging the call with Janelle. All I can tell you is I was rescued by a silver looking flying saucer. I don't know its origin nor who is operating it. I saw only one crewmember. He was apparently wearing a green pressure suit and he was tied to the ship by an umbilical. When we debarked from the ship at McMurdo it was so dark I really couldn't see much but I know he never raised the faceplate in his helmet. I don't know where the remainder of my crew are. They were taken off Enterprise before me. I was last to leave. They departed somewhere over northern Asia down toward Australia so they have to be on the ground somewhere in that area. That's about all I can give you for now," Paul stated.

"Thanks, Paul," Win said. "We'll give you a call when Janelle gets here this afternoon. I will contact her and give her a report on your status. I know she will be ecstatic when I tell her. Put Phil Weston back on the phone and we will finalize your flight out."

"Roger that," Paul said. "Here's Phil."

Jack spoke first. What are the answers to my questions, Phil?"

"We can plow the runway, put down the pulvamix and set up the lighting in about a week. JP-4 could be made available if it is necessary just let us know the requirement. We can light up the ice runway with what we have," Phil reported.

"That sounds great, Phil. Let's plan on that schedule. We will have a G4 at McMurdo next Tuesday. Just keep us advised. Did you copy all that Director Perry?" Jack asked.

"I got it all Jack. When can we set up a call with Paul and Janelle Anderson?"

"Give us a 15 minutes heads-up and we will put the call through," Jack answered. "We'll be in touch as soon as possible."

"Thanks for the good news, Jack. We at NASA really appreciate what you have done," Win said.

"If you need other transport later on, Omega Aviation is a good firm to deal with. They are experienced people and can get the job done. Talk with you soon," Jack said.

Monday, Mongolia (One day earlier)

Hank and Sally finally felt capable of standing. They were still in shock of what had just happened and had no idea where they were let alone which way to civilization. It was still early morning and the sun had not come up yet so they decided to sit on a log by the side of the road and wait for someone to come along. They were in a valley surrounded by trees and low mountains. They were thirsty and there was a small stream near them but they were not sure of the quality of the water so they passed on a drink. They had been sitting by the side of the road for about an hour and a half when finally the sun peaked over the horizon.

Hank turned to Sally, "Where the Hell do you think we are, Sally?" Hank asked.

"I know we were somewhere over eastern Asia when we were taken off Enterprise so we have to be in that general vicinity. Where that may be is anybody's guess," Sally said.

"I agree, Sally. This appears to be a main highway so somebody will come along sooner or later, so all we need to do is wait and I am sure someone will help us."

The temperature was rising and had reached 57°F and the astronauts were warming up a little. They still had their space suits on, which were a little uncomfortable but that was all the astronauts had to wear so they just sucked it up and put up with the inconvenience.

Sure enough about two hours after sunup, Sally spotted a horse drawn wagon coming down the road from the east. As the wagon approached the astronauts stepped out into the road and flagged down the driver. Obviously this was a farmer with a load of hay on his wagon. The astronauts knew beforehand that he probably didn't understand English so they made gestures indicating they would like a ride. The farmer was in awe at these strangers on the road dressed in garments he had never seen before and speaking a language he didn't understand. He could see they were not dangerous so he gestured for them to climb on the back of the wagon. Where they were headed was a deep mystery. Soon they came into a small settlement, about ten dwellings, which looked like round tents and not much else. This obviously was a poor village and indicated a possible poor country. There were no commercial businesses. It appeared to be all peasants trying to eke out a living from the earth. The astronauts still found no one who spoke English. They were offered a drink of water from an animal skin and being as thirsty as they were, they accepted. The water was clear, cool and refreshing. The people were genuinely friendly and curious who these people were. The astronauts were invited into one of the tent houses. As Hank entered, he observed it had a wooden frame, a wooden door and was covered with a material, which appeared to be a woolen felt. It was sparsely furnished and was one room. The astronauts were given fermented milk almost like yogurt for breakfast along with a flour biscuit. A heavy strong coffee was served as a drink. Through hand gestures Hank and

Sally tried to make these newfound friend understand just who they were and needed to find the American embassy. They tried to relax and accept the situation they found themselves in. These peasants saw how cumbersome their space suits were and they were offered some native clothing. They were both glad to shed their space suits for something more comfortable.

Alice Springs, Australia

Astronauts Burt Simmons and Michael Syong had been deposited on the road some fifty-five miles east of Alice Springs. Within an hour of their touchdown a bus out of the Aritunga Historical Reserve headed for Alice Springs had stopped and picked them up alongside the highway. It took them to Alice Springs and dropped them at the city police station. Since everyone spoke English they had no problem conveying their status of whom they were and what they needed to do. The police sergeant on duty put through a call to the American Embassy in Canberra for them. After someone answered he handed the phone to Michael.

Michael began, "This is Michael Syong. I am an American astronaut and would like to speak with your administrative officer."

The operator on the other end of the line answered, "Mr. Syong, standby. I will ring our administrative offices. May I put you on hold?" She asked.

"That will be fine," Michael responded

The administrative offices picked up and the operator asked to talk to Joshua Olson, embassy administrative officer. He soon came on the line and she began, "Sir, I have a Michael Syong on the line that claims he is an American Astronaut and he wishes to speak with you. Shall I put him though, sir?"

"Yes Nan." He answered. "I will speak with him."

"This is Joshua Olson," he began.

"Mr. Olson. My name is Michael Syong, I am an American astronaut who was on the space shuttle Enterprise. We had a serious problem and two of us were rescued about six hours ago by a flying saucer of unknown origin and were deposited outside Alice Springs. We are currently at the Alice Springs police station and need your help."

"Michael, that's a hard story to swallow. Are you sure you're not just Americans who are stranded and need assistance getting home," he offered.

Mr. Olson, I assure you we are telling you the truth and need your help," Michael said. "I would suggest you contact the State Department and verify my identity. My fellow astronaut's name is Burt Simmons. We will await your answer but if you would please call or send a message to NASA Houston and report us safe on the ground here in Australia it would be highly appreciated."

"Let me speak to someone there at the police station," Joshua asked.

Michael turned and handed the phone to SGT McTavish, "The embassy would like to speak with you, sergeant."

SGT McTavish took the headset, "This is Sergeant McTavish."

"Sergeant," Joshua began. "Could you describe the two people who are claiming to be Astronauts?"

"Sir, they are definitely Americans. They were picked up on the road just outside Aritunga Historical Reserve. They were dressed in space suits and were carrying their helmets. They have an American flag on their left sleeve and no baggage, identification or money on their person except for nametags on their flight suits. We have had one reported sighting of a UFO about the time they claim to have been set down on the Ross Highway. I believe their story and who they are."

"Okay, sergeant put Michael back on the phone," Joshua said.

"Michael Syong here again, Mr. Olson."

"Michael, I believe your story and here is how we will proceed. I will notify NASA Houston of your status. In the morning we will send our twin otter to pick you up and bring you back to Canberra. It is about a five hour flight so don't expect our plane until after noon. If you have any expenses just sign for them and ask that the bills be sent to us for payment. Is there anything else we can do for you at this point?" Joshua asked.

"No, sir. Burt and I appreciate that. We will keep the police here advised of our situation and location so if you need to contact us you can work through them. Thanks again sir," Michael said.

"You're welcome, Michael. We will be in touch tomorrow morning," he said.

Sergeant McTavish made a few phone calls and soon he turned to the astronauts and said, "I have talked with Dr. Sam Burns and he has agreed to put you up at his place for the evening. I will get one of our cars to drive you out to his house. It is only about a ten minute ride from here."

23

"Return to Civilization"

Canberra, Australia

Joshua Olson hung up after talking to Michael Syong. He drafted a message to NASA Houston and sent it via the state department communications system. He reported that Michael and Burt were safe on the ground in Alice Springs, Australia, and what his plans were to get them to the embassy in Canberra. He contacted his embassy pilots and briefed them on the mission for the next day.

Washington, DC

Jack still was closely monitoring the television for the NASA press conference. At approximately 11:15am Manned Space Flight Director for NASA, Winston Perry, came to the dais and stepped to the podium. He thanked everyone for coming and began his briefing of the media.

"I am pleased to announce that it appears that our Enterprise astronauts have been rescued by UFOs of unknown origin. I have personally spoken with Captain Paul Anderson who was set down at McMurdo Station in the Antarctic in the late afternoon Eastern Time yesterday. He is in good health and anxious to return to Houston. He was the last astronaut off the space shuttle. All others were rescued before him and are down on earth somewhere but have not been found as yet. We have no other information on this rescue or the whereabouts of our astronauts. As this situation develops we will keep you all advised. I will take a few questions."

"Director, Megan Keller, Fox News. Did Captain Anderson give you any details of the ship or aliens who rescued him?"

"No, he only described it as a silver disk and also indicated he had no view of the inside of the craft. I am sure when he returns to Houston and is debriefed he will be able to furnish more details." Winston added.

"Director Perry, is there any speculation within NASA what the origin of these UFOs might be?" The CNN reporter asked.

"No, there is no speculation and won't be until we debrief all the astronauts," Winston said. "No more questions for now we will have a briefing as we receive information." Winston Perry stepped off the podium and left the room.

Jack was listening to Fox News and they went into speculation mode. It appeared everyone was highly pleased that our astronauts had been rescued but the origin of the UFOs was high in the mode the news channels were now in.

The red phone behind Jack's desk rang and he answered. It was CIA director Bill Reynolds.

"I just saw the NASA press conference Jack. I guess we got off scott-free on that one," Bill said.

"Yeah, Bill. Nothing of any kind of report or description of our AFVs. I think we will be okay. Just have to wait and see," Jack said.

"Okay, Jack. Keep me advised of what you are hearing on the rescue of the astronauts," Bill said.

"Will do, Bill," Jack responded and hung up the phone.

Pitcairn Island

Tori Croft and Jody West were still in shock of what had occurred minutes earlier. They were still adjusting to gravity and were a little shaky on their feet. After a couple of minutes they regained their senses and discussed where they thought they were and what they should do. Off in the distance they could see a light they estimated to be a half mile. It was just a little past sunset and they decided to walk towards the light. It was a little difficult as they were still in their space suits but they managed. They appeared to be in a valley with no roads visible. They walked through the forest which consisted mostly of fruit trees. There were breadfruit, bananas as well as orange and lime trees, which they could easily identify. It only took them approximately fifteen minutes to cover the half-mile. Soon they approached a house. It was a small bungalow, single level, set up approximately two feet off the ground. It had a couple of lights burning inside and two people that the astronauts could see.

Tori approached and knocked on the door. A middle-aged woman opened the door and stood there shocked. She had seen her share of strange things in her life but this one beat all.

Tori spoke first. "Good evening," she said. "My name is Tori Croft, I'm an American astronaut. Do you speak English?" she asked.

The woman, whose name was Sarah Christian answered in the Pitcairn language, which was a combination of 18th century, English and Tahitian. "Verily, I speaketh English." She said. "What art thou doing here and how did thee get here?"

"Well how we got here is a long story but short version is we were rescued from space and the vehicle that rescued us set us down here. By the way where is here?" Tori asked.

"Thou art on Pitcairn Island," Sarah said. "Please come in and be our guest."

As they stepped up onto the stoop Tori introduced Jody and Sarah pointed to the gentleman sitting in the living room. "That my husband Fletcher," she offered.

Fletcher was shocked to see these two beautiful women dressed so strangely and entering into his home. He was trying to get a handle on who they were and how they got there so he asked the same questions Sarah had asked previously. Sarah was kind enough to fill him in on the who and how and he still seemed puzzled. They sat and talked. Tori and Jody told the whole story. Fletcher smiled and he then knew what had happened. Jody had mentioned space shuttle Enterprise and that lit up a bulb in Fletcher's head. He acknowledged and said he was aware of what must have happened because they received their news through their satellite dish which carried CNN.

The astronauts took off their cumbersome space suits and Sarah managed to find each one a blouse and shorts, which helped them relax a little. Sarah fixed dinner for all and they sat down to a feast of Spiny Lobster, peas, corn and arrowroot flour bread. Desert was a fruit platter with plenty for all. They continued their discussion during dinner and Fletcher came up with a plan of action. They would ride his four-wheeled ATV into Adamstown in the morning where there was a phone and they could call Wellington, New Zealand, and report their position. Fletcher told them the power went off at 10:00pm so they might want to go to bed by that time. In the second bedroom Sarah had a double bed, which she turned down for them. They settled in for the night about 9:50pm. They both tossed and turned and talked through the night. They tried to assimilate what just happened.

Washington, DC

On hanging up the phone from Bill Reynolds Jack turned to working on the plan to pick up Paul Anderson from McMurdo. He put in a call to Bob Avery at Omega Aviation Headquarters. When Bob answered Jack told him the ice runway would be ready on Tuesday so he instructed him to position a G4 in Christchurch, New Zealand, to be ready to fly to McMurdo. The crew would checkout Antarctic clothing and survival gear for the aircraft from the Polar Programs office at the airport. It was already Wednesday at McMurdo so Bob would have a day or so to get the flight underway and headed for Christchurch. Jack directed the crew to keep in contact with the Polar Programs office in Christchurch for any changes and update to their itinerary.

After hanging up the phone Bob called John Walker at the hangar in Salt Lake City and passed the requirement, which had been given to them. John Walker indicated he had Terry Richardson and Jerry Elliott available to pilot the flight to McMurdo and he would also assign as Navigator Ivan Wheaton as a back up for the flight. The G4s were all GPS equipped but sometimes the GPS did not operate at 100% in the high latitudes and Grid navigation might be required on the Christchurch-McMurdo leg of the flight. Terry and Jerry had more than five years Antarctic flying between them so they were well qualified to conduct this mission.

Ken Nichols called Jack from his basement office and asked if he was busy. Ken indicated he had new information on two more of the astronauts. Jack told him to come on up he would be waiting for him. Ken arrived in Jack's office and immediately began briefing him on what he had.

"I am tapped into State department's communication system and they forwarded a message from the embassy at Canberra, Australia, to NASA Houston telling them they had Michael Syong and Burt Simmons safe and sound in the embassy there. They had picked them up at the airport in Alice Springs," Ken said.

"That's good, Ken. It will probably fit right into our plans for Christchurch. I will need to call Director Perry at Houston Space Flight Center and discuss it with him. How about you keep in contact with all parties who are working on this situation. Keep me up to date on McMurdo when you get something," Jack said. "Also Ken I need you to contact Matt Beeson in Christchurch. We need to tell him about the Antarctic clothing and survival gear requirement and to activate Deep Freeze control for about a week. He'll probably need to recall a couple of his air traffic controllers to do that and will need a little lead-time. Brief him on the flight times and requirements so he is up to speed when Terry Richardson arrives in Christchurch."

Ken went back to his office and Jack placed a call to Director Perry at Houston. When he came on the line Jack offered, "Director, Jack Forester here. How are things in Houston.?"

"We are making progress, Jack. How are you progressing there in DC?" He asked.

"We have set up a G4 to be in Christchurch by next Saturday. We have two highly experienced Antarctic pilots ready to fly to McMurdo just as soon as we receive word that the ice runway is available to receive them. We expect to hear from them soon but I have been assured that they will be ready to receive the G4 on Tuesday, Christchurch time, so we have that situation under control. I was just informed that two more astronauts have been located in Australia and are now safe and sound at the embassy in Canberra. I think a good option would be to fly them to Christchurch and that way we could have the G4 bring them and Paul Anderson back to Houston at the same time. What are your thoughts Director?" Jack asked.

"That sounds like a great plan, Jack. It looks like the quickest and most efficient way to get it done. If Omega makes the flight on Tuesday when could we expect them to return to Houston?" Director Perry asked.

"I am only guessing but if they get it done on Tuesday they could leave Christchurch on Wednesday which would be Tuesday our time. Then fly to Tahiti, remain over night there on Tuesday and fly into LAX on Wednesday, change crews and be in Houston by Thursday next week. I believe that's the earliest it can be done," Jack said.

"That sounds okay to me Jack and I guess we can live with that. Maybe we will have more info on the other astronauts in a few days. What are your thoughts on that?" He asked.

"Director, I think we will find the other astronauts located in Asia somewhere within a few days. Please consider Omega Aviation for the mission to retrieve them. The director of operations at Omega, John Walker, is highly qualified to fly into Asia as he has had quite a few flights there recently and is quite familiar with the air traffic control and airports," Jack said.

"I like that plan. If you could ask Omega Aviation to schedule John to do that when we need to get that done I would appreciate that." Director Perry said.

"We can do that and, just for your planning and info, Omega Aviation has told me the G4 will depart for Christchurch tomorrow. I will be in touch when I hear anything more," Jack said.

"Thanks for everything, Jack. We'll be in touch."

Jack called Ken and briefed him on his just completed discussion with Director Perry and instructed him to pass the info on to Bob Avery at Omega Aviation.

Washington, DC

Two days had passed with no word from any of the other astronauts still unaccounted for. Jack was beginning to wonder what the delay was in the astronauts being found and reporting in. Ken came into his office early this Friday morning smiling just a little.

"Just got a copy of a message sent from the embassy in Wellington, New Zealand, Jack. Two more astronauts accounted for. They are located on Pitcairn Island. The astronauts have indicated the next transportation available for them off the island will be late Sunday. The MV Claymore II is the charter vessel for Pitcairn. It will take them thirty-two hours to reach the village of <u>Rikitea</u> on Mangareva Island. Then by local ferry to Totegegie Airport located some nine kilometers from Rikitea. All this is timed to connect with air service on Tuesday provided by Air Tahiti, which will take them to Faaa Airport at Papeete in Tahiti," Ken said.

"That looks really good Ken. Fits in perfectly with the flight schedule of the G4 out of New Zealand. Let's send a message to McMurdo and pass this information to Paul Anderson. I am sure he will be worried about his crew and this should help to ease his worries. I am sure I will hear from Houston on this one," Jack said.

Sure enough, later that day Jack received a call from Director Perry asking how this new revelation fit into the flight plan of the G4, Jack told him it would work out perfectly as the crew was scheduled to remain over night at Papeete on Tuesday and depart early Wednesday morning. The Director was pleased, as was Jack, that things were working out for the best.

Mongolia, Saturday Morning
Hank and Sally had now been on the ground for a little over four days. The native people who had taken them in were very friendly and took good care of them despite being unable to understand each other's language. Since they had arrived, no vehicles or any form of transportation had passed this settlement. Hank had been able to determine that they were in fact in Mongolia and which direction it was to the capitol of Ulaan Baatar. He had no idea how far it was but knew which way they needed to travel to get there.

Late Saturday morning the Lord smiled down on Hank, Sally and the settlement. A two-vehicle Army detachment rolled down the highway from the east and stopped for a coffee and cigarette break. There were one officer and seven enlisted men. As they disembarked they and the settlers began communicating in their native language. Hank heard them talking outside and stepped out to investigate. Sally was just behind him and soon they heard their first words in English. The officer had been trained abroad and attended two years at Sandhurst in the United Kingdom. The astronauts conveyed their situation to Lieutenant Gündegmaa and he in turn went back to his vehicle and relayed the situation to his base and commanding officer. It took about three hours before his radio crackled to life. His base was calling and soon he relayed to the astronauts that a MI-24 helicopter was airborne from Ulaan Baatar to pick them up and take them back to the city. It was about 4:00pm when a helicopter was heard approaching from the east. Hank and Sally gathered up their flight suits and soon were winging their way to the airport at Ulaan Baatar. On arrival they were met by a GM SUV, which had brought the American ambassador to greet them and return them to the American embassy. Ambassador Campbell shook their hands and invited them to take a seat in the vehicle. The vehicle was quickly underway and headed toward the embassy.

Washington, DC

Jack was in his office working on a Saturday when he received the word from Ken that the final two astronauts had been accounted for. The word was passed to Utah and everyone within the AFV program had a cumulative sigh of relief that all astronauts were safe and sound and back in American hands.

Director Perry had also been working overtime on this Saturday and after he was made aware of the latest development he had his secretary place a call to Jack's office just in case he was also working. Jack picked up on the first ring and Director Perry spoke.

"Jack, Win Perry here. Sorry to bother you on a Saturday but I had hoped you would be in your office. Are you aware of the status of our last two missing astronauts?" He asked.

"Hey, Win. Good to hear from you. I was just thinking about calling your office. Yes, I just received word that your two missing astronauts had been found in Mongolia and had been transported to the embassy in Ulaan Baatar. Shall we activate our plan to retrieve them?" Jack said.

"That's what I was hoping you'd say. How soon can we get the G4 airborne?" he asked.

"We can get the plane airborne within two hours after I hang up from this call. I know your next question and here is what I think. The crew should be in Tokyo about twelve and one half hours after they depart Utah. However, we still need to request overfly permission from the Chinese and Russians before we can fly to Ulaan Baatar. State is aware of how important this flight is so permission may well be granted by the time our crew gets to Tokyo. I believe John Walker will call for overnight crew rest and depart for Mongolia on Sunday morning. That will put them in Ulaan Baatar on Sunday Afternoon. Departure will probably be early Monday morning with arrival in Houston early Tuesday morning. That's the best I can give you, Win," Jack offered.

"I guess we here at the manned space center just want to get all our people back safely as soon as possible. We will just have to live with what's dealt us," Win said.

"We will keep you advised on any arrival times and possible delays if we get them. State will probably be our best source of information. Why don't you ask State to keep us all advised," Jack said.

"That's a good suggestion Jack, I will contact State and ask for updates for all of us. Wish the guys at Omega God's speed. Later Jack."

"Talk to you later, Win. Take care," Jack said.

Jack hung up the phone and immediately dialed John Walker at Omega Aviation. "It's a go for Ulaan Baatar John," He said.

"Roger that." John responded. "We'll be on our way in about fifty minutes."

"Keep us advised of your progress, John," Jack said. "State will be requesting overfly permission of China and Russia. We will send it via your cell phone by text."

"I understand, Jack. We are on our way," John said.

Bob Avery was advised of John's departure and he called the State Department for overfly permission of China and Russia as was his usual procedure. State told him they were aware of the urgency of the mission and assured Bob that they would press China and Russia to grant permission ASAP.

Sunday morning arrived and found Jack back in the office. There were too many things happening for him to take the day off. He had asked Ken to work Sunday also. When Jack arrived Ken was already there and had made some coffee. They sat down in Jack's office in the lounge area and decided to relax if that was at all possible. Ken told Jack they had received John's arrival message in Tokyo but had not heard from State as yet on the clearance. Jack told Ken to keep on State's case and see if he could hurry it up. They finished their coffee and Ken went to his office. Jack was sitting at his desk when the red phone rang. He picked it up. It was Admiral Bill Reynolds at CIA. "Jack, I thought I would catch you at the office today. How about bringing me up to date on what's happening?"

"Bill, here is the latest I have." Jack went though the McMurdo flight schedule, the Australian embassy delivery requirement of the astronauts to Christchurch, Pitcairn Island coordination and John Walker's planned flight to Ulaan Baatar and return to Houston. "Sounds like everything is going well, Jack," Bill said.

"You know Bill, there's an old Antarctic saying, when things are going well something will jump up and try to bite you in the ass. I hope that doesn't happen here. I would like to see things go smoothly for a change," Jack said.

"Aw relax, Jack. Everything will work out okay. We will monitor the news reports here and see what the media can dream up on the UFO story. I'll keep you up to speed if anything pops out at me. Talk with you tomorrow. Have a good day, Jack," Bill said.

Ken called Jack from the basement, "I have an arrival message of Terry Richardson and his crew at Christchurch. They are in contact with Matt Beeson. Matt is reporting his air traffic controllers will be on duty starting Monday morning and will have Deep Freeze Control operating by noon."

"That's great. Now contact Phil Weston at McMurdo and advise him of that, Put Matt in touch with Phil and have them coordinate the flight. Tell them both to keep us advised of what is happening. Also don't forget to advise Matt of the flight from Australia with the two astronauts onboard. It will be a Twin Otter from the embassy," Jack told Ken.

Late Sunday afternoon, State called Ken to verify they had obtained permission for John Walker to overfly China and Russia. They would follow up with a confirmation message. Ken dialed John's phone and sent him a text verifying over-flight permission. It was already early Monday morning in Tokyo and John was still asleep. He awakened about 6:00am local time, saw the text message and confirmed it with Ken with a return text. He also included his Tokyo departure time and ETA Ulaan Baatar. Ken received the text at home. He immediately contacted Jack and infoed State who in turn notified Ulaan Baatar via State Department communications. John also indicated he would remain over-night in Ulaan Baatar and depart early Tuesday morning, Monday eastern time.

Christchurch, New Zealand: Monday morning.

Matt rendezvoused with Terry and crew at the Antarctic clothing storage facility. They were fitted with a complete set of Polar Programs Antarctic outdoor clothing and gathered Antarctic survival gear for the aircraft. Terry remarked they never looked so good when they were flying for the U.S. Navy. This Antarctic gear was a big step up from what they were used to. After they left the clothing storage they walked over to Deep Freeze Control to see how things were going there. When they walked in the controllers were already up and testing the transceivers. They called McMurdo control, which came up loud and clear. Terry prodded the controllers to ask how they were progressing on the ice runway. Phil Weston came up on the frequency and reported that the ice runway would be ready by noon Tuesday to receive the G4. Terry inquired about JP4 fuel for them. He told Phil they would need about 500 gallons and that the McMurdo fueling crew should plan for a hot refueling. Of course, hot refueling meant no engine shutdown and all aircraft systems operating. Terry indicated they would spend as little time on the ground as necessary. His departure from Christchurch would be about 8:00am local time and time enroute was estimated to be about five and half hours. Matt told Phil that they might be able to get a couple of mailbags aboard but that would be the extent of cargo. Phil asked if there were any other requirements. Matt and Terry discussed it for a minute and determined that there were none. The controllers took command and signed off.

Tuesday came early for Terry and crew. They were up at 6:00am and ready to proceed to Deep Freeze Control by 7:00am. Terry, Jerry and Ivan entered Deep freeze control, said their good mornings and busied themselves filing their flight plan. This was old hat they thought as they had done it many times. The controllers at McMurdo had passed the weather forecast and winds enroute to Christchurch and Ivan plugged these into his flight plan. Within minutes they presented it to the Deep Freeze controllers who in turn coordinated it with Christchurch control. New Zealand ATC would control them down to Dunedin and then Deep Freeze would control them to 60°S where McMurdo Control would follow them the rest of the way to the Antarctic. Christchurch tower cleared the G4 for takeoff at 8:06am. They were off on their adventure to McMurdo.

24

"Precision Planning"

Enroute McMurdo

Terry leveled his G4 at 38,000' just twelve miles short of Dunedin. Over the VOR station at Dunedin, they were handed off to Deep Freeze Control. Ivan took control of the HF radio and made contact with Deep Freeze. They were headed for Campbell Island which Jerry had entered into the systems GPS. They were cruising at 575mph and were over Campbell Island in about forty-six minutes. They switched their compass to free directional gyro control and Ivan had the pilots reset the DG to grid heading 004°. Things on board were routine and soon they reported to Deep Freeze at 60°S. Deep Freeze switched them over to McMurdo Control and Ivan confirmed their status with McMurdo. At 67°S they entered nighttime. It was darker that a coal diggers fanny in a deep mine. There were few stars out and quite a few cirrus clouds above them. Soon they could see the white ice below and then the Transantarctic Mountains were visible. Since there were only two air traffic controllers wintering over, Williams Field Tower and approach control as well as GCA were not manned. McMurdo would do all controlling on the current frequency. At one hundred miles out Ivan reported their position and they were cleared down to1500'. Altimeters were reset and the weather report indicated high clouds above 30,000' visibility greater than fifty miles. Terry leveled the plane at 1500' grid heading 345°. They had set the GPS to bring them in between Ross Island and The Transantarctic mountains to the west.

At fifty miles out of McMurdo they saw the 50-gallon drums with flames coming out of them, lighting the ice runway. Terry turned port and leveled the wings heading grid 270°. He was lined up with the ice runway. Winds now reported light and variable. At five miles he slowed the plane and lowered the landing gear and flaps. At three miles he began his descent at 500 fpm and called for his landing lights. Landing checklist was complete and once again he slowed to touchdown speed of 123 mph. Over the threshold he bumped the throttles up and back to raise the nose slightly and slow his rate of descent to less than 200 fpm. He touchdown on the ice runway at 60' from threshold and put the engines into full reverse thruster mode. He hardly touched the brakes and stopped in about 4000'. What a beautiful landing he had just made. He taxied over to the loading area, swung it around to 090° grid and set the brakes when directed to do so by the ground director. He had Jerry move over to the left seat and directed him to remain in the aircraft. Terry and Ivan donned their red parkas and opened the door of the G4. At the foot of the stairs Phil Weston, Captain Paul Anderson and Ed Petrie of Raytheon Corporation, who was charged with operations at McMurdo, met them. The outside air temperature was cool—36°F but with light winds it was almost comfortable. They exchanged greetings and Paul said his goodbyes and thanked Phil and Ed for their great hospitality.

Terry directed him to get on the aircraft and take a seat back in the cabin. Meanwhile Ivan supervised off-loading of a few mailbags they had brought with them and then ensured the baggage door on the starboard side of the aircraft was secure. Ed's people had hooked up the refueling hose from the tanker they had driven down onto the ice pad and were hot refueling the aircraft. It was a very efficient operation and in less than twenty minutes Terry and Ivan were back on board where Terry assumed the copilots position and Ivan took up his navigator's station. The steps had been retrieved and door closed. Terry called McMurdo for flight plan clearance and takeoff. He received same and very quickly Jerry pushed the power levers forward for his takeoff roll on runway 09°g. At 4500' of roll Jerry rotated and pointed the plane skyward. In the cold temperatures the plane performed magnificently. They were soon level at 40,000' and cruising along at almost

600 mph. The winds that high had been mostly out of the west at 60 to 80 knots but crosswise to their track so they did nor hinder their progress nor aid them. At about the 2-hour mark into the flight they passed 67°s and soon were cruising in the bright sunlight. Ivan reported 60°s to McMurdo and once again they were switched over to Deep Freeze control in Christchurch.

The remainder of the flight was uneventful. Paul Anderson had been given a headset for the flight and he enjoyed listening to and just being around these professional naval aviators.

Pitcairn Island—Sunday evening
Tori Croft and Jody West had received word via Auckland, New Zealand, to get to Tahiti as quickly as possible and NASA would arrange transportation home. They had also arranged for NASA to pay for any and all expenses incurred by Tori and Jody so they had no worries as far as money was concerned. Fletcher and Sarah Christian made sure they were transported to the pier so they could board the Claymore II for their trip to Mangareva. On arrival at the pier they said their goodbyes and thanked Fletcher and Sarah for their friendship and hospitality. They boarded the longboat which took them out to the Claymore II. The amenities and accommodation were bright, clean and practical. The vessel accommodated twelve passengers in private twin share cabins on the lower deck. They had their own shared dinning and lounge area on Deck three, with plenty of books and movies and a 42" HD LCD television to help pass the time. They had heard the TV reports that Paul Anderson was in McMurdo and safe. They also listened to the speculation as to who had rescued them from space. All meals, bedding and towels were provided and snacks and beverages were available in the shared break room, close to the galley. The 32-hour trip passed fairly quickly and was pleasant. They arrived at Rikitea village in Mangareva and were then transferred to the ferry, which took them the 9 km to Totegegie Airport. They arrived at the airport in plenty of time to board the 9:00am Air Tahiti flight to Papeete, Tahiti. It was after lunch when they arrived and were met by the Consular Agent for Tahiti. He introduced himself as Jacques

Chirac. He stated that he had been instructed by the State Department to provide them with everything they needed. A G4 Gulfstream aircraft flying out of Christchurch, New Zealand, hopefully on Wednesday would pick them up. He had made reservations at the InterContinental Resort Tahiti for at least one night. Tori and Jody savored this return to civilization. After arriving in their room they both went to the shoppe in the hotel and were fitted out with a bikini swimsuit and a tropical outfit for street wear. The also purchased some high fashion sandals to replace what the Christians had given them. They would mail the clothing and shoes to Sarah when they reached Houston to replace what she had furnished them while on Pitcairn. They changed into their bikinis and went to the beach just outside the hotel, found a couple of nice lounges, ordered a couple of Mai Tais and settled down for some sun and relaxation.

Canberra, Australia

Michael Syong and Burt Simmons were more keyed up than normal. The prospect of finally beginning the road home was with great anticipation. They had both talked with their families back in the states and all had been relieved when they learned of their rescue from space. It was a joyous phone call and would be even more joyous when they held their families close and personal.

The embassy personnel got them on the road to the airport early after a hearty breakfast and they were looking forward to the flight to Christchurch.

Their pilots were U.S. Navy Lieutenant Commanders Charlie Martin and Casey Dykstra. When the astronauts arrived on the flight line Charlie greeted them and told them the flight would be about 4 hours, 45 minutes. They all boarded the Twin Otter and were soon winging their way to Christchurch. Matt Beeson, who briefed them on the current operation now in progress, met them at the terminal. Matt told them the pickup of Paul Anderson at McMurdo had been successful and the G4 was once again airborne and would arrive about 5:45pm. Since the astronauts were already located at the General Aviation operations terminal and it was 4:15pm, they decided to stay there and wait for the G4s arrival.

In short order the G4 was sighted on final for runway 33. They landed and taxied over to General Aviation for off loading where they were met by customs, agriculture and immigration. The aircraft and personnel were quickly cleared and began walking towards the terminal. Paul spotted Mike and Burt and they rushed to greet each other. Hugs and back slaps were exchanged and the astronauts showed real affection and caring for each other. They were overheard saying they couldn't believe they were safe on earth after the predicament they had been in. To whoever rescued them they would be eternally grateful.

Matt directed them to the White Heron Hotel, which was across the street from the General Aviation hangar. They all had reservations there for the night and would catch up on what had happened and what was planned for their future. Terry briefed them that they would be departing the next morning for Tahiti where he hoped they would pick up the other two astronauts.

Christchurch, New Zealand

Earlier Wednesday morning Terry Richardson had filed his flight plan for Faaa Airport, Tahiti. Soon after, they departed with their precious cargo of astronauts Paul Anderson, Michael Syong and Burt Simmons on board. Flight time to Tahiti would be 4 hours, 2 minutes. They crossed the International Dateline and were back in Tuesday but going east had changed three time zones so their arrival time was 5:30pm. They were met by Jacques Chirac, who took them over to the InterContinental Resort Tahiti where they too had an overnight reservation.

As they were checking in, Tori Croft and Jody West burst into the lobby. They knew Paul and the others would be there but not exactly when they would arrive. They spotted Paul, Mike and Burt, rushed over to them and once again hugs and expressions of love and affection for each other were made. They were overwhelmed with emotion at seeing each other alive and well. The conversation moved at the speed of light and everyone wanted each other's story and what they had been through the past week. Paul told them that Hank and Sally had been found in Mongolia after four days and were even now being airlifted back to Houston. They decided they would meet in the dining room in forty-five minutes and over dinner could then each tell their story. Terry, Jerry and Ivan made their own separate plans for dinner. There was a great seafood place just off the hotel grounds and they figured that would be a good place for them to dine. They would meet in the hotel lobby in about and hour and then walk over to the restaurant.

Ulaan Baatar, Mongolia

John Walker had left Tokyo, Japan, on Monday morning headed for Ulaan Baatar. It was approximately a 3 hour 30 minute flight. On approaching Chinggis Khaan International Airport he was cleared to descend to 6000'. They broke out of the clouds at 9500' and continued descending. Leveling at 6000' they completed the appropriate checklists and prepared for landing. Air traffic control cleared them to land on runway 32, which was 10,170' in length by 197' in width. John turned on final at five miles and began his descent to the runway at 3 miles. Over the threshold he slowed to touchdown speed. The landing was normal but at 2500' of roll the left wheel ran over a sharp object and the tire blew. The plane swerved to the left and John managed to keep it on the runway and bring it to a stop. He was able to then taxi the plane off the runway onto the mid field taxiway. Field services managed to tow the aircraft to the General Aviation Terminal.

John assessed the situation and determined that he would need a tire but that the wheel assembly would be okay and all that would be needed was the tire mounted and the wheel assembly reinstalled. He walked over to Korean Airlines maintenance hangar and negotiated with them to get a new tire and do the maintenance work. Meanwhile the U.S. Embassy in Ulaan Baatar was notified of their situation and that John Walker would keep them advised on the aircraft status and possible departure time. Korean Airlines personnel determined they could get a tire shipped in by Wednesday and have it installed in time for a late Thursday departure. John authorized the airline maintenance to do the work on the aircraft. He also left the phone number for the Ramada Ulaanbaatar Centercity hotel, which is where the flight crew would be staying. They had two days to tour the city and also stopped at the embassy and were introduced to Hank and Sally who were waiting anxiously to get back to Houston.

About 2:30pm Korean Airlines maintenance manager called the hotel and rang John's room. They told him the tire was mounted and the wheel reinstalled on the G4. John told them to send their bill to the embassy, which in turn would bill Omega Aviation. He notified the embassy that the scheduled takeoff time was 7:00pm local time. The embassy said they would have Hank and Sally at the terminal in time to board the aircraft.

John and his copilot checked out of the hotel about 4:00pm and proceeded to the airport by taxi. After arriving at the terminal they went over to the main terminal and ate a light dinner. They checked the Anchorage, Alaska, weather and filed a flight plan. Their time enroute would be six and one half hours and would put them in Anchorage about 8:30am Wednesday local time.

Hank and Sally arrived about 6:15pm and were greeted by John who told them to board the aircraft relax and they would be ready to taxi in about fifteen minutes.

Preflight was completed and the flight crew manned the aircraft, completed the checklists and started the aircraft. Departure was on time and soon they were winging their way to Anchorage. Their flight path took them over the Kamchatka Peninsula and they next crossed the International Date Line. The copilot checked in with Nome ATC who relayed their progress to Anchorage control. Touchdown in Anchorage was smooth and on time. The pilots and astronauts grabbed a quick breakfast, filed their flight plan and were once again airborne direct to Houston at 10:30am. Their ETA Houston was 7:00pm local time.

Papeete, Tahiti

The Omega Aviation flight crew had a great seafood dinner. The weather was warm and tropical as they walked back to the hotel. Terry stopped in the lobby and called all the astronauts' rooms and left messages indicating a mini-bus would be ready to take them to the airport at 4:30am. Their scheduled departure time was 6:00am.

Everyone was in the lobby by 4:25am and boarded the mini-bus for the airport. They all sat together in the airport restaurant and had a tropical breakfast of eggs, mangos and whole wheat bread. Terry and Ivan went to flight planning while Jerry took the astronauts to the aircraft. He preflighted the G4 and Terry and Ivan arrived shortly thereafter. They all boarded the aircraft and departed for Los Angeles International Airport. Arrival was at 12:06pm after being radar vectored all around southern California. They grabbed a light lunch and departed for Houston at 2:00pm. Time enroute would be three hours with arrival time as 7:00pm local time.

The flight went smoothly and Terry was under the control of Houston center. They were cleared to descend to 3000' where they were turned over to Ellington Airport approach control. Radar vectored them around to land on runway 01. About that time another G4 came up and checked in on the frequency. It was John Walker on the flight from Anchorage. It was still daylight so Terry called John.

"N60425 this is N60428, over," Terry said

"N60428 go ahead," John responded.

"Hey, John, how about giving NASA a well earned airshow," Terry offered.

"That sounds good to me. What is your position?" John said.

"We're south of the field about three miles. Here's what I propose. I will cancel my IFR flight plan and circle counterclockwise around the field at 1500'. Join on me and we will give NASA a low pass followed by a low break on runway 01," Terry said.

"Got it, Terry. I'm down to 3000' and in the clear. Break, Ellington approach cancel my IFR flight plan. I am proceeding VFR to the field."

"Roger 425 your IFR flight plan cancelled. Cleared to switch to Ellington Tower," ATC said

John had Terry in sight about three miles North of the field in a left orbit. He was heading south and joined on Terry's right wing in the parade position. Jerry Elliott called the tower and asked for a low pass and break for runway 01. The tower cleared them as requested. Terry lowered the nose of his aircraft as he continued his turn in to the runway. At one mile he was lined up on runway 01 and was down to 400', speed 250 mph. As he passed center field he called "28 break" over the radio and pulled up in a left break at 45° angle of bank. John counted to 10 and mimicked 28. Terry rolled out heading 190° and Jerry called downwind. John followed. At 1 mile past the threshold of the runway Jerry called the tower turning base and Terry began his 180° descending turn to final on runway 01. They were cleared to land. John next called turning base and followed Terry in his descending, turning approach for runway 01. He too was cleared to land.

After landing both aircraft were switched to ground control frequency. John joined on Terry's left wing and they taxied to the terminal in formation. Terry remarked to Jerry that John Walker was one great pilot and too bad he wasn't a naval aviator because he would have been a great one.

As they approached the terminal they saw the huge crowd waiting to greet the astronauts. Seems like every employee of the manned space center had turned out to greet them. Winston Perry and Pete Crown were up front and would meet the astronauts as they deplaned.

25

"Home at Last"

Houston, Texas

Terry and John brought their aircraft to a stop about 100' in front of and directly facing the large crowd. They set the brakes, shutdown their engines and quickly opened the boarding stairs.

Paul Anderson was the first to deplane followed by the other astronauts. On John Walkers' aircraft Hank and Sally stepped out into the warm fresh Texas air. Win Perry and Pete Crown were already walking quickly out towards the astronauts while the astronauts were in-turn closing the distance between them. The crowd was cheering and hollering welcoming them home. After greetings were exchanged on the ramp the group turned back toward the crowd where there was a microphone setup for some remarks. Before they reached that point all the astronauts family members broke through the barriers holding them back, raced to their loved ones, and embraced. There were many hugs, kisses and tears shed before Win Perry finally got to the microphone. There were a few media outlets covering the homecoming. NASA had made a late minute announcement of the arrival times of the astronauts, as things had been a little uncertain as to when they all would arrive. Win began his welcoming remarks but broke down in tears before he could finish. Pete Crown stepped up and finished the short ceremony. He acknowledged that no organization had ever been so thankful to have their astronauts returned to them safely as was NASA.

He completed his remarks with the announcement that no statement would be made by the astronauts until they had been debriefed. When he finished the media representatives began shouting questions at the astronauts but they were quickly ushered into waiting limousines and driven off the airport. The astronauts were given unlimited time to spend with their families and told to return to work when they felt rested and ready for debriefing.

Now the feeding frenzy started. The media, both written and electronic, wanted interviews with all parties concerned. Win Perry, Pete Crown as well as retired astronauts were all invited on air and gave interviews to the written media. The main questions were, "How did the astronauts get safely back to earth?" "Who were the beings operating the UFOs?" "Where did they come from?" Some of the follow on questions were, "When will the astronauts be ready to meet the press?" "What is their story?" "What is their mental attitude and approach to their rescue by unknown beings?" Everything was speculation with no hard facts. Win Perry was probably the most knowledgeable person on the subject as he had talked with Paul Anderson from Antarctica and gleaned an insight into what had happened but he was in the dark as to who and what. Local police were needed at the homes of the astronauts to keep the media away from bothering them. A few were arrested for trespassing but the still tried everyway they could to learn more from the astronauts.

The media kept up the constant buzz on the story. Jack Forester was pleased thus far as was Bill Reynolds. The AFV program was still under wraps and would remain so unless debriefing of the astronauts revealed something they had not counted on. The cover-up was at this point successful.

After about a week off the astronauts returned to the manned space center. Debriefing was the number one priority. Pete Crown and his deputy were designated to conduct the debriefing. Pete chose to use a group interaction style-debriefing scenario. This way all astronauts would be aware of what each of them had seen and heard in their rescue.

Pete started off the first session by telling the astronauts how they would conduct the debriefing then asked Paul to begin and the others to chime in when they had something additional to contribute along the way. He said the debriefing would be restricted to the flight portion of the rescue and asked that each astronaut write a report on the ground portion of their rescue so everyone could read their report.

Paul began. "Our first contact was a voice over the UHF transceiver. The pilot of the vehicle called us to get our attention. I looked out my side cockpit window and the saucer shaped vehicle was close alongside."

"Give us a description of what you saw, Paul," Pete asked.

"The vehicle appeared to be saucer shaped. I would guess approximately 50' in diameter. It was bulged out on top and bottom with a clear canopy centered on top. I could see two beings inside. It was silver in color probably a metallic color. There were no identifying markings on any part that I could see. The thickness of the vehicle was about 20' I would estimate. I answered them on UHF and the pilot or commander of that vehicle briefed us on how they would conduct the rescue. He indicated they could rescue only two of at a time and how they would signal us when to proceed to their vehicle. He did seem to know about our emergency escape oxygen system. Tori tried to call mission control but was unsuccessful. The pilot advised us that they had jammed all our other transceivers so we should not try to contact anyone. The vehicle then moved off out of sight and we all started to don our pressure suits in preparation to moving out of the shuttle. Hank and Sally were first up so they may be best to next give you their experience on this," Paul said.

Hank began his narrative. "After we donned our pressure suits Sally and I proceeded to the airlock chamber in the lower shuttle bay. As we entered the airlock chamber we observed a saucer hover over the cargo bay and lower a landing strut on the rear of the underside of the vehicle. The pilot locked the landing pad into the tie-down on the floor toward the rear of the cargo bay. We locked the door to the shuttle and waited for the lowering of the boarding ladder on the vehicle as we were told that was our signal to depressurize and move to and board the saucer. It took us a short time to depressurize at which time we activated our emergency escape oxygen system and proceeded to the rescue vehicle moved up the ladder and were met by a crewman. He directed us into seats on either side of the boarding ladder. After the boarding ladder door was closed the vehicle pressurized and our pressure suits deflated and we were able to breathe the air in the vehicle. I estimated it took fifteen minutes to descend without buffeting or heating of the vehicle by the atmosphere where the tricycle landing pads were lowered and we landed. The boarding ladder was lowered and we exited the vehicle. The crewmember once again assisted us in getting off the vehicle where we moved away from it. Sally and I sat on the ground for a few minutes until we readjusted to the earth's gravity. The vehicle then lifted off and went straight up for about 100' and then sped off to the east and accelerated to a very high speed. I did see it develop a green gas on the outside of the skin as it accelerated."

"Hank, did you see anything you could add to describe the crewman you had contact with?' Pete asked.

Sally chimed in, "Pete, the crewman had on a green pressure suit, a hard helmet somewhat like ours with a dark sunshield. I never saw a face or any features, as the shield was never raised. The gloves were twist-on similar to ours also. The crewman was attached to the vehicle by an umbilical, which must have supplied oxygen and communications. Before liftoff the crewman went back up into the upper section and our view was blocked so we couldn't see anything in the upper cabin of the vehicle. My other observations were the same as Hank's."

"Thanks, Sally. Who was next out of the shuttle?" Pete said.

Burt Simmons spoke up. "Mike and I were next out. The procedure was generally the same as Hank and Sally. Almost as soon as the first vehicle was out the second came in and locked itself onto the shuttle. We depressurized and moved quickly to the vehicle. Our experience was almost exactly the same as Hank and Sally." Tori Croft and Jody West spoke up and agreed that their experience was the same as the previous astronauts.

Paul Anderson added, "My only addition to the story was that my left glove developed a leak and I had to put the sealer in it which ate up some fifteen minutes before I could exit the shuttle. It took more time to get out of the shuttle and we progressed further in orbit after Tori and Jody left the shuttle and that is why I suspect I ended up in Antarctica.

When I left the vehicle on the ice of McMurdo Sound the crewman escorted me for about 300 yards I guess to make sure I was headed in the right direction and was adapting to gravity okay. He did activate my rescue strobe light and turned on my survival radio. I did notice the shape of the crewman was a human form. He had five fingered gloves, two legs and two arms. He never raised his dark helmet visor so I did not see any head or face features."

"While I'm mentioning Antarctica let me say those Naval aviators who flew me back from there are one fine group. I don't know how much experience they had flying in Antarctica but they were efficient and knew exactly what to do. They were in and out of McMurdo in about seventeen minutes and believe me it was pitch black and really cold. The flight back to Houston was highly professional and they handled that G4 like they were born in it," Paul said.

"Anybody have anything further to add to this story?" Pete asked.

Nobody had anything to add so Pete directed them to report to the flight surgeon for a complete physical and blood workup. He also requested that they get their ground rescue report turned in today so NASA could hold a press conference. He suggested that the press conference be held on Thursday. That would give the astronauts two days to get things turned in and paperwork in order as needed.

Win Perry and Pete Crown reviewed the video of the debriefing. It was a dull almost boring explanation of the astronauts rescue. There was nothing exciting and no description of the rescue vehicle and crew. Pete said the media would probably be disappointed except the ground survival and rescue would be more interesting. He said to Win he thought the astronauts would be ready for the press conference on Thursday. Win responded in agreement. Win then reported he had talked with the NASA director who in turn had briefed the science director at the White House. He had briefed the President on the whole situation. The president had called Paul Anderson, personally talked with him, and had said the he was extremely happy for the rescue and that they were all safe. He then talked with NASA director and asked him for his assessment on the rescue vehicles and their origin. The president got the same answer as everybody else. We really don't have any idea about the vehicles or their origin.

Thursday arrived and the press conference was setup in the press briefing room normally used for that purpose. A dais was setup with chairs setup for the seven astronauts and a monitor's position for Pete Crown. A microphone and pitchers of water had been set in front of each position. At exactly 9:00am the seven astronauts lead by Pete Crown entered the room and took their seats. They were all dressed alike in their powder blue flight suits with their nametags on their upper left breast and nameplates on the table in front of them. They looked sharp and ready to meet the press.

Pete welcomed all the media and thanked them for attending. He introduced Paul Anderson who he said would make an opening statement. Paul thanked everyone for their prayers and well wishes since they returned to Houston. He expressed his appreciation for being alive and said he was sure the other shuttle crewmembers felt exactly the same. He related the story of the rescue and how it unfolded. He went into great detail of the rescue vehicles and his personal observations. When he finished Pete indicated that he would recognize the media and then they could ask their questions.

The first question came from Megan Keller of Fox News. "Captain Anderson," she began. "What is your assessment of the origin and physical form of the aliens you came in contact with?"

Paul answered. "The vehicles were too small to be interstellar space vehicles. I believe they were scout ships launched from a mother ship from somewhere out in our solar system. As to their physical form I believe they were somewhat human shapes based on what I saw and heard. I do not believe they were humans from earth. From my knowledge of our technology I don't believe we have any industrial entity capable of producing the kind of ships we were rescued by. I know we are more advanced than other countries so I don't believe any country on earth could have produced those space vehicles."

"Could you explain further on your observations and analysis?" Megan asked.

"Yes, the voice communications were in good English however synthesized maybe from a language translator. They had two arms, two legs and five digits in their hands. They walked upright like a human and were coordinated like humans. They were also oxygen breathers," Paul said.

"Captain, Hans Butcher, CBC News, sir can you describe your reentry and how you got to Antarctica."

"As I told you about my glove problem, it took us further in orbit probably down across North and South America and across the southern Indian Ocean. When the vehicle detached from the shuttle they descended very rapidly and since Antarctica was the closest occupied landmass they set me down at McMurdo Sound just off Ross Island. I was about a mile from the base so I started hiking towards the lights. My strobe light was flashing and after about three tenths of mile a tracked vehicle came out from the base onto the ice, picked me up and deposited me on Ross Island at McMurdo base. I was given food and warm clothing and went over to the Chalet where I was given the opportunity to call Houston by the station chief Phil Weston. It took about a week to clear an ice runway on McMurdo Sound and the Gulfstream G4 from Omega Aviation out of Salt Lake City flew in and took me back to Christchurch, New Zealand. That's where we met up with Mike Syong and Burt Simmons who had been flown in from Canberra, Australia. That same crew flew to Tahiti where we picked up Tori Croft and Jody West and then they brought us to Houston. I will let the other astronauts tell you their rescue stories and their high adventures.

The press conference went on for about two hours. Each of the astronauts told of their survival and rescue after being deposited in the various places on earth. Each astronaut had about the same reaction to the space aliens as the other. They all agreed with Paul as to their origin and physical attributes. It was all speculation but the media now felt they had a reliable scientific source.

Pete finally called an end to the laborious process, thanked the media for their patience and with that the astronauts arose and left the room. There would be many requests for interviews and the story would go on for years. The lead headline from most media was "Astronauts meet space aliens!"

Meanwhile Jack Forester, who had watched the whole conference, shutoff his TV and leaned back and smiled. He was 100% sure the AFV program was safe and still undercover.

Bill Reynolds was in a good mood as he was also certain they had kept the genie in the bottle and nothing further would be discovered which could expose the AFV program.

Captain Paul Anderson retired from the Navy since there were no longer any manned space shuttle flights. As he was cleaning out his space suit he discovered a business card with Bob Avery's name and address at Omega Aviation. He pondered how that had gotten there. During the next month he was still bothered by the business card and decided that might be a good job opportunity.

At Omega Headquarters Bob Avery received a call from the gate guard.

"Mr. Avery there is a Captain Paul Anderson here to see you sir. What is your desire?" he asked.

Bob's first thought was "Oh shit," But he directed the gate guard to send him up to headquarters. He had better talk with him and get to the bottom of what was on Paul Anderson's mind. Perhaps the AFV program wasn't as secure as all involved had been led to believe. The next hour could blow the lid off of everything. Bob said a quiet prayer.

ABOUT THE AUTHOR

 H.J."Walt" Walter is a retired naval aviator who served four years in the Antarctic. He spent 22 years flying all types of naval aircraft including single engine props & jets, multiengine props & jets and the turboprop powered C-130. After retirement he earned his college degrees. A Bachelor of Science in Education, Bachelor of Science in Earth Science and Master of Science in Education. He also has three years of mechanical engineering at Purdue University. Taught high school Technology Education and Pre-Engineering at Canisius College and was also employed in the engineeering department of an aerospace corporation.